TURBULENCE

Louise Braithwaite

In Memory of Neil

Contents

Prologue: A Rough Ride

Looking back, perhaps 40 *was* a problem, after all.

It arrived innocently enough, in the February of 2011, well-placed to cheer the dreary days between Christmas and Easter. Kay approached it without much concern. It had always seemed to mark a turning-point (not wrong there!), of being that bit wiser yet, nowhere near "old" (or even middle-aged, these days).

Amongst the presents from her husband Phil was a wodge of money he'd saved to take her on a whistle-stop tour of Italy. This would be their first trip abroad together; Phil's first ever, in fact, as he'd never gotten round to sorting out a passport. It didn't matter too much; there were places nearer home that they'd both wanted to see, but it reached a point when they'd done it all – Scotland, the Lakes, Wales, the Cotswolds; and they'd been back to Devon and Cornwall, time after time.

They waited till Spring, to give time for Phil's passport to come through. Kay had helped him with the forms and arranged the flights ("you know me, love," he said, "I'm crap with all that"). Flying out of Liverpool to Rome, they hired a motorbike before riding on to Sorrento, then up to Tuscany where they spent time in Florence. They finished with a 3-night stay at Lark Garda, with a trip to Venice and night at the opera in Verona.

They arrived back in Rome on a high. Kay had been concerned that Phil might get bored with the galleries, and especially with the opera; but he'd gone with the flow, enjoying the coast and countryside and the opportunity for plenty of biking. They both agreed that they should do something similar for his 50th, in a few years' time – maybe the Netherlands or Belgium. But once they'd returned the bike, their good spirits were short-lived – almost from the moment of checking-in, their journey home was a nightmare.

For a start, the queue was ridiculously slow; then, when they finally got near the front, the couple immediately before them were arguing about the weight of their luggage. It was the same getting through customs, and they were starting to worry that it was close to the time for boarding; but it turned out the flight was delayed anyway.

They were due to leave at 10pm. It reached midnight before it was announced that, due to a technical hitch, their flight was regrettably cancelled; they'd be put on another tomorrow. By now too late to bother looking for a room for the night, they did their best to get some sleep in the departure lounge.

Next day was a little more straightforward – until getting on board to find themselves seated at opposite ends of the plane! By now they were too exhausted to kick up a fuss, but it wasn't ideal. They sat for half an hour without moving; not good for Kay, with her claustrophobia, and by the time they finally took off she felt quite sick. Once underway, it was a lovely flight, with little turbulence – until they reached Liverpool, amid a storm. They circled for twenty minutes, before the pilot tried to land - only to come whizzing straight back up.

"Just a cheeky tail-wind, there," the pilot announced, lightly. "We'll try another approach – but if that doesn't work, we may need to divert to Manchester."

Everyone groaned – then a woman started screaming, causing a panic as others burst into tears.

"Jesus Christ!" Kay heard – and couldn't help smiling as she realised it was Phil. "Someone tell her to put a cork in it!"

Thankfully, the pilot had more luck on the next attempt. Again, the plane sat for some time on the runway. It was twenty minutes before the doors were opened - worse this time, as people stood to get their bags, clustering at the end of the aisle. The screechy woman seemed to have made a quick recovery.

"Oh, I'm always the same," she laughed. "Drama queen, me!"

"Well, you need to rein it in," a man nearby remarked. "Scaring people like that…"

"Who the hell asked you?" the woman snapped, and her friend joined in an argument with the man and his wife.

Kay's head spun with the noise; it was getting hotter and more uncomfortable. "Look," she asked one of the stewards, "I know it's not your fault, but are we likely to be stood here much longer? I'm not feeling well."

"Only a couple more minutes. Do you need a glass of water?"

"No, thanks", she said (although a stiff gin wouldn't have gone amiss!).

Once they were finally off, they wasted no time in getting home, crashing out almost straightaway. It wasn't next morning that she checked her phone. There were several garbled messages from her mother, each one more frantic than the last. Hard to make sense of them all – but the main gist was that her dad was in hospital…

Part One: Grounded

Chapter One

"I'm sorry, Kay. I'd hoped it wouldn't come to this – but I'm afraid we'll have to let you go."

And there it was. Just like when she lost her dad; weeks, months, preparing for it; dreading it. Grieving before it happened; and now it had, there was a calmness; almost a relief.

"This is to explain our decision," Carol said, handing Kay a letter. "And what to do next…if you think we're wrong."

She opened and skimmed through it, briefly. Today's date – November 20th, 2015 – which was when her contract ended. Nothing she didn't expect.

"You okay, Carol?" she asked.

50ish, blonde and high-coloured, Carol was upbeat, jovial, almost always smiling. But, today, she wasn't so much serious as just plain *sad*; so unlike herself.

"I feel awful," she said tearfully. "I'll really miss you – we all will. And here's you, worrying about *me*!"

"Well - it can't be an easy thing to have to do."

"I can't believe I'm doing it at all! I'm so sorry to have let you down."

"It's not your fault."

"I tried as hard as I could, Kay, but…"

"Look, you did your best, Carol – and in fairness, I've not exactly helped myself."

"But after all you've had to deal with…and you were never off sick before. I suppose I'd just hoped we could turn things around. I'm sure you'd win if you appealed."

"I'll give it some thought."

Then, a moment or two of silence, both trying to take it in. 26 years…. Longer than she'd had her brother in her life - or Phil, for that matter.

"How will you manage?" Carol asked. "I mean, with being on your own now?"

"I've still got some money from the sale of Mum and Dad's bungalow, and I managed to get rid of the mortgage. So, I won't be out on the streets. Might starve to death, mind, but at least it'll be in comfort! Just kidding," she added, as Carol teared up once more.

"What are you like?" Carol managed a smile. "But will you *really* be okay, or are you just saying that to make me feel better?"

"I'll be fine. Just need to lay off the champers, eh?"

They both laughed. "At least you've not lost your sense of humour," Carol said. Then she handed her a bag, full of her belongings – books, magazines, a mug, a coaster. "I cleared your desk. Hope you don't mind?"

"Thanks," Kay said lightly. "That's great."

"I waited till everyone had left for the day– just so there wouldn't be questions. I only hope it doesn't feel like we're sneaking you out. You know the score. But in a few weeks, once things have settled down, we'll all get together. Doesn't feel right, not giving you a proper send-off."

"That'd be lovely… Something to look forward to." Another pause. "So – I guess this is it?"

They couldn't avoid walking past reception and catching sight of her workmates, interviewing clients. One of them – Anne Reynolds – looked up as she passed, and they exchanged glances. Kay nodded to her, and Anne, understanding her meaning, mouthed "Sorry."

"Keep in touch, Kay" Carol said, as they reached the back door. "And best of luck. Look after yourself."

She stood for a few moments – one final look at the building, before slowly heading away. Once she'd got around the corner, she took a few deep breaths before reaching for her phone.

"Jen? Just to let you know – I've had my meeting with Carol and, well – what I thought would happen, has happened…I'm ok… just feels a bit weird. But I can't say I didn't see *this* one coming…Great…if you've got time, I'd love to... See you soon."

Chapter Two

An hour or so later, she was with her friend Jen at their favourite haunt, Cuthbert's Bakehouse – a quirky, vintage-y, New York-inspired patisserie, a stone's throw from the Uni and cathedrals. Because this was all arranged last minute, they were too late to order afternoon tea; so, Jen had improvised and got a selection of cakes and scones to share, including their to-die-for Victoria Sponge. Petite, slightly built, Jen had an almost cat-like face with golden-brown eyes, jet black hair and slightly oriental features. Like Carol, she looked slightly tearful.

"None of that, now," Kay said with a smile.

Jen wiped her eyes. "It just seems so unfair. After all these years! It's hard to believe."

"Carol said the same. I really felt for her, to be honest. It was the last thing she wanted to do."

"I know she's not to blame, of course, but it just feels like it should never have got this far. Was there no way they could treat it as a one-off?"

"In fairness, Carol wanted to take it down that route – but I told her not to."

"But why…?"

"My choice, Jen. I just don't want everyone knowing my business."

"'Everyone' being Martin McGee?"

"Well – you know my feelings. And before you say it, you're right. I'm my own worst enemy."

"I'm not judging, hon. All I'll say is, it might be worth putting in an appeal. Lisa could help – have you told her yet?"

"No. I'll ring her tomorrow." Kay grinned. "Magoo's ears'll be burning - and mine if I don't appeal! She means well, but I won't be pushed into anything."

"Well, it's early days yet, anyway. But at least consider it? Once things have settled down, I mean."

"I will – although part of me is thinking it might be time for a change. It worked for you."

Jen had left the office five years ago, to set up her own Reiki and counselling practice; and although it had been somewhat slow to get off the ground, she was doing well. They'd both started work on the same day, back in 1989, as 18-year-olds straight from school. Lisa, a couple of years older, had shown them the ropes, and the three had become firm friends. A fiery trade unionist, Lisa was tough and no-nonsense, while Jen was mellow and wise. Although Kay knew Lisa had her back, it was Jen she'd always turn to first.

"Look," Jen said, handing her a parcel, "don't open this yet. Wait till you're on your own. Just a few bits and bobs I put together for you – I hope they'll help."

"Thanks so much, love – you're helping just by being here, believe me, and … Oh, God!" Kay sighed heavily, suddenly realizing the date. It hadn't registered with her when she saw it on the letter. "Funny how you lose track of time. It's just dawned on me now that it's the 22nd on Sunday. Phil's 50th."

"I'd thought of it, you know," Jen said, "but wasn't sure whether to mention it. I didn't want to upset you."

"It's just strange…by rights we should be biking around Bruges or Amsterdam now. That was always the plan."

"Oh, hon…." Jen sighed. "I'm worried about you. On top of everything else, now all this."

"Still in one piece, though, eh? Unless it just hasn't hit me."

"That's what bothers me. So, I'll be keeping a close eye - whether you like it or not!"

Later that evening, Kay opened Jen's parcel to find, amongst other things, a card with a stunning beach on the front; gleaming white, shimmering turquoise, backed with lush greenery. She guessed it was somewhere in the Caribbean but looking at the back she found it was Menorca. Jen's favourite place.

"So peaceful and relaxing," she'd say. "And ideal for biking. You and Phil would love it."

The card was blank inside, and she'd written a note:

"Just some bits to keep you going. As for the books…see what you think. Much love, Jen xxx"

There were four books in all – self-help tomes; as well as some crystals – jade, amethyst, rose quartz – the colours she loved. There was also a small package in bubble-wrap (therapy in itself!) containing a statue of a Thai Buddha. Jen kept a similar one in her Reiki room, which Kay had always admired.

Since being on her own, Kay had moved into the spare room, which she'd redecorated in a delicate duck-egg blue; the statue matched perfectly. Bedding, cushions, curtains were all in various shades of teal to tone in with the walls. Cool, tranquil, minimalist – as opposed to the noise and clutter of life with Phil. She placed the books on the bedside table, and the crystals in a trinket box on top of the chest-of-drawers. Then, instinctively, opened the third drawer down, taking out a box of old photos and two albums.

The first one she came across was from an office party, many years ago. There they were, the three amigos – JKL as they called themselves, back then – and a few others, including Anne, who'd nodded goodbye earlier that day. Plenty from her holidays with Phil. A windswept one of her at St Ives, early 2000's…another of Phil on the bike at Lake Garda.

She moved on to the albums. One had belonged to her parents. There were a few from their wedding day, early 1970. Her Mum, Dot: tall, fair-haired, slender, willowy. Her Dad, Frank: stocky, red-headed, with a thick moustache and ruddy complexion. Grandad Howie: thin and frail with his drink-ravaged face, looking much older than his 60 years. Dot with her siblings, Bob and June; all very alike, except that June was a lighter, almost platinum blonde. Bob – Dot's beloved older brother – was handsome and serious; and his glamorous young wife, Viv, looked a bit like Mary Quant, or a brunette Twiggy. No sign of June's husband Ray – perhaps he'd taken the photographs?

On to the next ones. Her brother, Andrew - chubby, rosy-cheeked, strawberry-blonde – in Sefton Park (around 1975, she guessed); there was a lovely one of them both near the statue of Peter Pan[ii]. Another, looking out across the river at Eastham Ferry – a favourite place for Andy, who always loved planes. Directly opposite Speke airport, it gave a good vantage point to watch the take-offs and landings.

Finally, her own wedding album. It started with herself and her dad – his auburn hair now a greyish, pale ginger, but still high-coloured and strongly built. Smiling broadly; Frank was never one to show his feelings, but didn't hold back, that day. Another of them entering the registry office; Jen and Lisa following behind, their elegant bridesmaids' dresses in a shimmery, delicate sky-blue. Phil and his brother, Pete, waiting as Kay and Frank approached; the beam on Phil's face at how she looked in her dress. Pete, still with his skinhead in those days, wore a grey suit and his permanent scowl. ("*Worst* bloody man, more like!" Phil's mate Col had muttered).

 Exchanging vows, signing the register – then with the gathering of friends and family outside the offices. Pete's wife, Jackie, and her sister Michelle - busty, blonde, and bouffant. Phil's friends in their biker gear (much to Dot's disgust); Robbo: tall, pale, lanky; Col: thick-set and stocky, with his bushy black beard. Kay with her parents; Frank still happy and proud, but Dot's face tripping her, even more than Pete's....

She and Phil, cutting the cake. Her copper curls were loose and natural; she wore a classic white dress and a bolero to match the bridesmaids, with a bouquet of mixed roses in pink, lilac, cream. As for Phil, this was one of the few occasions he'd ever worn a suit. It was navy and pin-striped, with a shirt in that same pale blue – open-necked, and no tie, of course (he wouldn't go *that* far!). But his beard was neatly trimmed, his long, dark hair neatly tied back; he'd scrubbed up well. The last one was in soft-focus – the two of them, smiling lovingly at each other, his arm protectively round her shoulder....

...She quickly slammed shut the album, stuffing it back in the drawer. Her face was drenched. What was she thinking?

Drying her eyes, she got herself into bed. She'd expected to crash out as soon as her head hit the pillow; but as she tried to drop off, her mind raced with the events of the day – and all that had led up to it.

Chapter Three

Andy had always loved to sing - and if it was in the back garden, at the top of his voice, then all the better! Especially "Come Fly with Me"[iii], which he'd learnt from their Uncle Tommy, and would belt out joyfully, whenever a plane passed by. He made up his own words: "Come fly on high, come fly on high away!" And then, the inevitable question: when could *he* go on a plane?

"Maybe one day," Dot replied - but was always too anxious to think of going abroad, let alone with Andy. As well as Down's, he had a heart condition and diabetes; there was always the risk he'd fall ill. She tried to compensate by taking him on the 20-minute bus trip to the airport, or over to Eastham – but just watching wasn't the same, he'd say. He wanted to fly. Much later, years after he'd died, Kay would feel guilty that he never got his wish. No-one was to blame, of course – but she was never a keen flyer, and wished she could love it, knowing what he'd have given to be in her shoes.

Other favourites were "I'd Like to Teach the World to Sing"[iv] (the Coke-ad version), and the "Top of the World"[v]. One day, she remembered, his song of choice had been "Jesus Christ, Superstar"[vi] - putting emphasis on the "Jesus Christ" with mischievous glee. It wasn't long before their neighbour, Elsie Maudsley, had knocked to complain - not just the noise, this time, but his "foul language."

"I'm so sorry, Mrs. Maudsley," Dot stammered. "It's from the musical."

"Can't say *I've* heard of it," Elsie sniffed.

"*Everyone* knows it!" Andy piped up.

"I think you've caused enough mayhem for one day, young man," his mother chided. "Now go inside, and stop being so cheeky!"

Their life, to many, would have seemed idyllic. Frank, in partnership with lifelong friend George Powell, made a good living as a plumber; he'd come from humble beginnings off Scotland Road, and knowing poverty as he had, put in long hours to ensure his family wanted for nothing. They had a cosy, three-bed house in leafy Mossley Hill – which, with different neighbours, might have been near-perfect....

On one side, there was Elsie, a 70-something widow who'd lived there since the 30s, when the houses were newly built. A committed Christian, she was a member of the W.I, and did all sorts of charity work – while privately disparaging those she helped. Next door to Elsie was Ethel Colman, her best friend and sparring-partner. While Elsie was plump and florid, Ethel was thin, grizzled, with a sharp, bird-like face - a bit like 'Terrahawks'*vii*' Zelda, as Andy would observe, ten years down the line. Rumour had it that Ethel's fiancé was killed in World War 1. As she never spoke of it, no-one knew for sure - but *something* had left her lonely and bitter, and she made little effort to hide her joy at others' misfortunes. A few years older than her "frenemy" Elsie, she was also one of the first residents of the road, having moved there with her widowed mother in 1934. For all their quarrels, Elsie and Ethel formed a united front when it came to passing judgement on neighbours who didn't quite belong. A month or so before the "Jesus episode", Dot had overheard them moaning about Andy. Such a noisy child, Ethel remarked – and she *did* feel sorry for Elsie, living next door, and having to put up with it......

On the other side was a married couple, Ron and Joan Banks - closer in age to Frank and Dot, but no less snooty than their elderly counterparts. Their daughter, Marianne – four years older than Kay – would later go to read law at Oxford. They talked constantly of how well she was doing, which Dot found insensitive, given Andy's problems. Nevertheless, Dot tried hard – *too* hard – to be friends with the wife. Wasting her time, of course, as Frank often tried to tell her.

"You don't understand, Frank," she'd say. "You're at work all day – I've got to talk to *someone*."

But Frank had no truck with any of them. Apart from their bitching about Andy, they looked down on Frank too, assuming him to be a ne'er do well because of where he'd grown up. (Dot, in her need to be liked, was prone to over-sharing – it always backfired). Kay, aged 5 at the time, could well remember the stifling "ladybird" summer of 1976, when the Banks' returned from holiday to find their house broken into - and the finger was pointed immediately at Frank.

She and Andy had finished their tea, and were watching "Blue Peter"[viii], when a policeman knocked. Of course, Frank had nothing to hide, as he'd either been at work or with the family; there was no time he couldn't account for. That was fine, they said, and they were sorry to bother him. "We had to ask everyone, Mr. Cooney. Just to be sure."

"No worries, son," Frank said calmly; but Dot struggled to keep her cool.

"I hope you're not accusing my husband of anything untoward!"

"Leave it, Dot," Frank sighed. "He's only doing his job."

Next day, Dot took Kay and Andy shopping in town. As they reached home, they found the two of them, stood there talking outside Elsie's house. They went quiet as Dot approached; then, after an awkward silence,

"Hello, dear," Elsie smiled. "Awful about poor Ron and Joan! This area's going downhill - it wouldn't have happened a few years ago, mark my words!"

"I know," Dot said. "It's terrible."

"Dreadful!"

"A disgrace!" Ethel agreed. "I just hope they catch whoever did it. I've a feeling it's someone from round here."

"I'm sure it is," Elsie said, still smiling. "Someone *very* close by, in fact. So - did the police call last night?"

"Yes – they spoke to Frank – said they had to ask everyone in the road. Did they talk to you?"

"No," Elsie smirked. "Why would they?"

"Oh!" Dot said, taken aback.

"Me neither," Ethel added. "I suppose they didn't see the need, really." She checked her watch. "Anyway - must be getting on. Bye, dear."

"Yes, bye, dear," Elsie chirped. "*Lovely* to see you."

"They think it's you," Dot fumed later to Frank. "And I wouldn't mind betting it was *them* who tipped off the police!"

"Look, Dot, forget it. It's all blown over now. You're more worried than I am."

"Yes, because it shouldn't have happened in the first place!" she said crossly. "Why are they like this with us, Frank? Looking down their noses – they're no better than us!"

"Does it really matter? I'd stop bothering if I were you. You've got enough to cope with as it is."

"Well, trust a man to say that! You've no idea!"

Chapter Four

More outgoing than her husband, but less self-assured, Dot lived on her nerves. It seemed to Kay, even at an early age, that her mother *found* things to worry about; and acceptance from the neighbours was at the top of the list. To be badly thought of was Dot's greatest fear. So strong was this that she often did favours in the hope she could somehow "make" them like her – bringing in their bins, fetching bits of shopping, inviting them for coffee-mornings. Then, inevitably, would be devastated when nothing changed

"Well, what did you expect?" Frank would ask, after Dot complained of feeling put-upon and used. "Traipsing round after them won't change things. Just ignore 'em – works for me."

To which Dot would respond, bitterly, that not everyone was a loner, like him, and that it was different for a man – women needed their friends.

As Kay listened, she often wondered if there might be something wrong with her; she too was a "loner". From how her mum spoke, how could you *not* want to be liked? Who could possibly *enjoy* being alone, or *not* want friends? And if they were horrible to you? … still better to have some than none. Kay, even at the age of 5, knew she didn't agree, and felt bad for this, as it seemed to mean she was somehow letting her mum down.

It was just that, given the choice of being alone, or with people she disliked, she'd take solitude every time. She enjoyed time with Andy, and loved her cousins in Scotland, Janice and Stevie – they were loud, exuberant, very different to herself, but also warm and kind. When they'd stayed in Exeter with Auntie June, she'd made friends with a girl next door called Lucia. They were inseparable for the two weeks, and she was heartbroken when they had to come home. Dot, for all her own need for companionship, completely missed the point.

"Honestly – all this fuss – you'd think your own home was a dump!"

The trouble was that, unlike her cousins and Lucia, not everyone meant well. Many of the kids from school (not all, of course; but *enough*) were mean-spirited and bullying – no different from the neighbours, in fact - and so she backed off and chose to play alone. While she never had imaginary friends, she did spend a lot of time in her head. She loved to read, paint, draw, and most of all, to create stories.

At a very young age, she'd gather her dolls and teddies in front of her toy blackboard: "Now, children – today we'll learn our alphabet." For some reason, she'd put on her Mum's housecoat, and a cushion on top of her head – presumably, she'd seen an old picture of a teacher in a cap-and-gown. Years later, she and Phil would laugh together as she shared the memory. "We could do it now," she'd said mischievously. "A bit of role play. But be warned – you'll get the cane if you're bad."

"Oh aye?" he'd grinned. "Is that a threat or a promise?"

As her reading and writing developed, she'd make up stories about her dolls and bears, creating personalities, interests, and families for them. Then, as she outgrew the toys, her great love was animals, especially cats. She'd always wanted one, but understood this could never happen, as Andy was much too scared of them. Instead, she'd make do with petting the ones that came into the front garden (while Andy stayed safely inside!). As with her toys, she created names for them, and tales of their adventures as they explored the neighbourhood.

She also read voraciously, starting with Enid Blyton and the like, before moving on to the classics. By her early teens, she'd read most of Dickens, the Brontës, Jane Austen. As she learnt more about the men and women who'd created the books she'd come to love, she thought how, when she was older, she'd like to do what they did; to write not just stories, but whole, proper novels.

For some, her thoughtful nature seemed a cause for concern. "Too quiet"; "shy and reticent"; "tends to daydream"; and (what irked her the most) "needs bringing out of her shell". One day (she must have been 8 or 9), she was called from class to have a chat with a man and a lady. She'd never seen them before, knew little about them – except that they were doctors, not teachers. "The doctors just have a few questions, Katie," Miss Franklin said. ("Kay" came much later, after she'd started work). They seemed nice enough, asking about her favourite lessons, who were her best friends?

"Charlie Moran," she replied.

They looked at each other, perplexed. "Not any of the girls?" the lady doctor asked.

"No," Kay answered honestly. "I prefer Charlie. The girls are mean to him. They call him Charlie Moron."

Although they were in different classes, Kay looked out for Charlie; as she'd always done the same for Andy, it was second nature. While she was somewhere in the middle of Set 1 (good at English, average at Maths), Charlie was in the remedial class, and found most things a struggle. He had little in common with Kay but, both being sensitive souls, they tended to stick together. With his thick NHS glasses and tatty brown hair, he was ridiculed, not just by the "scallies", but the "posh" kids who looked down on him. "Jilted John"[ix] was out at the time – inevitably, it rang out often across the schoolyard, with "Gordon" replaced by "Charlie". Kay sometimes found him crying alone.

"Never mind, Charlie," she'd say. "Come on – let's go back in."

As they walked to class together, "Love your new *boyfriend*, Katie!" the others teased; ("Take no notice," she said. "They're just jealous.")

… "Hmm…" the male doctor said, making notes. "I *see*."

They moved on to ask her about her stories and pictures. Could she draw one for them now? What she did was quite detailed – a young man with blue eyes, blonde hair, and a cheeky grin.

"Very good," the lady doctor said. "Is it anyone you know?"

"I'm not sure," Kay replied – but later realized it was probably how she imagined Andy grown up.

Did she enjoy school? they asked; and how well did she get on with her classmates? To the first she answered yes, she loved it (even Maths, which wasn't her favourite); and to the second - they were mostly alright, although there were a few she wasn't keen on - they picked on Charlie and some others. Did they ever pick on her? A bit – when she stuck up for Charlie – but she didn't care anyway.

"Okay," the male doctor said. "Nice to meet you, Katie. We'll let you get back to class."

Later, when Dot asked about her day, she mentioned about seeing the doctors, and how they'd asked her to draw the man.

"Oh, did they, now?" Dot said indignantly. And next day she was in the Head's office, demanding to know why her daughter was sent to the doctor, without asking her – and why was she being treated differently? Did anyone else have to go?

The Head, Mrs. Evans, explained that the psychologists had been brought in to look at another child who might need to go to special school. (Looking back, Kay wondered if this was Charlie, who did change schools a few months later). Since they were already there, she'd asked them to look at Katie, too; only because she seemed a little nervous, and didn't mix too well with the other children. And with her brother having Down's...they just had to be sure all was okay.

But (Mrs. Evans assured her) it turned out there was nothing to worry about. The psychologists had found Katie to be very bright – a bit too sensitive, perhaps, but otherwise, all was fine.

In bed that evening she could overhear Dot telling Frank. "Well, I said – of *course* everything's fine! She's in the top set, for heaven's sake! Oh yes, she said, she's doing very well. Good, I said – because I'd hate to think you were suggesting Katie has learning difficulties, just because Andrew does. No, not at all, she said - you're taking it the wrong way. But I'm not so sure."

"Bullshit!" Frank said gruffly. "They're just ignorant – like them bloody neighbours."

Dot sighed. "I know…but I do worry, Frank - about her being so quiet. I just wish she'd get on better with other kids. Apart from that daft boy Charlie, I mean."

"Oh, for Christ's sake, woman, listen to yourself! You're as bad as them! It wouldn't do if we were all the same, you know."

"No, Frank," she said, frustratedly, "you don't get what I'm saying. I just want to feel normal, that's all."

"Of course you're normal, you daft mare!"

"Not just *me*, Frank – I mean us - *all* of us, and – well, I don't know… I get the feeling people think we're not, and it's all my fault."

And then the usual argument, where Frank told her not to be so bloody stupid, and Dot said it was alright for him; *she* was the one they'd criticize. And on top of all that, there was enough to worry about with Andy. As she listened, Kay began to feel ashamed; it wasn't good to hear her Mum so upset, and to know that somehow, *she* had caused it. To be sent to see the doctor, when no-one else had to, and to have them try to work her out… Being so young, it was hard to put into words, but looking back she felt… a bit humiliated. *Less than*. That was it.

All she knew was that she had to change. As difficult as she might find it, she'd have to start spending less time alone. Otherwise, her Mum would keep worrying and blaming herself. Kay had never thought she was doing anything wrong, but she *must* have been, else why would Dot say, "they think it's my fault."? You only talked about "fault" when something was bad; so, she had to be better, for both their sakes.

Chapter Five

It wasn't easy, and many times she dearly wanted to go with her instinct – to back firmly away. Nevertheless, she stoically joined in as best she could, taking any rebuffs on the chin.

"Go away!" Millie Jones said, scornfully. "No-one asked *you*!"

Another girl, Susan King, must have noticed her embarrassment.

"Come and sit with us," she said kindly.

Gradually, Kay became the fourth member of Sue's tight-knit little group – the others were Julie Morgan and Sarah Blake. They were amongst the less cliquey girls at the school; at least Sue and Julie – she could never quite trust Sarah, and to begin with wasn't quite sure why. Just something a bit "off". Still, she surprised herself by enjoying being part of the gang, especially now Charlie had left. At home, she still had her alone time; but because she now had "proper" friends, her mum would stop worrying. It was the best of both worlds.

They moved to high school in 1982. The first two years were fine – the group stuck together, and life continued much as it had in primary. But then, as they went into different sets and took their options, the dynamics began to change; not for the better. Sarah made friends with a brash, loud-mouthed girl named Melanie Larkin. Before long, Mel was joining them for lunch. Kay had heard the term "fifth wheel" before – and as four became five, she started to wonder if this was herself.

It was little things at first. Mel took centre-stage at the dinner-table, and it was hard to get a word in edgeways as she regaled them with stories of the dramas in her life. How true all of them were, Kay really couldn't guess, but her friends were clearly taken in as they listened, mouths open in awestruck silence. Sarah seemed in in her thrall, laughing loudly at her smutty comments. As for Julie, Kay always got the feeling that deep down, she wasn't that impressed by Mel, but was afraid to tell Sarah what she thought. So, when Sarah would go on about how Mel was "such a laugh", she'd just nod meekly in agreement, while Sue said nothing at all.

Soon, Sarah (and to some extent Julie, and Sue) had become a clone of Mel. She started speaking in exaggerated scouse (she'd never sounded like that before), using words like "meffy", and "mingin'". They wore full make-up, including false nails and lashes, and thick foundation that had a definite orange tinge, with big hair, permed in the bouffant style of the time. They wore sheepskin coats, tucker boots and leg warmers in various fluorescent shades.

Kay's hair was always tied in a ponytail. Dot insisted she wore sensible shoes for school and thought 13 was too young for make-up. Compared with Mel and Sarah, Kay knew she looked hopelessly "uncool." It soon went from excluding her from the conversation, to jibes about her appearance; general remarks, on the face of it, but clearly aimed at Kay. Then there were the comments about the "snobs" in Set 1. She would shoot down anything Kay said in flames - accusing her paranoia and "taking things to heart" if she made any attempt to defend herself.

One lunchtime, Mel was furious to find a girl called Lucy Thornton sitting at their usual table in the canteen. Kay and Lucy were in the same English class but had rarely spoken. Withdrawn and painfully shy, Lucy generally sat at the back, head down, talking to no-one. Although most from the class were nice to her, many others from their year were unkind.

Kay smiled at Lucy as they reached the table. "Mind if we sit here?"

Lucy, smiling back, was about to answer; but her face dropped as she saw Mel glowering.

"It's alright," she murmured. "I'll move."

"Yeah," Mel snarled. "It's *our* table, so just *do* one, you freak!"

Close to tears, Lucy grabbed her bag and almost ran from the canteen.

"Look, she's left her plate! Dozy cow!" Mel grumbled, pushing it aside. Then, to Kay: "Next time, you don't *ask* her, you *tell* her!"

"There was no need," Kay said. "She was doing no harm."

"Oh, well, you *would* stick up for her – 'cos you're a freak, too!"

"She was the same in juniors," Sarah piped up. "There was this lad, Charlie Moran – Charlie Moron, we called him - you should've seen the state of him, Mel! And Katie was his best mate...."

This was all before they broke up for Christmas. Although the holidays were a welcome break, she couldn't enjoy them, because most of the time was spent dreading next term. On their first day back in the January, as they waited to go into Geography, Julie asked her about presents – what did she get? And what about her brother?

Andy's toys were often meant for much younger kids. Since Mel had joined the group, Kay told them as little as possible about her home life. Naturally, Mel has been gleeful to learn that Andy had Down's and was mean enough about him as it was. Not that Kay was in any way ashamed of him – she just didn't want to give Mel any more ammunition. But this time - thinking Julie was still her friend – she forgot herself, stupidly telling her that Andy's presents included an Etch-a-Sketch and Play-Doh, as he loved to draw and make models. Next morning at registration, she heard the laughter and whispering:

"So, what did *you* get, then?"

"An Etch-a-Sketch[x] and Play-Doh[xi]. How cool is *that*?"

"What the hell did you say to them?" Kay later confronted Julie

"Well," Julie said, stifling a giggle, "I only told Sarah..."

"Oh, great – then she told Mel. I should have known..."

And suddenly, there was Mel, in her face.

"Why?" she demanded. "Why *shouldn't* she tell me? We're all mates — we tell each other *everything*!"

"You're not *my* mate."

"*What...?!*"

"Look, Mel, I don't know what I've done, but you seem to keep having a go at me. And the things you say about my brother — it's not his fault he's..."

"A mong?" They all smirked.

"Leave him alone," Kay murmured — realizing, to her horror, that she was crying.

"Aw, don't be an arl-arse!" Sarah said — but she was still laughing.

"Alright," Mel said, "but lighten up, Katie! Mates take the piss. Deal with it!"

This was what Mel always did. Turned it around, so Kay was the one in the wrong — for being over-sensitive, not taking a joke like the others did...But with them, it was never like *that*. It was done with affection; the difference between laughing *at* and laughing *with*. Perhaps this was the problem. Maybe they were right - that she needed to "lighten up", and all she had to do was go with the flow. Laugh along. But...how to do this when they were mocking your brother? Agree with them? Join in...?

That was the difference. When it came to Kay, Mel's jokes were much more personal, and it always felt she was going for the jugular. What hurt most was that, while always unsure of Sarah, she'd been close to Sue and Julie. In the days before Mel, she'd sometimes invited the girls back for tea, so they'd met Andy more than once. It broke her heart to think of them using stories of the visits to keep Mel entertained.

Stronger than ever before was her belief that solitude was better than feeling lonely in a crowd. She began to see that her only mistake was to doubt this. Mel once suggested she go off on her own and be friendless, like Lucy. Kay was sorely tempted to take her up on it; because surely, your mates were supposed to help you feel happier, not worse. Otherwise, what was the point?

But there was such a stigma attached to always being alone, and this concerned her – not so much for herself as for her Mum. As he got older, Andy's behaviour grew more erratic; if Dot found out that things weren't going so well, she'd say she didn't need something else to fret about, or for Kay to add to her woes. For this reason, whenever Dot asked her about school, her response was always the same: "Yep – fine." Sometimes, she'd overhear Dot telling Frank how lucky they were with Katie; she never gave them a minute's trouble. Of course, she'd add, it had been a worry that she was so shy when she was younger; but now she was doing great, and had lovely friends…

"It's not just about that," Frank said, matter-of-factly. "They're supposed to be there to learn."

"Well, I know – but she gets good marks, too, and that's one in the eye for Joan next door. I get so fed up with all her bragging about Marianne."

"It's not a competition"

"I'm not saying it *is!*" Dot snapped. "Honestly, Frank! You never get what I mean."

But, in truth, Dot did sometimes make life a competition; wanted her kids to be the best-mannered, nicest, smartest; and as Andy was so often misunderstood, her hopes for this were pinned on Kay. Time and again, she'd been told her the same thing. Don't make waves. Put others first. Don't ever, under any circumstance, say anything to offend. Fit in, and above all, be *liked*. And as much as Kay loved her mum, she was beginning to resent it.

It was all so much easier at primary school. The bullies there hadn't bothered her because they didn't *matter*. But now - thanks to Mrs. Evans' doctors, and her mother's worrying - she cared, so much more than she wanted to.

The next few weeks were slightly better. While she still felt "out" of things, at least Mel seemed to have calmed down with the remarks. At around this time, Kay noticed on her way home from school that each night, the same lad seemed to be at the bus stop. She'd not seen him before – a couple of years older, fair-haired, quite good-looking. He was ultra-trendy and, at first glance, a bit of a scally, but friendly enough – smiled and winked when he saw her. Before long they'd started chatting; she found out his name was Gary (Gaz for short), and he lived in Garston with his mum and sisters. It did cross her mind to wonder why he got that bus, when Garston was in the opposite direction – but she thought little more of it at the time.

It wasn't that she was desperate for a boyfriend, and she certainly didn't want one just to gain street cred with Mel and Sarah. Even so, the attention gave her self-esteem a boost – *someone* thought she was worth getting to know, and although it wasn't about proving it to *them*, perhaps she did need to prove it to herself. So, when Gaz asked her on a date, she was quietly pleased.

They met on a Saturday afternoon, and as the weather was bright and sunny (if cold), Gaz suggested a walk through Calderstones Park. Kay told him more about Andy's disabilities, and he listened attentively, commenting that it must be so hard for her family. They stopped near some trees; he said he really liked her. Would she go with him?

Then he moved forward, as if to kiss her... and suddenly, from nowhere, peals of shrill laughter. Out they popped, from behind the trees; first Mel and Sarah, tears of mirth streaming; then Jill and Sue, also giggling, but looking decidedly uncomfortable. At first, Kay thought one of them had gotten wind of her date, and they'd followed her to the park to make a show of her. But, to her despair, she realized that Gaz was laughing too.

Then it dawned on her – Mel also lived in Garston; had a mum, an older brother, and a sister. This was obviously the brother;

looking at them now, together, she could see the resemblance. No wonder she'd been quiet lately, as she'd plotted this set-up as payback for being called out the other week.

There would be worse things to happen in Kay's life than this, but she never forgot it – the moment she realized some folks have no conscience. Until then, she'd believed that most, if not all, had it in them put themselves in another's shoes – harder to find in some than others, perhaps, but must surely be there *somewhere*. But now she saw her mistake; and that some simply couldn't do it. Even worse, there were those who could, but chose not to, because…just *because*.

Back home, she went straight to her room; said nothing to Dot, except that she'd been for a walk and started feeling sick (which wasn't untrue). Her mum thought she was too young for boyfriends and would be angry to know she went on a date - even if it *had* turned out not to be real. No doubt, Gaz would have told his sister everything Kay had said, in confidence, about Andy. But she was past caring. They'd done their worst. Like a dose of mumps or measles – once it got you, it couldn't touch you again.

Unbelievably (or maybe not), they still expected her to hang out with them. At lunch on Monday, she sat alone in the canteen; they all gathered round.

"Aren't you speaking to us?" Sarah demanded.

"Come *on*!" Mel said, exasperated. "It was just a *joke*!"

"Oh, forget it!" Sarah snarled.

They moved to the next table, where Kay could hear them sniggering. When Lucy Thornton came along, looking for somewhere to sit, she looked confusedly at Kay – then at the sneering girls.

"Sit here, Lucy, if you want," she said,

"Knew those freaks would end up getting together," she heard Mel, in a loud, staged whisper. But the comments soon died off; no reaction, no glory. Kay and Lucy were soon joined by Sue, who quickly became Mel's next target. In their new gang of three, they looked out for one another, and school became, if not exactly enjoyable, at least bearable.

Chapter Six

She started at the office just months after Andy's death; casual at first, but she within weeks she was offered a permanent post. Before long she was promoted to an advisory role which, though sometimes stressful, she always enjoyed. Once she'd settled there, everything fell into place – despite it not being the career she'd planned.

Her dream was always to study English Lit, and she'd had a provisional offer of a place at Leeds, depending on her grades. She'd wanted to take it as high as she could, maybe even to PhD so she could become a lecturer; she preferred this to the idea of teaching in a school. But what she really wanted, more than anything, was to write. She knew this wouldn't be easy, so teaching would be how she'd make a living – but becoming a published author was the long-term aim. After the bullying, her stories took on a darker, grittier feel, and when she was 16, she started plans for what she hoped would be a novella. She spent a long time working on her plot and characters, then began to put together a rough draft.

But when Andy died, everything stopped in its tracks. April 22nd, 1989 – two months after Kay had turned 18, and a week to the day since Hillsborough. Both her parents were in a bad way, but Frank quickly put a lid on it, because when Dot saw him like that, she became frightened and agitated. She needed him to be strong for her, she said, or she'd never get through it. And so he was – stoic, indomitable, as always. But Kay would never forget what she saw on the night of the funeral. Not realizing she was watching, her father wept silently; his whole body shook, face crumpled with anguish.

Knowing that Dot couldn't cope with Frank's grief, Kay kept her own well-hidden – and when she did find her feelings coming to the surface, nipped them in the bud by reminding herself that Andy was at peace; it was his time; she should think of what was best for him, not herself. Inside, she didn't truly believe it. Andy might have had his problems, but he had such a zest for life, and could have had at least a few more good years. But she knew that dwelling on this would finish her off; and if she was going to be there for Dot, she couldn't let that happen.

Dot's life was never easy. She was just 14 when her mother committed suicide; and years later, her dear brother Bob died the same way. Their mum's family, the Edwards', had a long history of depression. Dot's grandfather also died young; thought at first to be a tragic work accident, but the coroner delivered an open verdict. Kay had looked at the family tree, taking it as far back as the 1830s, to the North Wales village they hailed from. She was fascinated but saddened at what she found: in each generation, at least one man (and the occasional woman) had died young; cause of death "misadventure".

Owen Edwards and Gladys Thomas – Dot's maternal grandparents - had married in 1914; and when Owen went off to the first war, a few months later, Gladys was already carrying Dot's mother, Dilys. The family moved to Liverpool from their village of Mostyn, near Holywell, towards the end of 1918; a fresh start, as Owen returned from war, one of the lucky ones to have survived. What he'd been through he never spoke of; and, by all accounts, his general demeanour was even-tempered.

The Edwards' bought a house in the "Welsh Streets" area of Dingle; sadly run-down, these days but, at the time Owen and Gladys moved in, a respectable, "skilled" working-class district. When Kay looked on Ancestry[xii], the 1911 Census gave occupations such as joiner, clerk, policeman, builder. Once, out of interest, she and Phil went to look at the house. While sorry to find it boarded-up, they could tell it would have been a cosy, if modest home; a far cry from the cramped tenement where Frank grew up. By comparison, the Edwards' home was palatial.

Owen was a train driver - a reasonably well-paid job for those days. They were an upright, churchgoing, Welsh Chapel family, and this, no doubt, was why Dot was such a stickler for manners and "decency". Dilys was almost 7 when her sister Olive was born; and from what Kay could gather, they had quite a good life, and were happy enough, until their father's death in 1928.

Dot described her grandmother, Gladys, as a formidable lady, and Kay could see why. Left alone with the two girls, she got by as best she could, taking in dressmaking to supplement her widow's pension from the railways. They had enough to manage, but life was certainly harder than before; and after struggling on for a while, she decided to use the spare room to take in a lodger.

Howell Lloyd – the son of old friends from Mostyn – had come to Liverpool, like many Welsh students, to train as a teacher. A rather shy young man, who'd seldom travelled beyond Holywell, he found city life intimidating. His homesickness was so severe that he was on the verge of giving up his studies, when his mother suggested he rent a room from Mrs. Edwards. It might help, she said, to be around friendly faces.

Howie was 19 when he first joined the household, in 1930; Dilys, at 16, had just left school and started commercial college. He was with them for two years – and Gladys had no inkling of how close he and Dilys had become. She was furious one morning to find them in bed together; even more so to find they'd been courting in secret for months. Well, there was nothing else for it, Gladys said sternly – he'd have to marry her. After all, what if he'd got her pregnant? Neither disagreed, and so a few months later they were wed, shortly before Howie took his first teaching post. But as it turned out, it would be 18 months before they had their first child, Bob, in 1934; then Dot, in 1936, and June, just before the second war.

Howie's teaching career was put abruptly on hold. He chose to go in the navy and was away for the duration; he had a few narrow escapes and was torpedoed several times. After the war, when Dot was 9, they moved from their grandmother's to the suburbs – an elegant, four-bed detached in Woolton.

Unbeknownst to Dilys, their lifestyle had come from moneylenders. Howie's wages from teaching were good, but not brilliant, and there was no way he could afford the deposit on the mortgage. Rather than settle for somewhere slightly more modest, he went to a loan-shark, then kept borrowing from others to pay it back. As the interest on the loans mounted up, there was a trip to a casino, in a desperate attempt to win enough to settle them all. Sadly, things didn't go as hoped and, now completely out of pocket, he borrowed even more. Meanwhile, the mortgage wasn't paid – the letters from the bank were considerably less threatening than the bullying tactics of the loan sharks, and he tended not to read them, anyway.

Dilys had no clue until the lenders started knocking. Dot could recall being told to stay as quiet as possible, and on no account to answer the door. She also remembered sitting on the stairs with Bob and June, listening helplessly to their parents' rows about money. The trouble was, neither could cope with life, so there was no-one to steer things in the right direction. Dilys was showing signs of severe depression, while Howie was a kind but feckless man. He'd never truly enjoyed teaching, and a lavish lifestyle increasingly became his refuge.

Dot was 11 when the net finally closed in. Howie got a beating from one of the loan sharks, while another took most of the furniture. A final warning about the mortgage was issued by the bank, but as Howie ignored the letters, he was unaware. One day, Dot returned from school to find the house was being repossessed. Defeated, humiliated, they packed their bags to return to Gladys, who thankfully was willing to take them in.

But, although they were always grateful to Gladys, her generosity was sadly marred by her harsh attitude. She was furious with Howie, understandably – but also with her daughter, for not keeping him in check. She never let either of them forget how stupid they'd been in losing their home, or how much they were beholden to her. Howie buried his head even further in the sand, and to escape his mother-in-law's tongue-lashings, was out of the house most of the time. While Dilys suspected more casino trips, Gladys thought he was cheating, and was convinced she'd seen him in town one day, with another woman. She lost no opportunity in telling Dilys, who broke down and said she didn't want to hear it.

"Well, that's too bad," Gladys snapped. "I'll not have you saying I didn't warn you!" Each time Howie went out she'd say the same thing: "Ah, there he goes! Off to meet his paramour!"

This went on for a few years – during which time, Dilys fell into deeper despair. She'd spend whole days without getting out of bed, or weeping alone in the front parlour; until, one autumn night in 1949, she would finally end her life.

Howie, broken and guilt-ridden, now turned to drink; while Gladys, in her own grief, was even angrier than before.

"That's right!" she'd sneer. "Sit there snivelling. Never mind that this is all down to *you*!"

Whilst he normally avoided conflict, Howie was bolder in drink., retaliating cynically that Gladys, of course had *nothing* to do with anything, had she? Sniping, judging, belittling; maybe he *wasn't* the best husband, but she too had played her part. And so, it went on… the two of them stuck in the midst it all: 14-year-old

Dot, and 11-year-old June, who back then was extremely shy. To make matters worse, Bob, now 17, had left home to fulfil a lifelong dream of going to sea. Bob had looked out for his sisters from a young age. A sensitive lad, clever, resourceful, and wise beyond his years, Dot often said Kay was just like him.

Impressed by his father's tales of the navy, Bob joined up as soon as he could. This wasn't without much soul-searching, as he felt so guilty for leaving the girls. Eventually, Howie took him aside, telling him not to hold back, else he'd end up like himself, with a messed-up life and career he detested. Deep down, Dot knew her father was right (for all his faults, he was self-aware). Still, she couldn't quite forgive him for encouraging Bob to go. Their mother's death was easier to deal with when Bob was around – but now, although he wrote every week, they were lucky to see him twice a year.

As she left school and started work at Irwin's[xiii], the bad luck showed no signs of ending. During a robbery at the store, she was hit over the head and knocked out cold. She spent time in hospital with head injuries and was plagued by migraines for years to come. But worse than that was how it affected her nerves. Already vulnerable, it made her jittery and perpetually anxious – how Kay always knew her to be.

Dot's first love - a police officer named Sam Stonehill - was a cold, controlling man, whose behaviour bordered on emotional abuse. They were together for eight years, but Sam refused to "name the day". Weeks would pass without her hearing from him, then he'd turn up, demanding she drop everything. They all told her to ditch him; Gladys and Howie (for once in agreement); Bob, June, and her best friend, Irene Jenkins; but she stuck it out, thinking this was the best she could get.

It wasn't just the family who thought she deserved better. Ray Burgess lived a few doors away and had long had his eye on her.

"Look, Dottie," he'd say, "why don't you dump the Laughing Policeman, and come out with me?"

"No thanks, Ray," she'd reply, firmly. "And I've told you before. I'm happy with Sam."

But even without Sam, Dot would never have gone out with Ray. For a start, he was shorter than her, and she was already conscious of her height. The other problem was Gladys, who pitied Ray's mother for having a "tearaway" for a son. In fact, Ray was a decent chap, with a good job in engineering – but he rode a scooter and looked like Buddy Holly. Amy Burgess was as strait-laced as Gladys, and often moaned about her youngest with his "shocking" clothes and music. And his brothers were so sensible…

Of course, Gladys wasn't happy when, eventually, it was June who got together with Ray. After a few rebuffs from Dot, he picked himself up, moved on, went out with other girls – until he realised one day that Dot's younger sister was just as pretty and, although quiet, had a dry sense of humour. Before this, June had been so timid he hadn't noticed her. But lately, she'd begun to grow into herself; at least in part because of her job as an optician's receptionist, where she had no choice but to talk to the customers. Every so often, Ray – short-sighted since childhood – would come into the shop. He chatted her up a few times, before it clicked with him who she was.

Just as June and Ray got engaged, Sam ended things abruptly. Dot was devastated to learn he'd been cheating for years with a fellow police officer named Jessica Jervis. Again, she had no-one to turn to as it all fell apart; Bob, by now, had left the navy for a cargo superintendent job ashore, but he'd also married Viv McIlroy. Dot had no time for Viv, who she thought completely unsuited to her brother. Apart from being too young for him, she was loud and "common," as Gladys called her, "an upstart"; adding that "if her arse was encrusted in diamonds, she'd never be a lady." Dot had to smile; Gran was quite rude in her old age.

June's confidence had blossomed, and Dot, increasingly resented this. In what seemed like no time at all, June had gone from painfully shy teen to self-assured young woman, with plenty of friends and a lot to say; and now, as she and Ray were wrapped up in their wedding plans, it felt as though she didn't need her sister at all. Kay, who got on well with Auntie June, had always thought this unfair of her mum. Yet she couldn't completely blame her; everyone was moving on with their lives, while poor Dot was stuck at home with Gran.

Luckily, Dot still had a few friends left, despite Sam's best attempts to isolate her. She'd stayed close to Irene, who encouraged her to get out and about again, and not think of herself as "on the shelf". Irene's boyfriend George was Frank's best mate – they were both apprentices years ago, and had worked as plumbers together ever since. Perhaps, Irene suggested, they could go out as a foursome?

"Oh, I'm not sure," Dot said. "After everything with Sam…"

Irene sighed. "…you can't trust men?"

Dot nodded sadly. "Gran says they're just like children, and never to rely on them, and…oh, I don't know! Look at Dad… then Sam…I can't help thinking she might be right."

"And what about your Bob?"

"I know, Rene – but there's too few like him, more's the pity."

"Look, I'd be the same," Irene said. "But you can't keep letting Sam ruin your life. Frank's a decent bloke." She smiled. "They're not all like the Laughing Policeman, you know!"

It took a while – but Irene went on so much that Dot eventually gave in. If nothing else, it was a change from night after night with only Gladys for company. So, she went along, although still apprehensive - and not just for the fear of being let down. She would never admit this to Irene, but it did bother her that Frank was from such a poor area ("I know," she said to Kay, years later, "I was a snob, wasn't I?"). And on top of that, a Catholic; not that it mattered to Dot, but it certainly would to Gladys… and if she disapproved of Ray (her friend's son!), she was sure to disapprove of Frank! But still - she could at least go and meet him; and if she wasn't keen, then no harm done.

As it turned out, Frank was just as Irene had described him. Maybe he didn't rock her world, but there'd been more than enough drama in her life thus far; and a peaceful, if uneventful existence, was more than good enough for her. Surprisingly, Gladys didn't protest. Perhaps she'd softened with age, or hadn't taken it in (at nearly 80, she was increasingly frail and becoming forgetful); but when Dot was upfront with her about Frank's background and religion, she never passed comment.

At heart, the Cooneys weren't so different to the Edwards' and Lloyds; they had the same work ethic, and belief that, however much or little you had, good manners cost nothing. The tenement in Burlington Street was neat and spotless – just like her Gran's, Dot thought, but in miniature. Like Dot, Frank had lost his mother at a young age, and spent many years living with his grandmother. His parents, Joe and Mary-Ann, struggled to raise their family during the depression; Joe, a casual dock labourer, found it hard to get work - while Mary-Ann sold fruit and veg, as well as cleaning jobs to keep their heads above water. Never very well (she'd had rheumatic fever as a child), all this would take its toll, and it didn't help that they lived in damp, crumbling court housing. She died suddenly of a stroke when Frank was 5, in 1936.

Her mother, Nancy (known simply as "Nin") had gained more space since her youngest son had left to get married, so she brought them to live at her new flat on Burlington Street (luxurious, Kay guessed, after the courts). Frank and Joe had been there ever since; apart from when Frank and his sister, Teresa, were evacuated to a farm in Wales. They were sadly ill-treated and would soon run away to return to Nin.

By the time he met Dot, Frank seemed the archetypal confirmed bachelor. At 37, still living with Joe and Nin, he was content with work and a few close friends. He went for a pint with his father or George; but otherwise, was happy with his own company. Nin, at 81, was a little older than Gladys, but spritely for her age. Tiny, with snow white hair, she wore a shawl, like many of the older residents, and had a happy, friendly manner; while Joe, like his son, was steady and quiet. Dot felt at ease straightaway – and a little ashamed for imagining the worst.

Teresa was pleasantly surprised when her stoic, reserved brother announced he was engaged. Two years younger than Frank, and much more gregarious, she'd been married for ten years to a Glaswegian named Tommy Devine – a jolly man who lived life to the full. Teresa had moved to Glasgow after her marriage, where they lived with their children, Moira and Stevie. Kay always had fond memories of their visits.

Dot and Frank were married in January 1970 – eighteen months after June and Ray, who had since moved down south with Ray's job. Howie, meanwhile, had got a flat in Wavertree, close to Bob and Viv. After the wedding, Frank moved into the house in Dingle, where Dot continued to care for Gladys. Kay was born there in 1971 - then Andy, the following year.

Gladys died the month before Andy's birth. Most of her savings went to her younger daughter, Olive; the rest were split between Bob and June, while the house went to Dot – as a thank-you for looking after her these past few years. Frank was making good money and had managed to save a good bit while living with

Nin – so, when they came to sell the house, they were able to buy the new one outright, despite it being in a sought-after district like Mossley Hill.

This all should have marked the end of Dot's troubles, but it sadly wasn't to be. In 1976, Howie (now 64 and still a heavy drinker) had been unwell for some time; but dealt with it, as ever, by pretending nothing was wrong. He ignored all suggestions of going to the doctor until, close to his retirement, he collapsed in class one morning. He was rushed to hospital where he was diagnosed with liver disease, too advanced for treatment, and was dead within months. Bob, who was close to his father, became severely depressed - which, in turn, put pressure on his marriage. He ended his life in May 1977, shortly after separating from Viv. Dot would never completely recover from the shock; and now, after everything, to lose her son....

Of course, going off to Uni was now out of the question for Kay. She couldn't think of leaving Dot – and besides, she didn't get the 3 Bs needed for Leeds. The offers through Clearing were all too far away; eventually, she was accepted on a course at John Moores (Liverpool Poly as was) but as it was now well into the first semester, she'd have to delay till next year. She decided to get some work-experience in the meantime; and when temporary post as a filing clerk came up, it seemed ideal.

When the permanent job was offered, she took it without hesitation, ringing the Poly to say she didn't need the place, after all. By now, she realised she no longer wanted to study or write.

She hadn't put pen to paper since Andy died. At first, she thought this might pass, but she'd tried many times, and nothing would come. Besides, she'd settled in so well at the office. She hit it off with Jen and Lisa straightaway, and the three were soon out in town most weekends – something she had never imagined she'd enjoy so much. Just months after being made permanent, she got the promotion. It was all going as well as she could hope for. Why fix what wasn't broken?

Chapter Seven

She was 22 when she met Phil. He and his brother Pete were working next door at the time, building Ron and Joan's conservatory. The Banks' had always used a local company, Osborne Constructions; but the owner, Ted Osborne, was 70 now, and winding things down. He'd given them a list of builders, including the Wainwrights – brothers from St. Helens, who were "a bit rough around the edges", he said, but first rate at what they did.

The Banks' got in touch with a few from Ted's list, but in the end decided on the Wainwrights. Ron had been impressed with them – they charged reasonable rates and seemed to know what they were talking about. Pete was a joiner, and Phil (or PJ, as he called himself) a bricklayer. But, like Ted, both seemed to be able to turn their hands to most things. Joan went along with her husband's choice, but wasn't happy, as she confided to Dot over the garden fence.

"Ron thinks he knows best," she grumbled, "but I think they look like cowboys. Ted was right about them being rough – I'm surprised he recommended them, really."

When they arrived to start the job, Dot took an instant dislike to them, having already made up her mind after her chat with Joan.

"Well, I can see what Joan means. They look shifty, to me…"

Frank rolled his eyes. "Yeah — but Joan says 'jump', you say 'how high?'…"

"Oh, *shut* up, Frank!"

Kay and Frank exchanged glance. They'd both seen Dot upset by Joan so many times over the years, yet Dot remained friendly with her, and influenced by everything she said. But much as Kay disliked "Joan-next-door", she couldn't help but agree that the brothers *were* a bit on the rough side. They clearly didn't get along, and could often be heard shouting, arguing, and swearing at each other in their broad Lancashire accents. The angrier they were, the thicker their accents seemed to be - occasionally slipping into "old" Lancashire, with words like "thee" and "thy". It was a while before Kay worked out which was which - when they weren't hurling insults, they only ever called each other "Our Kid". They looked and behaved nothing like each other; you'd never have guessed they were brothers, let alone twins.

One was short and stocky, and seemed abnormally muscular, like a body-builder — clean shaven with closely cropped hair, almost a skinhead. He chain-smoked, even as he worked, and was sullen in manner; scowled a lot, spoke little, except to admonish the young apprentices, who he called "a pair of dopes". His brother, by contrast, was over six feet tall — also powerfully built, but more naturally so. His dark hair was long and wavy, and he sported a thick, bushy beard; obviously into metal, with his studded belts and wrist bands, skull-and-cross earrings, and plentiful tattoos. He seemed as jovial as his brother was surly and appeared to have a good rapport with the two young lads. His brother seemed to resent their camaraderie, and would ignore them, fuming in silence.

"You're too soft with 'em," Kay once overhead him saying. "I'd sack 'em, if it were just up to me!"

"Fuck's sake, our Kid, cut 'em some slack! We all had for't start somewhere – even you!"

The two lads, Lee and Darren, *were* a bit daft, it had to be said – loud and silly, constantly playing the fool. But in fairness, they were very young, 16, maybe 17 at most. The bearded one kept them in line – although he had a laugh with them, they seemed to know when they were going too far. They had scant respect for his brother, resenting his harsh, over-bearing attitude, putting up two fingers behind his back, and calling him "mard-arse" and "smile-awhile". One Saturday, as Kay sat reading outside, the four of them ate fish and chips in the Banks' back garden (Ron and Joan were out, of course – Joan would never have stood for *that*!).

"They laughed at us in 'chippy," Darren grumbled, "'cos we asked for fish 'n' split. Said they'd never heard of it."

"Well," (the bearded brother's voice), "they wouldn't round here, you muppet!"

(A "split", as Kay would learn, was St. Helens-speak for chips and peas).

"They don't call it a split? Bloody stupid, that!"

"Yeah," Lee chimed in, "Scousers are weird!"

Then Darren launched into a ridiculous impersonation of a scouse accent (it sounded more like Brummie!) – egged on by Lee who roared with laughter.

"Eh! What's a split, laaaa? …"

"Pack it in now, lads."

"Yeah - I'll 'split' you in a minute!"

"Oh, crack a smile, our Kid! But just watch it, lads. Or 'neighbours might hear and have a pop at you."

"No chance!" Darren scoffed. "Have you seen 'em? They're ancient! 'Cept for that girl next door, who never lets on…"

"Speak for yourselves – she lets on to *me*. She's a nice girl."

"Yeah, but you *would* say that, PJ, 'cos you bloody fancy her!"

"No way!" Lee howled. "She's a *minger*!"

"Now, I'm warning you, lads, pack it in! I'll not tell you again!"

"See?" Darren crowed. "You *do* like her! I *knew* it!"

Kay got up furiously and went to the fence.

"Just so you know, I can hear every word. And you're no oil painting yourself, by the way!"

"Shit!" Darren said, while Lee stared at the floor in shame. The short, stocky brother muttered under his breath, and the bearded one – PJ – looked mortified.

"I'm so sorry, love. We were just takin' 'mick, but it got out of hand…" He glared at Lee. "Well? What d'you say?"

"Sorry," Lee mumbled. "I were just windin' him up…"

Kay nodded curtly. "Fair enough."

"Thanks, love," PJ said. "They're good lads, really – just need for t' grow up a bit." Then he grinned; and she couldn't help but notice he had lovely, warm brown eyes – and perhaps the nicest smile she'd ever seen.

"I'll have to go in," she said quickly.

"Aye, love," he winked, "see you later."

"Not if I can help it," she thought; and avoided walking past them for the whole of the next week, leaving earlier for work, and staying later than usual to make sure they'd gone. She knew they'd be there the following Saturday, of course, and so, despite the warm weather, she stayed indoors.

She felt stupid and annoyed at herself for being upset by those daft lads; as hard as she tried to put bad memories to bed, you could never completely wipe them out. But it wasn't just that; it was how they'd teased their boss about her. Was he in on the joke? He might have told them off in front of her – but, in private, maybe the four of them laughed about the "minger" …But then, the way he'd looked at her…All she knew was that she didn't feel comfortable – and was angry at the fact she found him attractive, despite herself.

He'd never be her type. She didn't like beards, couldn't stand metal, and hated Neanderthals like *him*. He'd be a sexist pig, no doubt; swore like a trooper; smoked like a chimney – and yet…There were those eyes; and *that* smile…. Which he obviously used, she thought, to draw the women in! Well, it wasn't going to work with *her* – and if she didn't walk past, she wouldn't give him the chance to try.

The doorbell rang. As she answered it, she was mortified – and secretly pleased – to see him stood there.

"Sorry, love – mind if I use your bathroom?"

She looked at him suspiciously. Was this a wind-up? Had his stupid mates put him up to it?

"Can you not use Joan's?"

"Can't get in – she's been in there bloody ages. Must be having 'crap of her life!"

Kay couldn't help but smile at the thought of this.

"Look, I'm not being funny, love, but can I come in? I'm bloody desperate!"

She looked at the time – Dot would be back soon from the shops and wouldn't be happy… "Go on – but be quick…."

He rushed up the stairs, then she could hear him in the bathroom – it sounded like a waterfall, followed by a herd of baby elephants as he clumped noisily around before the toilet flushed and he came back down.

"Aw, thanks – you're a life-saver, you."

"You're welcome," she said coolly.

And there it was again – the Smile. "Not seen much of you this week – if I didn't know better, I'd think you was avoiding us! You're not – are you?"

She didn't reply.

"Look, love," he said, "all that, last week – they didn't mean owt. Just showing off. Said it more for t' get a rise out of me, than owt else."

"I know. As I said – it's ok."

Then, for a moment, an awkward silence.

"So," he asked, "got much planned for 'weekend?"

"Oh, you know – this and that."

"You out tonight, then?"

"Not sure, yet. Are you?"

"Maybe – see how 'mood takes me." He winked. "Any-rode – thanks again, love. See you."

"Bye, then," she said, as she shut the door, and hated herself for how good she felt.

In an hour or so, he was back. "Would you believe it – I *still* can't get in 'bathroom!"

"Oh, come *on*!" But she could feel herself smirking. "You're pushing your luck now, mate."

"Got you laughing though, eh, love? Come out with me tonight – and I promise I'll stop mithering."

"And what if I've got other plans?" she teased. "Do you expect me to drop them, just for *you*?"

"'Course not – but you said you didn't, when I asked before…"

"I said I didn't know – and as it turns out, I haven't. But that's not the point – I *might* have done."

"But if you've not – then what d'you reckon?"

"Well – I suppose just the once can't hurt."

He grinned. "Nice one."

"I mean it, though – it really is just once – and don't even *think* about mithering again."

"Scout's honour."

Then she heard Dot (now back from shopping) from the living room. "Katie? Is someone there?"

She sighed. "Best get back in."

"I'll knock at 7," he said.

She shut the door. "It's okay, Mum. They've gone now."

Chapter Eight

She got changed – kept things casual, but not too scruffy, either. No dark colours – she wanted to look the least like a rock chick as possible. She wore her hair up, as she often did back then, but had pulled it into a much tighter, more severe bun than normal. With it down, she looked soft, feminine, receptive; everything she didn't want to be with this man, because – as she kept reminding herself – he *wasn't* her type …

Still, as the time drew near, she felt herself getting nervous. The thought crossed her mind that he might not turn up – and that he'd be in the pub with his two young pals, laughing about how she fell for it. Come on, she rebuked herself – that was years ago, and besides, it was *school.* Just three years since she'd left, but already it seemed a lifetime. And Gary Larkin was just a kid…. Trouble was, though, some men never grew up…. and how humiliating to sit there, watching the clock, waiting like a fool. She'd give it ten minutes. Fifteen at most…

Then, just before 7, the doorbell. She quickly grabbed her jacket – not that she wanted to appear over-eager; more because her mother would have less chance to quiz her…

"I'm off out," she called. "I'll see you later."

"Hang on, Katie - you never *said* you were going out."

"It was all a bit last minute."

"So, who…?"

"Look, Mum, I'm in a hurry…"

"But…"

"For God's sake, Dot," Frank snapped. "Stop giving her the bloody third degree! She's not a kid."

No doubt, Dot would have had something to say to that, but Kay didn't wait any longer to hear it. She opened the door and, to her horror, saw a Harley parked outside – and PJ (she still, at this point, didn't know his full name) wearing leathers and a crash helmet, and handing one to her.

"Put this on, love," he said, "and we'll get going."

"On *that*? No chance."

"You'll be okay – I'm careful. Been riding for years."

"If I'd known, I'd never have said I'd go."

He sighed. "I'm sorry, love. But honestly, you'll be safe. I know what I'm doing."

She could see the curtains twitching, and her mother's face at the window, aghast at the sight of the bike – and who she was with. What would be worse? she asked herself. She could go on the bike or stay here and debate it, giving Dot time to come outside and make a holy show of her. It was no contest. If she went, there was sure to be a row tomorrow, but that was nothing new. Dot always seemed upset at her nights with Jen and Lisa. Why did they have to go *out*? she'd say. Couldn't they come to the house instead? She could make sandwiches….

It was never easy, especially after Andy. Kay did her best to protect her from worry – whilst still, somehow, balancing this with a life of her own. She was lucky that the girls understood – making sure they got a cab together, and that they left not too long after midnight (when the night was just beginning for most!). Kay felt awful at first, but Jen told her not to be silly; what were friends for? None of this ever seemed enough to reassure Dot - and if Frank hadn't backed her up, she might never have gone at all.

Given the choice, Kay would prefer to argue later, in private, than out here on the doorstep, in front of this man (who, despite not being her type, she rather liked, anyway).

"Okay – I'll give it a go."

"Nice one!"

She put the helmet on and sat behind him as he started the bike. Just hold on, he instructed – and as they got going, she looked back briefly to see Dot, hand on hip, at the front door; her hunch had been right. They turned into Queens Drive, heading off towards Sefton Park - and she thought, briefly, of her trips there with Andy. They rode past the park, through Aigburth Vale and onto Jericho Lane, which led them to the waterfront and Otterspool Prom - another park childhood haunt.

"So," he asked, "what did you think?"

She had to admit that, despite her fears, she'd enjoyed the ride far more than expected. He'd taken care and – as promised –

did indeed know what he was doing; and although she'd felt nervous, she found it exhilarating. He looked pleased.

"I knew you'd be fine. Come on – let's go in."

The pub was part of a chain, serving standard, but decent, bar food. She had a good look at the menu, but he didn't bother; said he knew what he wanted. In the end she went for steak and chips with a glass of red – which he insisted was his treat.

"No, honestly," she said, feeling uncomfortable – she'd never liked the idea of feeling beholden to anyone; and if she let him, what might he want in return? He seemed to read her mind.

"Look, love - I don't expect owt, you know."

"I know…I'm just independent. It's how I am."

"Oh aye?" he chuckled. "Women's libber?"

"Yes," she replied briskly. "Is that a problem?"

"'Course not. I'm all for it. But, if I ask, I pay. That's how *I* am."

She couldn't help but smile. "Alright - but just to keep you happy! And I'm getting dessert."

The service was swift, and the steaks arrived not long after. As they ate, they found out more about each other. He lived with Pete and his wife Jackie, he said, along with their twin sons, Craig and Carl. He and Pete were also twins; it ran in the family. They'd never known their father; and their Mum, Pauline, was just 16 when they were born in the St Helens mining village of Sutton Manor. Their grandad and uncles were all colliers, the last in a long line. They'd lived with their grandparents until, when they were 8, Pauline had a huge falling-out with her mother, and the three of them moved to a council flat. They were there until they were 12, and it wasn't the best of times.

Their mother drank and neglected them. The flat was in a tough neighbourhood; the lads struggled to fit in and were bullied as newcomers – which wasn't helped by their often-unkempt appearance (there was seldom enough money for food, let alone new clothes). After three years, Pauline dumped them back with their grandparents; she couldn't cope anymore and had found a new man who didn't want to be saddled with kids. She'd done them a favour, really, he said – they were happier with their nan and grandad than they ever were with *her*.

They stayed with them for many years. Pete married Jackie when he was 19; she was 17, and already pregnant with the twins. They all lived in their grandparents' tiny house off Jubits Lane in Sutton Manor – five adults and the two "little 'uns", as he called his nephews. Nan died in 1988, then Grandad, months later. By this time, the brothers had set up business. Pete bought the house they lived in now, which was in a better-off part of Sutton, on a modern housing estate near Sherdley Park – another place Kay remembered from childhood, when they'd been to the St. Helens Show.

PJ had suggested getting his own place, but Pete said there was no point – they were fine as they were, so why change things? So, despite not getting on, they'd kept living together, because they always had. It was just easier. No wonder they were tough,

Kay thought – their lives had been so hard, and she really felt for them. And it couldn't be easy now, the way they argued...

"Must be difficult," she said. "Living and working together."

Again, he seemed to know what she was thinking. "Well – you'll have heard us having a pop at each other. It's not great – but then, when we're home, it's Jackie and 'lads who get it in 'neck. Don't get me wrong – I love him because he's our Kid, but I could fuckin' swing for him, at times. If we wasn't brothers, we'd never be mates."

"Sounds a bit like my mum and Auntie June. Always at odds over something – and I'm afraid to say, it's usually Mum who starts it."

"I noticed she were giving me daggers before. Will she have a go at you later? For coming out with me, I mean?"

"Most likely."

"Sorry, love – I didn't mean for t' cause any hassle."

"No, don't worry. She gets anxious about anything happening to me, that's all, and she's probably panicked at seeing the bike. But Dad's great – he'll make her see sense."

"That's good – I wouldn't want you getting grief 'cos of me."

The waitress cleared the table, and they got desserts – which he bought, despite her protests.

"Okay then," she said, rolling her eyes. "But I'm paying next time..."

"Hang on – I thought there weren't gonna be a next time?"

"Nothing wrong with keeping an open mind," she smiled, as the coffees arrived. "I've got to ask, though. Was that true what you said about Joan, taking all that time to have a crap?"

"First time, yeah. Second time – no," he smirked. "I were just pushing my luck, as you said. Had to think of *some* excuse to come back and ask you out…"

"Of course, if I liked Joan, I'd think you were *just* a bit naughty, saying something like that. But, as I can't stand the woman, I think it's hilarious!"

"Not being funny, but she looks at us like something she trod in."

"That's Joan for you. Mum likes to think she's a friend, but the times she's had her in tears…Always moaning behind her back and passing comment about my brother having Down's – although in fairness, she wasn't the only one."

"She puts me in mind of that Mrs. Bucket^{xiv}!"

"Dad says the same! And Ron's just like Richard. Anything for a quiet life. She likes to make out it's the other way around, though. 'Ron always thinks he knows best,' she says to Mum."

"And your mum still speaks to her?"

"I know! I can't get my head around it!"

"Didn't know you had a brother. I've not seen him about?"

"He passed away - four years ago, now."

"Shit – it's bloody rough, is that."

She sighed. "It's okay. I've learnt to live with it. But it was awful for Mum – she'd cared for Andy all his life, and she was just so lost without him. Still is, really…I guess it's why she worries so much. It was a lot worse for her than for me."

"Hard for you too, though, love. Bloody hell! Don't get me wrong, our Kid does my head in, but I'd be gutted if owt happened to him."

"I won't lie, it wasn't easy. But I needed to be there for Mum - so I had to just try and get on with it."

They finished their coffee.

"Thanks," she said, "that was lovely. And listen - if I seemed a bit off when you first knocked – well, I'm sorry. It just takes me a while to be sure of someone."

"Don't be so daft, love. After all, you didn't know me from Adam. Wouldn't blame you if you'd sent me packing! But I'm glad you didn't."

She smiled. "So am I."

They took a stroll along the Prom before heading back. The evening was starting to draw in, and the sunset gave some stunning views across the river to Wirral.

"I go over for a ride, every so often," he said, "and sometimes to Wales. We should go one day, if you're up for it."

"I might just take you up on that."

They walked further on. After a bit of cajoling, she found out "PJ" stood for Philip John (his middle name was for his grandad, Jack). Could she call him "Philip" instead? she asked – she liked it better.

"Call me what you want, love," he grinned, "as long as you come out again."

"Well," she said mischievously, "you might live to regret saying that – Shit Face!"

"Walked into that, didn't I?" he laughed. "You're a bloody case, you!"

"A women's libber, and a bloody case – are you sure you can handle it?"

"I'll cope," he said, before giving her a kiss that took her breath away.

It was hard and passionate, tender and gentle, all at once. She'd never been kissed by anyone with a beard before (after all, she didn't *like* men with beards – or so she thought). She found she was enjoying it; she'd expected it to be rough and coarse, but instead it was beautifully soft, almost luxurious.

The feeling she had was one of safety, yet excitement; that, for once, nothing would go wrong – and that she was okay, just as she was.

Chapter Nine

This feeling lasted – and, for all his rough-hewn ways, he was the perfect gent; kind, considerate and fiercely protective. The biggest challenge back then was getting past the criticism, the judgemental looks, the comments that it would never work, because they were so *different* .... Although she got on well with most of her workmates, there were the odd few who mistook her reserve for coldness – and she knew full well that they made snide remarks when he picked her up from work on the bike.

"I must say," Maria Troughton remarked, "Phil's not at *all* what I expected."

Annoying as they were, Maria's comments about Phil were no surprise. Not so well-liked as she chose to believe, Maria irritated many (especially Lisa) with her condescending manner. Jen, who'd worked with her in Accounts, had tried to be tolerant – but soon backed off (to Kay and Lisa's relief) when she tried to gate-crash their nights out. Less expected, and more upsetting, was Lisa's reaction. Ironic that she should, for once, agree with Maria - albeit for very different reasons.

It was no secret that Lisa had little time for men – with some justification. Her dead-beat ex, Barry, had dumped her just before she had their daughter and had never contributed a penny. But it wasn't just Barry; Lisa's own father was a waste of space who'd cleared off when she was a baby. Perhaps some *were* different, she said – but she was sick of trying to find them.

"You do know what they're like?" she asked, on learning that Phil was a biker. "I mean, how sexist they are?"

"I know they get a bad name," Kay said – after all, hadn't she had doubts of her own? "But I can only take as I find. He's got a good group of mates, and yes, I suppose they *are* a bit wild – but they're some of the kindest people I know."

Lisa softened. "Well, I hope you're right. I don't want you to get hurt."

It took a few months, but Lisa did eventually come around – which was just as well, as Kay had enough on her plate with Dot. When she'd got home after that first date, she'd half-expected her mum to still be in the doorway, hands on hips, waiting for her. But the house was in darkness, and her parents were obviously in bed.

Next morning, it was clear they'd fallen out. Dot made breakfast without speaking to either of them – her face the way it had been last night on the step. She clattered and banged the dishes around; and the more she did it, the more pointedly Frank ignored her. He smiled when Kay joined him at the table.

"Morning. Did you have a good night?"

"Morning, Dad. Yeah – we just had a meal at the Otterspool. Nothing wild."

"He seems a decent fella," Frank said – as Dot gave him a look to kill. "Had a few chats with him when I've gone past. Not sure about his brother, though; I've let on a couple of times, and he's just blanked me." He finished his tea. "Anyway – I'm off for me walk."

"See you in a bit, Dad," Kay said; Dot never answered.

After he'd left, she didn't say a word to Kay – just carried on cooking in resentful silence, before putting in front of her a huge Full-English.

"Thanks, Mum – but you didn't have to go to any trouble. I could have just done myself some toast."

"Well, you might have said something!" Dot snapped.

"You didn't ask, though – you did it before I had a chance. And I'm not saying I don't want it – it looks lovely – I only meant, to save you some time."

Again, Dot didn't reply – just gave her a reproachful look as she made a pot of tea. Kay sighed. "Look, Mum, I can see you're not happy. And it doesn't take a genius to guess why."

"Well," Dot said bitterly, "don't worry about what *I* think. As your dad said – it's none of *my* business…"

"Come on - I'm sure he didn't mean it like that."

"Didn't he."

"You know Dad – he's a plain speaker. He probably just meant…" – that I'm old enough to make my own choices, she was going to say; but decided it best not to go there. "The thing is, Mum, I'd feel much happier if I had your blessing."

"Why does it matter? You'll just do what *you* want, anyway."

"And is that so awful? It *is* my life," she pointed out, gently, "when all's said and done."

"Oh, as if I'd forget *that* – when Dad, and Auntie June, and everyone else keeps reminding me! You know, when we lived with Gran, she said that if you live under someone's roof, you should abide by their rules. But you're not allowed to say that these days."

"Times have changed, Mum."

"Yes; more's the pity."

"Would you like me to get a place of my own, then?"

"Of course not!" Dot looked crestfallen. "You young ones have this obsession with going your own way…And you've got a nice home here, so I don't know why!"

"Because of what you said – about your house rules." She paused. "And because it's what people do."

"So you can do as you please, you mean!"

"Look," Kay said, as patiently as she could. "I understand, more than you think. It's still so hard, after Andy – and I know you'll be terrified about the bike. But we're getting nowhere with this. I really think we should wait till things have calmed down."

"Well," Dot sniffed, "you asked why I wasn't happy."

"I know. I thought we could sort things out – but it's not the right time."

"It'll *never* be the right time. He's not for you, Katie!"

"You don't know him."

"And you do? You've only been out with him once!"

"Yes, and I'm keeping an open mind – but you've never even *spoken* to him!"

"I don't need to. I can see what type he is."

"Oh, Mum. You've got a short memory. You were really hurt when the neighbours said things like that about Dad."

"But that's different – your father's nothing like *him*! All those tattoos!" She shuddered. "Anyway - you'll do as you like, as always. But don't come to *me* to pick up the pieces when it all goes wrong!"

"Oh, no worries," Kay said cynically – angry at herself for rising to it. "It's the last thing I'd do."

Chapter Ten

Eventually, the comments at work would die off; while Lisa admitted she'd got Phil all wrong and apologised for being so negative. "I thought he'd be a real hard-case," she said, "but he's as soft as anything underneath, isn't he? I'm sorry, Kay – I didn't mean to think the worst."

For Dot, though, it would be a long time – years into their marriage, in fact – before she accepted Phil. One of the many things she disapproved of was that, at 27, he was five years older than Kay – despite there being the exact same age-gap between herself and Frank. When Kay pointed this out, she replied – like she had that Sunday, over breakfast – that it was just *different*.

Then there was the bike – for obvious reasons – and, of course, the tattoos. No-one could deny that he had many; and combined with the wild hair and beard, leathers and studs, it *did* give the impression of the stereotyped "hard-core" biker. His friends looked just the same; but, as Kay had said to Lisa, a kinder, gentler group would be difficult to find. She tried explaining to Dot that Phil had been bullied in his younger days (as had most of his pals) and looking tough was just a way to protect himself. All to no avail.

It was no surprise to Phil that Dot wasn't his number-one fan – he'd picked up on it that night when she'd been at the window, and when he came to the house, her manner was cold and clipped. When he asked why, Kay was as up-front as she could be, without hurting his feelings. Her mum didn't understand about bikers, or Metal, she said; she lived in the past, expecting lads today to dress in suits, like the young men of her youth.

For Kay's sake, and to keep the peace, Phil toned things down a bit when he visited; although he'd never wear a suit (his wedding day was the exception), he did put on a shirt, left off the jewellery, and tied his hair back as neatly as he could. But Dot's manner remained frosty. It made no difference, because – however much he smartened up - he still had the bike, and "those dreadful tattoos." Eventually, they'd admit defeat and come to accept that Dot's mind wasn't for changing – and, hard as it was, they'd to have to accept that.

When it came to Phil's friends and family, Kay found herself accepted straight away – except by Pete, who showed the same resentment as Dot did towards Phil, never speaking to her at all. As Phil pointed out, though, Pete was the same with everyone; so, it was impossible to tell if it was actual dislike, or just indifference. While Kay completely understood that their upbringing (or at least, the part of it with Linda) had toughened them up, there were different ways to show toughness – and Pete's way had very little warmth or softness behind it. Hard as nails, inside and out – or so it would seem; it wasn't always so, as Kay would discover. Like herself, the brothers were no strangers to being bullied – in fact, they'd gone through much of their childhood feeling like outcasts.

Their mother's neglect had been pretty bad; by Phil's admission, the two of them had been filthy. As they got a bit older, they tried to keep clean and look after themselves as best they could, but this wasn't easy. Pauline often didn't buy basics like soap, and because the bills weren't paid, there was frequently no electricity – or hot water. There was little they could do about the clothes she got them, which were poor quality, tatty and ill-fitting. They were laughed at mercilessly – often by teachers, as well as other kids. Phil, being the bigger and "gobbier" of the two, stood up for himself and his brother, which earned him the reputation of a trouble-maker – a "wrong 'un", as he called it. He gave as good as he got, including with the staff.

On one occasion, there was an altercation with the woodwork teacher, Richard Toale. "You're a gobshite, Wainwright," he said with a smirk – pleased at the fact it rhymed. "Or, should I say, Wain-shite!" It soon caught on amongst the kids – and the worse it got, the harder Phil fought back. Pete, on the other hand, was small and, in those days, very timid – and for this reason, suffered much more. To make matters worse, their diet was appalling; Pauline never cooked, and they pretty much lived on chip-barms or "splits". Because of his short stature, Pete piled the weight on, which of course was more ammunition for the bullies. It made Kay think of Roland from "Grange Hill[xv]"– although Pete at least had his brother.

They were still in Juniors when they'd moved with Pauline to the flat. The ridicule they'd got at their new primary school was bad enough; their only real friend there was a shy and sheltered boy named Danny Cooper, a fellow newbie and outsider who was close with them for a while, until they outwore their welcome with his mum. But it was nothing compared with high school – and Toale wasn't the only teacher to make their lives hell. Similarly looked down upon were two lads from a local children's home. One was Philip Robinson, the other Colin Blackwell (whose older brother, Ed, had recently been expelled). They soon palled up with Phil and Pete – perhaps the one good thing to come from those dark days, as they became (for Phil, at least) lifelong friends; and despite hating school so much, they had some laughs together. To avoid confusion, Phil started using "PJ" – although the other Philip usually went by "Robbo".

Life improved for Phil and Pete when they returned to their grandparents; but, although now well-fed, cared-for and *clean*, the cruel nicknames persisted. The lads, along with their two pals, spent more and more time bunking off and hanging out with Ed and other kids from the home – who were mostly metalheads, although a couple of punks were also in the mix. It was at this point, Phil said, that he really started getting into music, and dressing as he did now. It was a way of sticking two fingers up at those who mocked him. They called him scruffy, so he was scruffier; laughed at his messy hair, so he grew it long and more unruly. But, while Phil loved to rebel, Pete – as it turned out – wanted nothing more than to conform. He only hung out with their mates from the home because there was no-one else; secretly despising them and admiring the bullies.

When they were 15, Phil had another set-to with Toale. This time, it ended up with Toale hitting him across the head, while Phil responded by punching him in the face. Toale went ballistic, telling him he'd be out the door – as if *that* was a punishment, Phil laughed; did they think he *wanted* to be in that shithole? And he saved them the bother of expelling him, by never setting foot in the place again.

Pete now found himself alone, and at the mercy of the bullies. Col and Robbo bunked off nearly all the time – not that Pete cared about them, anyway – but without Phil to back him up, things quickly got much worse, as taunts gave way to physical violence. The teachers said it served him right - perhaps he'd finally start to look after himself, instead of leaning on his brother; their grandparents said the same, in a kinder way.

Pete began to spend every spare minute in the gym. During the Easter holidays, he took crash lessons in boxing. This wasn't long before he'd leave school, but he'd planned to enrol in a carpentry course, and knew some of the bullies would also be going – and if he didn't act now, things would never change. The more he worked out, the fat turned to muscle; and as he got physically harder, his attitude toughened up too. Before long, Pete was accepted by lads who'd given him a bad time; and as they all moved over from school to Tech, life finally began to look up. Kay had to give him credit. Whatever his failings, at least he'd had the guts to turn things around.

Sadly, as Pete gained in confidence and stood up to his tormentors, he became more like them – which, as Kay saw it, was the huge difference between him and Phil. Perhaps there was much truth in the old cliché – that what didn't kill you made you stronger – but the brothers used their strength in completely opposing ways. For Phil and his mates, it was about justice; they'd all had the rough end of the stick, at one time or another, and wouldn't see anyone go through the same. For Pete, on the other hand, it meant belittling others – including (much to Kay's anger) his own sons.

She had an idea that Pete took something to build up physical strength – steroids, or maybe testosterone. From the sound of it, his surliness was nothing new; and even in his timid younger days, he'd always had that scowl. Their Nan often chided him for it, Phil remembered: "Straighten your face, our Peter," she'd say; "or 'wind'll change, and you'll stop like that." Clearly, the wind *had* changed, as Kay couldn't think of a single time she'd seen Pete smile.

And yet, much as she couldn't take to him, she felt sorry for the boy that Pete had once been. Maybe he hadn't been likeable – but really, could anyone blame him for being sullen? Would anyone in that situation *truly* feel like smiling? For this reason, as well as for Phil's sake, Kay tried her best with Pete. The one thing they had in common was their taste in music – Pete mainly listened to Ska and reggae, which she loved and had grown up with. She made a real effort to engage with him, but the most response she got was a grunt if anything at all. And somehow, she felt just like little Janet from "Grange Hill", in her fruitless attempts to befriend Ro-*land*.

She got on well enough with Jackie and Michelle, and took instantly to Craig and Carl, who were thankfully nothing like their father in personality, despite being the image of him. Carl was a livewire, while Craig was sensitive and easily hurt by Pete's cutting remarks. Phil constantly had words with him about how he spoke to his sons. He thought the world of his nephews, who adored him – which caused considerable conflict, as Pete was jealous and would watch resentfully as the boys did play-wrestling and rugby tackles with their uncle.

She sometimes joined them for their Friday "chippie night". They had beer with their fish and chips; and in drink, Pete changed from sullen and brusque to downright nasty. He'd turn on them, one by one – Phil, Jackie, Michelle, then Craig and Carl. Kay would wonder when her turn would be, but he said nothing to her – instead just giving her a filthy glare when he thought she wasn't looking. If she could, she tried to avoid going when they were drinking. Hard work though he was, she preferred Pete silent and morose to drunk and belligerent.

As for Phil's friends, she was welcomed into the fold straight away – just as Phil and Pete had been, all those years ago. Most, but not all, had been at the children's home, although friends of friends had joined the group over the years. Some had bikes, and a couple were in bikers' clubs, but Phil never was – too many rules, and he preferred to do his own thing. They were a wild bunch; a merry, warm-hearted band of rebels and misfits, fiercely loyal to one another, who'd never "fitted in" and never wanted to. Kay was treated as one of their extended family. Anything went; if you respected them and let them be, they'd accept you without question. Kay dearly wished she'd had friends like this at school and was glad for Phil that they were in his life and had been there for him when things were so hard.

Chapter Eleven

As time went on, the one thing they both wished for was more privacy. Being round at each other's houses wasn't ideal, and it would be a few months before things got intimate. Apart from anything else, Kay was apprehensive. She had little experience (the nearest she'd got to a serious boyfriend was Simon Shaw from Human Resources, which fizzled out after a few dates), and dreaded her first time; but Phil was patient and gentle and made it as good for her as she could have hoped.

Christmas came and went and was not the best as they'd spent it apart. They both knew what the atmosphere would be like if he came to hers; it wouldn't be much better at his, as Pete was bound to be drinking. A few months back, they'd managed to get some time to themselves when Pete and Jackie had taken the boys to Center Parcs[xvi]. It was lovely, but over too quickly.

"You know what we need," Phil said. "Our own place."

This was on New Year's Day, mid-morning, as they ate breakfast at a greasy-spoon near Col Blackwell's place in Earlestown. They'd stayed over with Col, who'd had a house party; most of the gang were there, and it had been a good night.

"I know we've not been together long," Phil added – obviously aware he'd taken her aback. "But I love you, Kay. I want you to be with me." He paused. "So - what d'you reckon?"

Of course, she wanted to be with him, too - but if things were hard with Dot now, she could only imagine how it would be if they moved in together. On top of everything else, there'd be the question of what "people" thought – Auntie June, George and Irene, Joan-next-door...

She sighed. "It's not that I don't want to..." She tailed off – and he knew, without her saying any more, exactly what it was.

"Now look - if you're not ready, no problem. We'll wait as long as you need - but you can't keep letting her hold you back."

"She doesn't mean to. It's just the life she's had – and she misses Andy."

"So do you..."

"I know – but he was her whole world. And you're right, it *is* hard for us all, but with Mum... You know, when Andy died, she still wasn't completely over Uncle Bob. It was twelve years earlier, mind you, but they were really close. So, don't get me wrong – I know how difficult she's being – but I can't hurt her. It'd be the last straw."

"I do get it, love. I know it's hard."

"The other thing is, she's old-fashioned – and, rightly or wrongly, she gets bothered about people judging. Not that anyone would, but… it's how she grew up. She'll never change."

"Of course," he said with a smile, "she'd have nowt to worry about, if I made an honest woman of you."

"Oh, yeah," she laughed. "You, in a tuxedo?"

"I'd wear one for you, though." Then she realised he was deadly-serious. "Marry me, love. We've both been through some crap in our lives– but it stops now. I'll look after you."

They'd only been together for five months. It was all very quick; yet Kay knew, straightaway, what her answer would be. Despite the conflict with Dot, these past months had been the happiest of her life. While not the "bad boy" so many expected, her man was a free spirit; and now here he was, committing to her for good. Not because she'd tried to tie him down or "tame" him, or any of that crap – but because he *wanted* to. She knew nothing about bikes, and he had no interest in books; but it didn't matter. They both loved music, animals and being in nature, and what they shared, they made the most of. He brought her out, she calmed him down, without either trying to change each other. They were as they were - and that was all good.

As for Dot... There had to be a point where she stopped letting Andy be the excuse for everything. Sooner or later, things would need to come to a head. Their last row was just the day before, when Kay told her they were spending New Year with Phil's friends. Well, she said – it was up to *her,* if she wanted to be with strangers, instead of her own family...

"To be fair, Mum, they're not strangers - they're our friends."

"*His* friends."

"Does it matter?"

"Yes - because you're staying with these people, and I can just imagine what they're like! And you're only young – you should be with friends of your own."

"So," she snapped, "if I was out with Jen and Lisa, there'd be no problem? That's funny – because you usually see your arse!"

"What a thing to say! I bet you've learnt that from *him*!"

(In fact, she'd "learnt" it from Frank.).

She heard the bike pull up outside. "Look, I'm not arguing anymore. I'm going - I'll ring you at midnight."

"I'll be in bed." Dot pulled childishly away as she tried to hug her. "It's not worth staying up – so don't bother."

"Fair enough," Kay sighed. "I won't, then. Happy New Year."

As much as she tried to avoid it, it always ended up like this. It wore her down. She just wanted what most people did. A place of her own; good, genuine friends; and now the right one had come along, a man to share her life with. Was that so wrong? Already, she'd given up her dream of going to Uni – she wasn't giving up Phil.

"Well?" He anxiously awaited her reply.

"I can't see why not," she smiled. "In fact, there's nothing I'd love more!"

Chapter Twelve

The next months flew by; an exciting, but difficult time, predictably with plenty of tears from Dot. But at least they had Frank on-side. It tuned out he'd had a savings account for years, which was all for Kay. Initially, he'd planned to surprise her with the money when she started Uni – but when that didn't happen, he decided to keep on with it until she got married, whenever that was. They used most of it towards a modest but classy wedding, with the rest going towards the deposit on a house.

They found a starter home on a modern estate, not unlike Pete and Jackie's; the location was ideal, opposite Broadgreen station and alongside the motorway; a short bus ride from her parents, without being on the doorstep. Kay could jump on a train to the office, and Phil could get on the '62 and be in St. Helens in no time. It was in good condition, but some of the décor wasn't to their taste, and Phil couldn't resist making a few changes. With Col and Robbo's help, he spent much of his spare time working on it and had it ready with a few weeks to go.

Meanwhile, Kay tried to involve Dot in the wedding as much as she could, in the hope she'd enjoy it - which might in turn lead to a change of heart. But, on top of everything else, Dot was upset that the guest list was shorter than she'd have liked and left out the neighbours (especially Ron and Joan, who were bound to take umbrage). She also disapproved of the choice of music; she was fine with "Claire de Lune", which Kay would come into – but not with what they'd walk out to, which was "Sweet Child o' Mine"[xvii].

The date they'd set was September 4th – little more than a year after they'd met. Kay had her hen-do a week before the wedding, on August bank holiday weekend – a spa break in Edinburgh with Jen, Lisa, and other friends from work; her old school-pal Susan King, and Jackie and Michelle. To include Dot, she also organised an "oldies'" hen night with June and Teresa for the eve of the wedding – which ended up as more of a family get-together, with Frank, Ray and Tommy going along too, as well as Stevie, who'd brought his parents down from Glasgow. Phil decided to have his stag-do on the same night and wasn't bothered about a weekend away; the Swan with his mates was fine for him.

The family were staying at a travel lodge further along Queens Drive, and Kay had booked a table at the Beefeater[xviii] attached. Sadly, though unsurprisingly, it left her wondering why she'd bothered; but still, she knew she'd feel worse if she hadn't at least tried. The atmosphere was tense and heavy, relieved only by Tommy and Stevie's banter. Dot was silent, distant, and had nothing to eat or drink. She had a headache, she said; no doubt brought on by all the stress. Conversation was a struggle, and Stevie tried to lighten things by talking about his new car.

"Have you never thought about driving lessons, Katie?" he asked. "Gives you so much freedom."

"Well," Kay began, "I..."

"No, she hasn't," Dot interrupted. "I've always said to Katie, I don't *want* her to drive! It's too dangerous. And now she'll be going on that bike all the time. I'm dreading it!"

("Sorry,") Stevie mouthed. Kay shrugged. ("You weren't to know.").

"For goodness' sake, Dot," June said crossly, "don't be so silly. Ray had that scooter when we were first courting. We were perfectly safe."

"But that was years ago, June – the roads were quieter. Besides, Ray was nothing like..."

"Mum," Kay warned, "not now. Let's just try and enjoy the evening."

"I can't help how I feel, Katie. I've tried, but..."

"You haven't *really* tried though, have you, Dot?" June said. "You were just the same when our Bob married Viv."

"Yes," Dot snapped, "and look how *that* turned out!"

"Oh, come on – you can't put all the blame on Viv. Bob had his problems, after all."

"Don't you dare say that about Bob! He was the best brother anyone could have asked for."

"I'm not saying he wasn't - I loved him too, don't forget. But he did have his issues."

"*Issues!* The only *issue* was that stupid girl! I tried telling him, but would he listen? And I knew I was right, like I am now!"

"Alright," Frank said sternly, "knock it off, both of you."

"And anyway, "Dot went on, ignoring him, "what would *you* know about it? You were off, swanning about with Ray, while I was looking after Gran. Not a thought for anyone else."

"Hang on," Ray said, "June did her bit. And it's not *our* fault if you wanted to stay in, pining over the Laughing Policeman!"

Thankfully, the waitress arrived to clear the plates. "Any desserts?"

"No," Kay sighed. "I think we'd best call it night."

They got a cab home in sombre silence – and once in the house, Dot burst into tears. Kay managed to get her sat down on the sofa, where she continued to sob inconsolably.

"I'll make some tea" Frank said. "You try and calm her down."

Probably best to let her cry it out, Kay thought; and just sat with her – not a word – until the weeping finally subsided.

"June's too fond of her own voice," Dot said at last. "And she wouldn't say boo to a goose at one time, you know – Ray asked me out before he ever noticed *her*!"

"I know, Mum."

"Talking like that about Bob! As if it was *his* fault he… And I know she was close to him too – but Bob and I were inseparable as kids. I don't think June understood that – or maybe she was jealous. But one thing I'm sure of, he'd never have left me for no good reason."

"Look, I know how much it hurt you," Kay said. "I think June just meant it's never that simple. And I'm not saying the break-up with Viv didn't play a part - but there could have been other things going on for Bob, that no-one knew about."

"Maybe - but even so, I *knew* she wasn't for him, Katie. Her family were dog-rough."

"That doesn't make her a bad person, Mum. From what I remember, they were happy to begin with – and Viv was always kind to me and Andy."

"Yes, but you were only a little girl…" Dot sighed. "I suppose June was right, in a way – Bob did have a lot on his mind. I don't think he ever stopped missing being in the navy, and it hit him more than anyone when your grandad died. But still… I just think, a decent girl would have stood by him, and not run away at the first hurdle."

"That can happen in all walks of life - no matter how well-off you are."

"It's not just about money, Katie. And no doubt you'll think I'm a snob - but it's how you're brought up. I mean, look at your dad. He came from a poor family, but they were honest – hard-working. Whereas Viv… I don't mean to sound unkind, but some people just aren't like *us*. It's not that they're bad – they've just never been taught the right way, so they don't *think* like us. A different breed." She teared up again. "When I tried to warn Bob, he thought I was interfering. And now, it looks like history's repeating itself."

"You know, I can't speak for Viv - I don't know enough about her life to make a judgement. And yes, Phil did have a bad childhood; his mum was a waste of space. But he spent a long time with his grandparents, and they were salt-of-the-earth. Just like Dad's family, really."

Dot was silent.

"Look, Mum – we're all tired, and we've got a hectic day tomorrow. Let's go up and get some sleep."

It took her a while to drop off. Her last night: she'd have given anything for it not to be like this. If only Dot could meet her part of the way. Not even half – a quarter, an eighth, would be better than nothing.

"I know you'll disagree, Frank," she overheard. "I just had this image of her walking down the aisle with a lawyer or a doctor."

"Like Marianne's fella, you mean?"

Ron and Joan's (soon-to-be-ex) son-in-law was a surgeon - and serial womaniser.

"Look," Dot bristled. "I'm not wrong to want the best for her."

"But it's for *her* to decide what that is. And she could do a lot worse. He's got a good trade, and he's a grafter. And he thinks the world of her."

"It's just not what I wanted."

"It's not about what *you* want…"

"So, you'll be saying all this when she has an accident on that bike?"

"If it wasn't the bike, it'd be something else… aw, come on. Don't get upset again…."

It turned out Phil's stag-do hadn't gone to plan, either. Pete, after a few drinks, picked an argument, which was nothing new – but Col was furious with him for ruining Phil's night, and they nearly ended up coming to blows. Despite everything, the wedding itself went well, and they truly had the best day they could have hoped for. They settled easily – comfortably - into married life; and for many years, were mostly happy. Until one day they weren't.

Chapter Thirteen

If she were to pinpoint where it all went wrong, it would be a few months after her 40th – when they returned from Italy to the news of her dad taking ill. Still exhausted from that dreadful trip home, they jumped in Phil's van and rushed over in a panic to the Royal. They found Frank on A and E Majors. Dot was there and, in truth, she looked much worse – pale and drawn, with red, swollen eyes. Frank, on the other hand, was sitting up, calm and relaxed.

"You had us worried there, Dad."

Phil winked. "Too much partying, eh, Frank?"

"I'm fine!" Frank laughed.

"You did give us quite a scare, though. Mum said it might be a stroke?"

"Well, you know how your mother exaggerates."

"I'm *not* exaggerating, Frank!" Dot said crossly, through her tears. "It's what the doctor told us – I *heard* him!"

"A mini-stroke, he said."

"But what if it happens again? They said your blood pressure was up."

"Yeah, but they're giving me pills for that. They'll sort it out."

"I hope so." Dot turned to Kay. "I couldn't get in touch," she said reproachfully. "Every time I rang, it was that stupid voicemail."

"I know, Mum," Kay sighed. "I'm so sorry. The flight ended up being cancelled – then the battery went on my phone."

"But I was worried sick! I thought something had happened to you, on top of everything else..."

"There were nowt we could do, Dot," Phil said; she didn't reply. She'd softened towards her son-in-law over the years, but there was still a feeling that they tolerated each other, rather than being the best of friends – and that it wouldn't take much for old tensions to re-appear.

Frank stayed in hospital a few days longer. He'd had a funny turn during his usual Saturday trip to the bookies', and another customer had called an ambulance. The paramedics had found his blood pressure to be through the roof, at 230/120 - not just high but "sky-rocking", they'd said, and without hesitation had taken him in. The test results showed he did indeed have a stroke – only a mini one, as he'd guessed, but he'd still need to treat it as a warning. They let him home once his blood pressure was under control; but although he tried to get back to normal, he'd never be quite the same.

At almost 80, Frank was still resolutely independent – walked everywhere, went for his paper each morning, the bookies' every weekend. He and George had carried on working well into their

70s, then gradually wound their business down, still taking occasional jobs for a few more years. Once he'd retired for good, he and Dot moved to a bungalow in Childwall, which was ideal for them – within walking distance from Kay and Phil, and much smaller and easier to run.

Dot had slowed down over the years, and because Frank had more time on his hands, they shared the housework between them – although Kay had noticed more recently that Frank seemed to be doing the lion's share. Dot was finding it hard to stand too long, without her back aching.

"We can always come over and help," Kay said. "Just let us know what you need."

But no, Frank said, he preferred to do it himself, if he could – he felt better if he stayed on his feet. For a long time, Kay felt guilty that she hadn't been more forceful in getting him to accept the help; he'd clearly overdone it.

"All you could do were offer," Phil said. "You did your best."

"Did I, though? I just think I could have insisted - not taken no for an answer."

"I don't reckon he'd like that – you know how he is."

As the months passed, she noticed two things. The first, sadly, was that Frank was less keen to go out. As Kay observed him, she guessed it was a fear of falling; since the stroke he'd been much less steady on his feet and had begun to shuffle as he walked, spilling drinks and dropping food. To Dot's despair, conversation was non-existent; he spent most of the time asleep.

The other was that when she visited, she was not so much lending a hand, as single-handedly running their home. Not that she minded helping. Dot - now in her mid-70's - was bound to be slower; that was to be expected, and now Frank had to take things easier, Kay understood she'd struggle. But there were still lighter tasks which, if she took her time, she could manage – or, at least, *had* been able to, before Frank's stroke. The whole thing had thrown her into a state of total panic, where she doubted herself and her abilities; never over-confident to begin with, she now seemed crippled by acute anxiety. Deep down, Kay knew that the right thing to do would be to challenge her mother - albeit as gently as she could - and encourage her to stay active.

The problem was, when she tried this approach, it never went to plan. What was "supposed" to happen didn't; and if Kay took a step back it would be Frank, not Dot, who'd end up doing more. So, what could she do? She didn't want him to have another stroke, so she soldiered on. It was easier all round.

Chapter Fourteen

Frank's decline grew steadily worse. After some persuasion, he paid a trip to his GP, who sent him for a scan at Broadgreen. The results came through a few weeks later – almost a year to the day since he'd had the stroke – and he was called back because, as it turned out, it wasn't the best news he could have hoped for. Although it was just a min-stroke, it had done more damage than they'd ever imagined.

The specialist they saw got straight to the point and told him – quite bluntly – that he showed all the symptoms of Parkinson's. Usually, Frank appreciated the honest, no-nonsense approach – he always said he hated "bullshitters". But, this time, the doctor's forthrightness was not welcomed. Frank wasn't just taken aback – he was furious.

"No chance!" he shouted. "You don't know what the fuck you're talking about!"

"*Dad!*" Kay chided him. "No need! It's not *his* fault."

While Frank could be brusque, on occasion, she'd never seen him lose it like that before. She thought of that old saying, that you could take the boy out of Scottie..., and imagined him growing up – tough, street-wise – in the Liverpool slums.

"Don't 'Dad' me!" he snapped. "I know a pillock, when I see one!"

"Alright, Frank," Phil said, "pipe down – 'bloke's just doing his job."

The doctor sighed. "Sorry to have shocked you, Mr. Cooney – but sometimes, it's best not to beat around the bush. Now, I know this is hard to take in..."

"Hard to take in? I'll *never* take this in, I'll tell you that! *Parkinson's...*" Frank shook his head. "I was fine, up till last year. You don't just get bloody Parkinson's out of nowhere!"

Then the doctor explained that it was a certain type – the correct name for it was "Vascular Parkinsonism". In fact, it wasn't "true" Parkinson's, but had a set of symptoms that looked the same – unsteadiness, shaking, to name a few – and it was caused by damage to the brain, following a stroke.

"And I see from your records, Mr. Cooney, that you did have a stroke, last year."

Frank's rage suddenly subsided, and he now looked close to tears. Kay squeezed his hand.

"Can it be treated?" she asked.

"Well," the doctor said, "I won't lie – it's not something that can be cured. But, with the right medication, it can be controlled. It's not easy, but you can live with it."

"I don't *want* to live with it!" Frank said bitterly. "I'd rather be bloody dead, than have that!"

"Come on, Dad – we'll get you through it." While she tried to sound encouraging, she didn't push the point too much; it was very raw, and he'd need time to adapt.

"Yes," the doctor agreed, "there's plenty of help and support we can give. I'm going to put your name down for some physio – and prescribe some tablets that will help you manage the symptoms." He wrote a prescription. "I'm letting your GP know that I'm giving you these. Now just to warn you – if you happen to feel worse through taking them, stop at once. It's unusual, but always possible."

Without further ado, they got Frank home, stopping off at the chemist on the way. Kay went in with the prescription, leaving him with Phil in the van. They'd had the van for a while now, using the bike only for day trips and holidays; it was much easier for Phil's work and the shops. They'd recently started taking Dot shopping, too – another thing she was finding hard.

"He kept saying he doesn't believe 'em," Phil said later that evening, "about him having Parkinson's. And I don't reckon he'll take them pills, either – doesn't need 'em, he says."

"Well, it'll take a lot for him to get used to this. I'll need to work on him with the tablets. And I'm going to have to spend more time there – they'll need me more than ever, now."

Phil sighed. "Yeah - but mind you don't overdo it, love. You're there loads as it is."

"What else can I do though, Phil?" she said, aware she sounded defensive. "They're really struggling. I can't exactly leave them to their own devices, can I?"

"Alright - don't get wound up with me, love. I'm not having a go at you."

"I'm not *getting* wound up!" she snapped. "I'm just saying."

"That's all I were doing, too."

They were talking in bed, as they often did, curled up together — but now she felt herself pulling away.

"Hey - don't be like that. I didn't mean owt bad."

"I know that." She softened. "And I'm sorry if I sounded a bit off. My head feels about to explode!"

"No wonder – you're meeting yourself coming back. And it's all on you. Just wish I had more time fort' come and help."

"It's not your fault, sweetheart, you can't be in two places at once. I guess it's just harder when you don't have siblings. Like Stevie and Moira – they did everything together to sort things out, after Uncle Tommy died."

"I know what you're saying, love. But – and I don't mean this badly – do you not think Dot could do a bit more? Don't get me wrong, I know her back's bad, but it's like she can't even think for herself, these days."

"You're right – I probably need to be cruel to be kind. But I'm worried it'll all end up falling to Dad. And it not just her back that's the problem – she's completely lost confidence."

"But she'll not get it back if you keep doing everything."

"I know – but right now, Phil, she's terrified of losing Dad, so she's clinging on to me. And I can't blame her. I'm scared myself, when I stop and think about it; I just can't imagine him not being here. So, imagine how Mum feels, when they've been married 42 years? I'm just looking out for her."

"Yeah - like I'm looking out for *you*."

It turned out Phil was right about the tablets – the next time Kay was visiting, she found them in the bin.

"That doctor told me not to take them if they make me feel worse," Frank said. "Well, I had one, and I felt terrible!"

"You're supposed to give them more of a chance than that, Dad," Kay sighed. "He meant over a few weeks, not just a day."

"But I don't need them - I was saying that to Phil. I think they've got it wrong over this Parkinson's. They don't know what they're on about."

"So, how do you know they don't?"

"How do you know they *do*?"

"Probably because they're specialists…? I'm not saying that makes them perfect, but they must have *some* idea."

"All I know is, I haven't got Parkinson's - just like that funny turn wasn't a stroke."

"Oh, Dad..."

"No, it wasn't!" Frank insisted, starting to sound belligerent again, as he had at the clinic. "I'd have known if it was! You know, I reckon they're just fobbing me off. All this crap about 'living with it'. I don't see why I should! I bet you there's a cure for whatever it is, and they just don't want to waste their time on an old codger like me."

"So, what do *you* think it is, then, Dad?" she asked – naively thinking he might back down, if she called his bluff. But not a chance.

"*I* don't know– I'm not a doctor, am I? But one thing's for sure," he said firmly. "It's not bloody Parkinson's!"

Chapter Fifteen

As time passed, Frank's symptoms accelerated; he began to have frequent falls, and to spill hot drinks and scald himself. Dot would often call her in work in a panic because he couldn't pick himself up. At first, Kay and Phil had tried to manage it between them, going as soon as they could to get Frank off the floor. Phil was more than willing to drop everything – but at times the jobs were out in Warrington or Wigan; near enough, but not so much that he could get there in a matter of minutes. Apart from that, he might not hear the phone if the site was noisy, or he was engrossed in something.

Luckily for Kay, the office wasn't far on the train – she could get to Broadgreen station within five minutes and walk to the bungalow in another ten. But if clients were booked in, she had to make sure the appointments were cancelled, or someone could take them over, and it wouldn't look good to be doing it all the time. Carol was more than understanding, but she'd never play on that. She suggested to Dot that it might be quicker to call an ambulance and get the paramedics to lift him.

"I've tried that," Dot said. "But I get flustered on the phone. They ask too many questions."

In the end, Kay got a "lifeline" installed for them, so that, at the press of a button, a central office would be alerted – which solved the problem of Dot's reluctance to call 999. She also organised carers to call twice a day, which didn't go down well at first – especially with Frank.

He was becoming more and more irascible, and Kay, in turn, was losing patience with him. Of course, she felt sorry for all he was going through – could only imagine what it would be like for an independent soul like her father to become so frail. But if he'd *only* see reason about the meds…. life would still be far from perfect, but it had to be better than *this*.

Each time he fell, it was harder to recover. Eventually, he hurt himself enough to be taken to A and E - and following a week on a "frailty unit", as they called it, he was sent for three weeks' re-enablement. After this he got caught in a cycle - hospital, rehab, then back home, where he'd be okay for a few days before falling again; each time worse than the last, and harder to recover. Before long, the doctors began to suggest he might be better in a care home. Kay realised this was true; but in her heart she didn't again want this for Frank and knew how unhappy he'd be. She tried to warn him.

"Well," he snapped, "they can piss off! I'm going nowhere!"

He remained adamant –nobody could force him to go anywhere against his will, which, at that point, was still true. He still knew what he was doing; and, until he didn't, he had every right to live where he chose- even if he *was* a risk to himself. But, as time went on, Kay began to see all the signs of vascular dementia; she'd read up on it and found it could be common with this kind of damage to the brain.

It broke her heart to see her quiet, stoic father become bitter and paranoid. To make matters worse, he seemed to know who they all were, and exactly where he was. Kay would then begin to doubt herself. Maybe it *wasn't* dementia; perhaps he was just angry at his situation, and taking it out on them? Certainly, to begin with, the doctors were convinced he could manage his own affairs – he knew his date of birth, the month they were in, the name of the Prime Minister...Later, Kay would find out that this type of dementia could be different to Alzheimer's; and a person might seem lucid, while gradually losing all sense of perspective.

Before learning all this, she struggled to understand Frank's behaviour. It hurt deeply to think he knew how it was affecting them all – it seemed so callous. Yet at the same time, she knew something was amiss; it just wasn't *him*. She pushed the doctors to take a deeper look at his mental state, but each time the answer was the same; Frank had all his faculties, and what she was witnessing was just a stubborn, cranky old man.

But as she watched him deteriorate, she knew she couldn't believe this. His extreme paranoia wasn't normal – if it really wasn't dementia, was it a breakdown? He became convinced they were all "in league" with the doctors against him; that they were plotting his downfall, and the grand scheme was to get rid of him - a home, an asylum, or even dead, deciding his tablets were poison. Eventually, it would reach the point where she knew he'd gone for good; and although it would be six months before he passed for real, it was, for her, the day her father died.

In the summer of 2014, he went for yet more rehab at a home he'd been to the year before. Although this was something he was never ecstatic about, he usually accepted it, albeit grudgingly. But this time was different. He had a glass of water in his hand, which he kept banging furiously, while muttering away to himself.

"Stop that, Dad," she said. "You'll end up breaking it."

"I'll do what the fuck I want!" he growled; a look of pure hatred on his face as he caught sight of one of the nurses. "She wants me dead, that one!"

"Now come on, Frank," the nurse said, as lightly as she could "You've stayed here before – you know we're not like that."

"I know you're *poisoning* me, with them pills!" Then he started banging the glass again, shouting that he wanted the police.

"Dad," Kay said desperately, "this has got to stop..."

"*This has got to stop!*" he mimicked. "You're just like the rest of them."

This time, the glass smashed in his hand. He picked up a shard and lunged forward, as if to try to stab Kay with it. She moved quickly back.

"Lenny!" the nurse called out to one of the male carers. "Can you give me a hand?"

Lenny, seeing at once what was happening, came running over, joined by another, younger carer named Josh.

"What's all this, then, Frank? Let's calm down, eh?"

"Fuck you," Frank spat at him.

The carers managed to prise the glass from him and, after a struggle, got him into the wheelchair; Frank was shouting and ranting the whole time. They whisked him away – and Kay sat for a moment, the tears streaming.

"Do you want a cup of tea, hon?" Liz asked.

"No, thanks," she muttered. "I just need to get home."

"Is your fella picking you up?"

"Not tonight. He's working late."

"Would you like me to ring him?"

"No!" she said quickly. "No... thanks...I'll call a cab. It's what I'd planned to do."

Of course, Phil would have picked her up – he did most nights. He'd offered that evening, but she knew they were hoping to finish the extension they were working on, so she said no, she'd be fine with a taxi. And now she was glad. She didn't want him to know how bad things were in case he tried to discourage her from going so much; and as hard as it was, there was no way she could give up on Frank.

Chapter Sixteen

"So, how is he?" Dot asked, when Kay visited next evening. She went most nights, sometimes with Phil, sometimes alone, depending on his work; alternating between the two when Frank was away. It was mostly Kay and Phil who visited Frank – Dot had tried a few times but got too upset. Frank's illness made her crippled with fear, and as it progressed, she became more dependent on Kay than ever before. At the same time, her mobility deteriorated further, and she seemed to grow more physically frail, barely leaving the house.

The worse things got, Dot became trapped in a bubble of denial. She'd ring Kay in tears about everything Frank did; when he fell or had an outburst. Yet, she shut her ears to any suggestion of dementia. Of *course* it wasn't - that didn't happen to a man like Frank!

"So," she repeated, "how's Dad, Katie?"

All too easy to sugar-coat things, but she'd have to face it one day... "To be honest, Mum – not great."

"What do you mean?" Dot said in a panic - as shocked as if she'd never known he was ill.

When it came to it, Kay couldn't bring herself to tell her what happened with the glass. But she couldn't pretend all was fine, either. "Just very agitated. I mean, I know he's been wound up a lot, lately, but he said some terrible things to me."

"Well, I know he can be abrupt. But he doesn't mean it."

"This was more than abrupt."

"Look, Katie, I think you might be taking it the wrong way."

"You weren't even there, Mum – how do you know?"

"Because - well, you were always touchy. I mean, you were such a moody teenager..."

Kay knew exactly what she meant; all those times she'd struggled with what was going on at school....

"Thanks for that, Mum. If you must know, I was being bullied."

"Oh! Well, you never *told* me that, Katie!"

"No - I kept it to myself to save you worrying! Thing is, it's just the same now. *I'm* the one dealing with Dad, because you can't handle him having dementia - to be told I'm being silly, and over-sensitive!"

"I didn't mean it like that," Dot said tearfully. "And besides – he hasn't *got* dementia!"

"You keep telling yourself that, Mum."

Then Dot broke down, and Kay felt like the world's worst.

She got home, only for the evening to end in another row. With all that had happened, she'd completely forgotten she'd asked

Jen over for dinner that night and found Phil chatting with her in the lounge. He'd made coffee but hadn't started the meal.

"Sorry, love," he said, "wasn't sure what you wanted doing."

For Christ's sake – couldn't *anyone* think for themselves?

"Don't worry," Jen said, "I know how things are. Just coffee and a biscuit will be fine."

"Honest to God!" Kay said irritably to Phil. "Did you not even think to put any bloody *biscuits* out!"

"It doesn't *matter!*" Jen laughed awkwardly, to try and lighten the mood. "I didn't mean...you know, I'm not *bothered* about biscuits – it's just a figure of speech..."

"I'll get 'em," he said gruffly. "Or she'll be on my case all night."

"I feel awful," Jen said. "Hope I didn't put my foot in it?"

"It's not you, lovely – it's him, and Mum, and... everything else."

"Look, the last thing you need right now is to be worrying about me. You're under enough pressure as it is." hand-and-foot on me!"

Kay felt herself tearing up. "It was awful with Dad last night...," They heard Phil coming back in from the kitchen. "But look, Jen, I've not told Phil. I'd rather he didn't know...."

Phil brought in a plate of digestives, and more coffee for them both.

"Jen doesn't take milk!" Kay snapped.

"Honestly," Jen said, "please don't worry. I come for the company, not the food!"

"Glad someone's talking sense, Jen. She might listen to you. Can't do right for doing wrong at 'moment, me." Phil sighed. "Any-rode – 'rugby's on in a bit – I'll go up and leave you to it."

"You must think I'm a right cow," Kay said, once he'd left the room again.

"No - but I do think you're close to breaking-point with your dad - and the smallest thing can push you over the edge."

"I hate being like this, Jen. Phil's doing his best, but... he's such a typical *man*, at times. Come-day bloody go-day! And when you're already tired, and wound-up..."

"Look, Kay – I know you don't want to – but do you not think it'd be best to tell him how bad things are with your dad? It might help if he knew just how much stress you're under."

"You're probably right. But I can just imagine what he'd say...and that would just lead to more rows, which I don't need. It's lovely that he's so protective – but I can't not see Dad."

"Surely he wouldn't try and stop you?"

"No, but he'd say perhaps I shouldn't go as often if it's upsetting me, and to give myself a break."

"And would that be so terrible?"

"I keep wondering that. But if I went less, how could I explain it to Mum? I'd never hear the end of it! Things aren't easy with her right now, either. I love her to bits, but she's driving me mad! Sometimes, it's less hassle to just get on with it."

Jen stayed about an hour. Once she'd left, Kay went up to join Phil, watching rugby in the bedroom.

"How are they doing?"

"Alright," he grunted. "Surprised you're speaking to me, after how I screwed up before."

"Ah.... yeah... I did over-react a bit."

"A *bit*? You tore me head off for nowt!"

"I'm sorry. I had a row with Mum – that's why I ended up late. She just won't accept how ill Dad is."

He softened. "I know, love. But you'll solve nowt by taking it out on me. It's Dot who wants telling."

"It's not that simple, Phil. Believe me, I've tried – I get nowhere. And I don't know ...am I wrong, for wanting her to face facts? I just know how bad it'll be when the worst happens - and I've a feeling that'll be sooner rather than later."

"Come here." He pulled her next to him and they lay together, holding each other, as they always did – until things were right.

Chapter Seventeen

They'd been having a lot of these flare-ups, lately. Besides Frank's illness, the business hadn't been doing quite so well. There were peaks and troughs, and at that moment they were pretty much working flat-out – but during the quiet times, it wasn't uncommon for Phil to find himself idle.

In fairness, he could never be called a slacker. He'd always done his bit around the house, and for a long time, it was more than enough. Not only did he work longer hours, it was a hard, physical job; and when Kay looked at some of the men from the office, she knew how lucky she was. These were guys who lifted nothing heavier than paper, yet frequently expected their wives to run around, frantically doing everything.

They'd always had their routines and way of doing things, which suited them both. It was, by and large, a happy and peaceful co-existence, although life was never without its ups and downs and disappointments - especially their lack of success in trying for a baby. They'd considered IVF, but this, of course, was now out of the question – on top of everything else, the stress would be too great, with no guarantees. Instead, they made the best of what they had. They were close to Phil's nephews, especially Craig, who often stayed over with his mates after a Saturday night out in Liverpool. They'd smile as they came down next morning, at the sight of half a dozen kids (goths, moshers and metalheads all), draped across the living-room floor. Phil made bacon butties (the one thing he cooked well, apart from his door-stop toast), and Kay would invite them to stay for Sunday lunch. These days they still saw a lot of Craig, who had now settled down with his girlfriend, Sophie.

But now it seemed that, bit by bit, their old life was slipping away. They never went for trips on the bike anymore, and Sunday lunch had also fallen by the wayside. Saturday nights out had likewise come to a standstill because, after spending the day on the Frank and Dot's housework, she was she was always too worn-out. Phil helped her when he wasn't working, but usually managed to break something – including Dot's favourite crystal vase, a Royal Doulton[xix] and a wedding gift from Bob. To give him his due, he felt awful, and insisted on looking for a replacement straightaway – but Dot was still inconsolable.

In the end - a few more accidents later - she said it might be quicker, and easier, to just do it all herself; but then felt resentful if he'd been home all day. Not that he sat there twiddling his thumbs - he always had some DIY project on the go. But sometimes, it seemed like he was putting so much work into jobs that, in all honesty, didn't really *need* doing; and what she did need was for him to make a half-decent attempt at the day-to-day stuff.

She missed cooking more than anything. It had been a way to wind down after work, with music in the background, for the hour or so before Phil got in. (He was "chief bottle-washer" - an arrangement which, until now, had worked fine). But these days he was often home already, and while he always got something on the table, it was usually take-aways – not ideal if they were watching their money. He was more than willing to learn to cook, he said, if she showed him what to do. As there was no time for that, she wrote it down, step by step, for him to follow - but he never did; and the food was often burnt or raw.

He once attempted a beef casserole, with the idea it might be easy, being all in one pot. They had in all the veg they needed, but no meat, which was fine, he said – he'd go out and get some braising steak. Instead, he bought an expensive cut and almost destroyed it. She found the packaging later in the kitchen: Tesco Finest fillet.

"Honestly, Phil," she said angrily, "don't you look at *anything*?"

She felt awful for admitting it, but sometimes his rough, clumsy, *male* way of doing things got on her nerves; and qualities she'd found endearing seemed to grate on her. There was no doubt that she thought a lot – probably too much at times – and was a worrier, not in the same way as Dot (who worried for worrying's sake), but because she had foresight and could envisage how things might unfold. Phil, on the other hand, had an attitude of cross bridges as you came to them. Kay had always enjoyed their differences – his cheery, free-wheeling ways, and the contrast with her own introspection. But now, increasingly, she found herself confiding in Jen - not as well as, but instead of him.

Chapter Eighteen

A few days later, the social worker decided Frank could go home. A balding, middle-aged man named Mervyn Price, he was polite enough, but with a hint of sarcasm that suggested an underlying arrogance; a light, casual way of making a person feel small. He rang Kay in work to let her know that Frank could leave rehab that afternoon.

"You're joking? You do know what happened on Friday night?"

"Oh – that. Yes, they did tell me." And to her fury, he laughed.

"Glad you find it funny," she said coldly.

"No," (still laughing), "you're taking me the wrong way. It's just, that's perfectly normal. Old people get frustrated, and unfortunately, their loved ones get the brunt of it."

"Sorry, but this wasn't normal – you'd need to be there to see what I mean."

"The problem is, though, Frank can act for himself. And the fact remains that if someone can manage their affairs, they can't be forced into a home."

"But he *can't* manage… Oh, what's the point? You're not going to listen, are you?"

"Look, Mrs. Wainwright - as I've just explained, your father has capacity, so there's really *nothing* I can do. So – I just need to get the home-care package reinstated, and he'll be ready to leave."

This got worse. "You mean you've not done that already?"

"No. But stop worrying. It'll be fine."

That afternoon brought a call from the home. Could she go over? There'd been another situation with Frank....

It turned out he couldn't go straight home, after all – they'd need at least three days to put the care package in place. Unfortunately, Merv had already told him he was being discharged that day – and on learning he had to wait, Frank exploded again. He thumped the old man sitting next to him in the lounge, and there was another incident with a glass. Just as they'd done on the Friday night, Lenny and Josh had to restrain him. He was leaving anyway, he said – he'd sign himself out.

Kay thought, briefly, about ringing Merv to give him a piece of her mind – but there was little point. It would solve nothing, and she'd just get more of that smarmy attitude which, right now, she felt too worn down to deal with. She'd need all her reserves to cope with Frank.

When she arrived, he was in his wheelchair, coat on, bags packed, good to go and smiling warmly – Friday's antics completely forgotten.

"I'm glad you've come. I can go home, now." He lowered his voice. "They're trying to bump me off, you know."

They got down to the business of Frank signing himself out, which he just about managed to do, with Kay signing as witness – she had no choice. The black cab she'd travelled in was waiting outside, and the driver had got the ramp ready for the chair.

"Where are we going?" Frank kept asking throughout the journey.

"Home, Dad…like you wanted."

"Oh, aye." He nodded, reassured. "That's right."

They reached the bungalow; the driver brought the wheelchair to the door. Once inside, Kay helped Frank out of the chair and into his seat, while Dot looked anxiously on.

Frank, meanwhile, was glaring suspiciously at Dot, and around the room. The bungalow, though smaller than their house in Mossley Hill, was just like it inside; the lounge almost a replica of their old one, cosy and traditional with a red, amber, and gold-patterned Axminster, rust-coloured sofas, plentiful ornaments and plush furnishings in the warm tones of the carpet. Nothing had changed since Frank had been away, but he looked in turn confused, frightened, then furious.

"What's up with you, Frank?" Dot asked him crossly. "What are you *staring* at?" She turned to Kay. "What on earth's wrong with him? I thought he'd be glad to come home!"

"He's not himself, Mum. This is what I was trying to tell you."

Frank looked at her with a mixture of hurt, betrayal and pure rage. "*Liar!* You said I was goings *home!*"

"You *are* home, Dad. This is where you live…with Mum…remember?"

"Never been here in me life!" he thundered. "Tried to trick me, didn't you?"

On the coffee table was a crystal vase – the one that Phil had bought to replace Bob's. Frank threw it viciously to the floor; it shattered into tiny shards.

"Frank!" Dot shouted. "What's the *matter* with you? Now just stop it, do you hear?"

He glared again, with the same look of hatred that Kay had seen with the nurse.

"Shut it!" he snarled. "Shut your bloody mouth!" He banged fiercely on the arm of the chair.

Dot burst into tears, while Kay briefly shut her eyes to try and calm herself. During this time, Frank had got himself up and out of the chair, and they watched helplessly as he began to smash ornaments and glasses from the cabinet.

"Make him stop this, Katie," Dot wept. "I'm not well. My chest hurts."

"It's okay, Mum – I'll get it sorted."

She called for two ambulances - one for each of them. Dot's symptoms were, most likely, brought on by anxiety, which often happened when she felt she couldn't cope; but best to be on the safe side. Then she tried to ring Phil – "this person's phone is switched off…" Assuming he was still at work, she decided, as a one-off, to ring Pete instead.

"Yeah?"

"Pete…it's Kay." Silence. "Is Phil there with you?"

"Gone home. Finished ages ago. I'm eatin' me tea."

"Oh…okay, sorry to…"

He hung up. She felt the tears again, and wondered why; what else did she expect? She rang their home number and panicked when there was no reply. Where the hell *was* he? What if, on top of everything else, Phil had been in an accident?

"Please make him stop, Katie! I feel terrible!"

"Help's on the way, Mum," Kay said, wiping her eyes. Then relief, as Phil called her back.

"Sorry I missed your call, love, I were just in 'shower…. Everything ok?"

"Not really… Dad's going berserk, Phil, I'm really frightened – he's smashing things up."

"Shit. Where are you? Are you with him in that home?"

"No," she sobbed, "he's at the bungalow. They let him sign himself out this afternoon."

"Oh, fuck! I'll get over now."

Frank, meanwhile, had just picked up another vase and fallen on it, badly cutting his arm. He kept struggling, and failing, to get himself up.

"Shut your mouth," he snarled again at Dot. "Shut your bloody mouth."

Phil arrived at the same time as the ambulances, and was chatting to the paramedics as they came in. Frank was covered in blood from the smashed glassware; but despite the state he was in, they concentrated on Dot first. She'd mentioned chest pain, and best to be safe, they said. As Kay and Phil waited for Frank to be seen to, they finally managed to calm him down, and his rage burned itself out.

"So, am I going home now?" he asked mildly. He stared in bewilderment at the blood pouring from his arm, the shattered glass around him.

"Soon, Dad," Kay said. "You need to get to hospital first, though. That's a nasty cut you've got there."

"I know," Frank muttered. "It's that woman. She batters us."

Then it dawned on Kay that, by "home", Frank meant Burlington Street – and in his mind he was nine years old and running away from the farm in Wales. Her heart broke for him as he pleaded, "You won't make us go back, will you, Nin?"

"No," she managed. "Of course not."

By the time he'd been bundled into the ambulance, Dot was already on her way to the Royal. Kay and Phil followed on in the van. They were asked to stay in the relatives' room, where they sat for what seemed like hours - until, finally, a doctor came out.

She could tell from his face it wasn't good. Had Frank kicked off again, and really hurt someone, this time? Perhaps they wanted to section him – which, of course, Dot would never agree to....

"There's no easy way to say this," the doctor began. "Your mum took ill on the journey to hospital..."

Hang on... this was about her *dad*; they'd only brought Dot in as a precaution. Her head whizzed again, as she struggled to process what she was hearing. She was aware of Phil squeezing her hand.

"*What?*" she heard herself stammering. "What do you mean...?"

"I'm afraid she suffered a cardiac arrest. The paramedics did all they could, before taking her to Resus..."

"But...she'll be ok...?"

The doctor shook his head. "They worked on her for an hour but were unable to revive her - and she passed away. I'm so sorry."

Chapter Nineteen

For a good while, Kay struggled to recall what followed. Some bits were clear, but much was blurry, with large parts that were completely blank.

Vague, fleeting memories of her varying moods – tears and panic, alternating with numbness and apathy; disbelief, anger, followed by a sudden, rational calm. Her fear at being asked to formally identify the body, and relief to find that Dot looked peacefully asleep. She hadn't visited her in the funeral parlour; Dot had regretted seeing Howie, so always said she'd prefer to be remembered as she was.

She was aware there'd been a post-mortem, and that she'd had to speak to the police – the details were foggy, except that they'd told her it was nothing to worry about; just a formality, because it was so sudden. She also knew that, somehow, she'd managed to hold it together to arrange the funeral; and to write a eulogy, which she was determined to read on the day. Amidst the shock and grief, there were some pockets of happiness, at just how kind people could be, and the way her friends and colleagues had rallied around, with lovely cards, texts, Facebook messages, and some beautiful flowers.

But she'd blocked out most of the funeral. All she knew was that she'd stood up to begin the eulogy, which went well at first, until it reached the part where she mentioned Andy, then she got too upset to carry on. Phil would have taken over from her, she guessed, but her recollection ended as she went to sit down. At the back of her mind, the faintest memory of being at the pub afterwards, but little beyond that, apart from who was there and who was missing. Uncle Ray was recovering from an operation, so he couldn't make it; Auntie June had travelled alone on the train. Moira had brought Aunt Teresa, but Stevie couldn't get time off work., and there was Irene Powell, (but not George, who was full of flu), Jen and Lisa, and most of the gang from work. But who they sat with, what they ate, what they talked about – no idea.

Over the weeks and months that followed, bits started slowly coming back to her. That horrible, sinking feeling when the hearse arrived, which worsened as they followed in the car. "The Waltz of the Flowers" from the "Nutcracker", as they entered the chapel; the first hymn ("Morning has Broken"); the vicar inviting her to join him at the front – but after that…nothing.

She couldn't force herself to remember, she knew that much. It was clearly too hard to deal with, right now – and would come when she was ready.

Once the funeral was over, she began slowly to recover her memories. She ran the gamut of emotions - but mostly what she felt was a deep, crushing guilt. The post-mortem had shown that Dot had an undiagnosed heart condition. It may have been something she'd developed recently, but she could also have lived with it for years, even since she was born, and had taken its toll as she reached old age. Along with the arthritis, it had likely played a large part in her problems with mobility, and would no doubt have affected her confidence, too. No wonder she was needy – she was genuinely ill!

It had crossed Kay's mind, more than once, that Dot might be exaggerating – not just on that last, awful night, but ever since Frank's stroke. And perhaps there *was* an element of truth in this. So often, Dot had called her in a panic – *this* has happened, *that*'s happened – and Kay would rush over, only to find it was something and nothing. It was so much easier for Dot to turn to her, than try to cope herself; and entirely possible that she was making more of things, so Kay would spend more time with her. Even so, it would be hard to forgive herself for having doubts.

"There's nowt to forgive, love," Phil said. "You did all you could. She couldn't have asked for better."

"I know he means well," she said to Jen, "But I don't think he gets it. It's not about how much I did – it's about me thinking the worst of my own Mum! And not realising how poorly she was. If I'd just kept my eye on the ball…"

"And how could you do that, with your dad being so ill? You're only human, Kay. No-one can pick up on everything."

"I know…When I think of it, I did tell her, loads of times, to go to the doctors. But no, she'd say, it's too much bother - as if she didn't want to help herself – and that put doubt in my mind. But I should have *mad*e her go, and not taken no for an answer."

"She may have got upset if you'd forced her," Jen pointed out. "It might have made things worse."

"I guess you're right. That's probably what Phil meant – he just doesn't put it as well as you! But his heart's in the right place, and I know I should give him a break."

Gradually she'd learn to be easier on herself – and on Phil. Things began to improve; yet *something* wasn't quite right. All she knew was that it seemed to be linked to the funeral – which, by now, was the only thing she couldn't bring to mind. What was she blocking out? Perhaps the sadness of the day was just too much. That would make the most sense – yet she couldn't shake off a feeling that, alongside the grief, there was embarrassment, even shame; and that Phil had somehow let her down.

The one thing she could recall, faintly, was that at the pub, June mentioned a scare with Ray's operation. Who else did they chat with? She tried to think...and again, it faded away. They'd all be sharing memories of Dot – was this where Phil had slipped up? Had he said the wrong thing? After all, he knew Dot's failings only too well.

Really, this was all speculation - but time and again, her mind kept coming back to it. She thought of asking Jen, or maybe June, exactly what happened, but couldn't bring herself. Much as she wanted to know, there was a part of her that also recoiled from it. She needed her own version, no-one else's; and to remember it herself, or not at all.

Chapter Twenty

Early in the new year, Frank slipped quietly away; less than six months after his wife. During this time, he'd been in and out of hospital, and the plan was to find a permanent home. Kay had a few places in mind, but it never got that far – he kept getting chest infections, ending up back in hospital every few weeks, and starting the whole process from the beginning again.

Frank had finally - too late – been given a diagnosis of vascular dementia. Following that last night in the bungalow, he was placed on a "frailty" ward, where he had a psych assessment; and, to Kay's relief, they saw him at his worst. He'd been aggressive towards the nurses and had also started undressing in front of other patients; for his own dignity, he was moved to a side room. He'd been doing this when the psychiatrist arrived and, unlike so many others, she didn't just dismiss it as the typical eccentric behaviour of the old.

Soon after this, Frank was moved to a respite home in Toxteth, while Kay began her search for somewhere long-term. Within days, he was back in the Royal, after picking up a water infection which spread quickly to his chest. Somehow, he managed to recover – and went for yet another round of intermediate care, this time in Knotty Ash. He never mentioned Dot – and it was unclear if he knew she'd died, or even remembered her at all. Both Kay and Phil agreed it was best not to tell him. He was distressed enough already, and if there was any chance at all of him taking it in, no good could come of upsetting him even more.

The home in Knotty Ash ticked all the boxes – as well as being within walking distance, it had its own specialist dementia unit, and was clean, bright, with large, comfortable bedrooms. It was unlikely that Frank really knew or understood where he was; but in his more lucid moments, he didn't seem to hate it, which had to be a good thing. Once his three-week period of respite was up it was decided he could stay for good.

Christmas and New Year came and went - not quite as hard as expected. At least things were relatively quiet, and Frank as settled as they could hope for. But, a few days into January, she got the call. Frank was back in the Royal; the care staff had brought his lunch and found him slumped, unresponsive, in the chair. Another chest infection: she'd been told last time that he'd never get through another, so she knew what was to come.

Within half an hour, it was all over, and happened in a moment, without them even realising he'd passed. They'd been sitting with him, holding his hand, when a nurse came over and looked at him - "I think he's gone," she said quietly, and fetched a doctor, who confirmed it with a sad nod of the head.

Of course, she wept – they both did - but this was nothing like losing Dot. She couldn't begin to compare the two. She missed the man her father had been; but had grieved so much for him while he was still alive, that now, mixed in with the sorrow, was a deep sense of peace.

She thought the funeral might bring back memories of Dot's. They used the same undertakers, and it was held in the same place – the Rosemary Chapel at Springwood Crem, then on to nearby Allerton Hall (known to all as "The Pub in the Park"). Yet still, nothing would come.

But, if her dad's send-off was anything to go by, there was no need to worry. The whole day was perfect for Frank. Although Kay wrote the eulogy, she asked the celebrant to read it; after last time, she wasn't taking the chance. The celebrant was humanist, which was what Frank would have wanted, having long given up on Catholicism. There was no mention of religion during the service, which focused on Frank's early life; meeting Dot, his work as a plumber, and his patience and stoicism; asking everyone to remember these qualities, not the difficult years towards the end.

At the pub, the atmosphere was light-hearted. Kay enjoyed catching up with Stevie, who this time had managed to get time off, and Uncle Ray, now fully recovered from his op. George was there with Irene and had plenty of funny stories of Frank in his youth and their years as apprentices. As quiet as Frank was, he'd had a good sense of humour, and had played his fair share of practical jokes (all harmless) on unsuspecting newbies.

As for Phil – Kay was ashamed that she'd imagined the worst. No-one could have been more supportive, only leaving her side to keep the guests topped up with food and drink; wouldn't let her lift a finger.

It was just weeks later that Phil and Pete decided to close the business. They'd been struggling for a while, and Pete had now been offered a permanent job with a local joinery firm. As the business began to fail, the relationship between the brothers – shaky at the best of times – worsened to the point they might fall out for good if they carried on trying to work together; hard on them both because, for all their fighting, they loved each other dearly. Phil signed up with an agency, and thankfully began to get work straightaway – casual, but better than nothing.

But then it seemed their luck might have changed. Out of the blue, the estate agent called to say there'd been a cash offer on the bungalow, which had gone on the market when they knew Frank wouldn't return home; a pleasant surprise as she'd expected it to take much longer. It went through in a matter of weeks; just shy of £80,000, well enough to finish their mortgage. There was still a chunk left over, so they knew they'd manage, whatever happened with Phil's work; and most importantly, had a roof over their head no matter what. She took it as a sign of better times to come. Perhaps 2015 might just be their year!

To celebrate, they headed out of town and across to the Wirral for lunch in an old country pub, where they started to make plans for his 50th - now just 9 months away. They both agreed that a party was out of the question; it would have to be a joint one, and somehow, they couldn't see Pete being up for that. They also agreed that they needed a break; Amsterdam or Bruges, or perhaps a road trip to take in both. And as they started to look forward, she felt, for the first time in months, content – even happy.

Bit by bit, it seemed like they were finally getting their lives back. For a while now, intimacy between them had become infrequent. Phil had been as patient as when they first met, but she knew he missed it – they both did – and she hoped that as things picked up, this too would start to improve. One night, as she drifted towards sleep, she could hear him pottering about downstairs, locking up, then was aware of him curling up next to her.

"Still awake, love?"

"Yeah," she murmured. "Just about."

He held her close, spooning and nuzzling the back of her neck, and she was instantly aroused as he tenderly stoked her breasts. Feeling her responding, he pulled her gently but passionately towards him – she enjoyed the feeling of her head on his broad, hairy chest, and of his hardness, as it pressed through his boxers against her thigh. As the kisses got deeper, more urgent, she felt herself melting into him; and then...

She suddenly remembered everything.

Chapter Twenty-one

She pulled sharply away.

"I can't," she muttered.

"I'm sorry, love," Phil said, looking slightly bewildered. "You seemed so relaxed, and... look, I weren't putting on any pressure…"

"I know," she said flatly. "I thought it felt right, but..."

Then, before she could say any more, they the cats, Jazz and Jet, meowing to go out and scrambling at the front door.

"I'll see to 'em," Phil said.

"No!" Kay almost snapped. "I'll go."

She got out of bed hurriedly, pulling on her dressing gown, and was off downstairs like a shot. Once she'd let the cats out, she put the kettle on. She heard Phil call down, "Are you not coming back up, love?"

"There's no point – I won't be able to sleep."

"Look, I'm really sorry if..."

I know – you said so before – and you didn't. It's fine."

"And you're sure you're okay?"

"Yeah."

Although, at that moment, she thought she'd never be okay, ever again....

Since her mother's death, she'd had many of these sleepless nights. Learning to meditate had helped, and lately she'd found techniques to quieten her mind. She'd often end up doing what she had tonight – coming downstairs, making a drink, and listening to chilled-out music on her headphones. This usually helped her to calm down, so when she returned to bed there'd be more chance of her dropping off.

But not this time. In a split second, it had all come back to her – every detail of Dot's funeral. And her hunch was right; Phil *had* let her down. On the face of it, it wasn't earth-shattering - just the feeling that, on this worst of days, he wasn't truly there for her, and (even harder to take) wasn't even *trying* to be.

It was fine at first. As the hearse arrived, she felt, for one moment, that perhaps she couldn't do it.

"We'll get you there, love," Phil had said, gently. "You're stronger than you think. Come on..."

He walked her to the car, helping her in and out of it, and leading her into the chapel and her seat; his arm around her as they listened to the minister's introduction. But then, as she got up to do the eulogy, things changed in an instant.

She kept it light, remembering the happier times. But at the mention of Andy, she felt the tears suddenly welling up, as her throat seemed to contract and swell – she tried to get the words out, but they wouldn't budge.

"Would it be best if your husband took over?" the minister asked kindly.

She nodded, still unable to utter a word; then looked over at Phil, expecting he'd get up, bring her gently back to her seat – then calmly start reading from where she'd left off.

Instead, he sat there like a rabbit in headlights. His eyes wouldn't meet hers. He mouthed something to Jen - "can *you* do it?", most likely – before turning away. He bent his head and, for the first time in all the years she'd known him, she saw him floored, afraid – ashamed.

In fairness, not everyone could speak in front of people. It was difficult to imagine Phil being shy, but for all his bluster, he did have his quiet moments, and was much more sensitive than others may have thought; especially about anything that made him look foolish. He'd done a speech at their wedding, but that was different - he *knew* he'd be doing that. Not that he was ever one for planning. He hadn't written anything down; but still, in his own mind, he must have had at least *some* chance to prepare.

But this would have been unexpected; after all, she'd been so adamant that she'd do it herself. And because it wasn't *his* speech, she could see he might panic about messing up. She understood that and would have been okay with it – if not for what came next. As she'd sat back down, all she'd needed was to be back in his arms - but he just continued sitting there, looking down; looking away.

"It's fine," the vicar said to Phil, who didn't reply. "I can it. And I'm sorry. I didn't mean to put you on the spot."

"No," Jen said, "I'd like to. If that's okay?"

"Of course!" the vicar smiled.

All she could say was, thank God for her wonderful friends. It was they who held her as she broke down at the end, when the coffin began to move behind the curtain; and who stood with her afterwards, as she greeted everyone at the door – while Phil just lurked about in the background, head still down.

They got back in the limo, which drove them on to Allerton Hall – at which point June, who'd stayed calm throughout the service, suddenly burst into tears. Kay spent most of the short journey consoling her; Phil remained distant and detached, and still not a word from him. The car pulled up outside the pub, and he trailed behind as they walked in, June on Kay's arm, Teresa and Moira close by. Once inside, she got June settled with a drink and a plate from the buffet, and found it helped to be focused on someone else.

"I'm so sorry, Katie," June said, drying her eyes. "Here you are, looking after me – and you're the one who's lost your Mum!"

"Don't be so daft." Kay managed a smile. "I don't see it that way. She was your sister – we both loved her."

"It's so strange – as you know, we often didn't see eye to eye, even as kids – yet…I just can't believe I'll never see her again. And being back at Springwood, after all these years – brings it all back about Bob."

"Of course it would."

"I suppose it all got on top of me – and I just wish Ray was here. I've been so worried about him, too. It was touch and go for a moment, during the op."

It turned out Ray's heart had stopped, suddenly, in the middle of the procedure on his eye, and it took a few minutes to get him back. They'd worked quickly, and there was thankfully no lasting damage – but still, it was a real shock, especially as Ray enjoyed the best of health. He was recovering well, but had to take things easy, which he'd never had to do before. Just days later, they got the news about Dot. Poor June – and now she was trying to get through today without the man she loved. Kay knew how she felt.

As Jen, Lisa and the girls from work got to the pub, Phil headed straight to the bar. He stood the whole time, alone, nursing a pint – not any point did he come to sit with them, or even come near them, until they were ready to leave.

"I'll put 'kettle on, love," was all he said when they got in. Still no eye contact. She didn't answer – just headed upstairs, and then – she guessed she must have crashed out, as it all became hazy again. All she knew was that she was desperate for sleep, and too worn-out to think of anything else; and that when she woke, the whole thing seemed like a distant, horrible dream. As for Phil, he was back to his old self – as if there'd been nothing amiss.

It was so out of character. She'd never seen him like this before, in all their years together – and what a time for it to happen! Perhaps that was it. Had the pressure gotten to him? Maybe she'd expected too much – but then if you couldn't expect your *husband* to be there…. There was no problem if he couldn't finish the eulogy – his *reaction* was the issue. It had clearly hit a raw nerve, and he'd started acting…*guilty*.

So – what would there be to feel guilty about? She was sure there was more to this than just nerves and had an idea what it might be. And if he couldn't put how he felt to one side, for her sake – then where did it leave them?

Chapter Twenty-two

They were both in work the next day, so she waited till the evening to speak to him – best to be straight than let it fester.

"You're not yourself, are you?" he said as they finished their meal. "You've hardly spoke to me, since we got in. If it's not over last night, then what is it, love? What's going on?"

"I don't know, Phil – you tell *me*? You were right - I *was* more relaxed, and I was hoping we could get things back…how they were. But then, this thing popped into my mind – and don't ask me why it happened then, it just came from nowhere. But it was something about Mum's funeral, that I'd completely forgotten; and now I'm not sure what to think."

Straightaway, it was back – the "rabbit-in-headlights" look. "If it's about not doing that reading," he said at last, "I told you I were sorry – and I thought it were all okay."

"To be honest, I don't remember – but that's nothing new. So much has come back to me in dribs and drabs."

"It just threw me, love – and I thought it were best if Jen did it, in case I made a mess of it. When I said that, you – well, you seemed to get where I were coming from. It's not for everyone, you said."

"I know - but it doesn't excuse the way you were afterwards."

"What d'you mean? I didn't say owt wrong, did I?"

"No – more like nothing at all! I didn't get a hug, an arm around me – and then you just disappeared to the bar."

"Well…" he stammered, "I …I were just a bit on edge… and your mates were with you, so…"

"So, I didn't need *you*?" Sadly. "I don't know; perhaps you're jealous of the girls – and acting like that to prove a point…"

"Come on, love – what d'you take me for? I know I screwed up. For what it's worth, I'm really sorry - and I'm not just saying that. But can we not try and put it behind us? I feel awful, but I can't change owt, can I?"

"You could still tell me why," she persisted. "I mean, if you weren't feeling pushed out, then what *was* it?"

"Look," he snapped, "I can't keep apologising for ever! There's nowt more I can do – so just get off my case, eh?"

"Get off your case?" she repeated, incredulously. "Of all the days for you to let me down – and now, you want me to get off your *case*? Well, I'm sorry, Phil, but this isn't going away. I need you to be up-front."

"And I *am* being!"

"You know," she said, "perhaps I'm wrong, but…look, I need to ask you this. Did you hate Mum?"

"Oh, for fuck's *sake*!"

"Maybe *that's* why you didn't want to do the speech! I mean, you'd feel like a hypocrite, standing there, saying nice things, when you couldn't stand her. Then later, at the pub, perhaps you were too embarrassed to face everyone? After all, if someone mentioned it, it might have come out – what you *really* think…No wonder you were on edge!"

"No, love – you're way off-beam!"

"So, put me straight, then. Just be honest."

"I've told you - I *have* been!"

"Look," she went on, "If you weren't her biggest fan, I wouldn't blame you. I know she wasn't over-nice with you at first. But she was my *mum*, Phil! And whatever you thought of her, you needed to put that aside, and be there for me. I'm not wrong to ask why you didn't."

"It weren't about her," he muttered. "And I…I couldn't…." He trailed off.

"Couldn't what?" she asked. "Just *tell* me, Phil. We'll work it out."

"I couldn't…I can't – Look, I can't deal with this. I'm going for a walk – let things calm down."

"Yeah," she shot back, bitterly, "that's it. Lose the argument and walk away."

She hated herself for being like this – whatever she felt, this wasn't the best way to handle things. It was almost as if she were watching herself from a distance – like it was someone else –

and didn't like what she saw. Then, before she knew it, she'd said it.

"I'm beginning to think Mum was right. Perhaps I *could* do better than you."

His whole body seemed to crumple – and she'd never forget the look on his face. Of course, she didn't *mean* it. She so wanted to be wrong, but his behaviour seemed to confirm her fears – fobbing her off; shutting her down. And she'd said it, partly from frustration, and partly to shock him - so perhaps he'd realise how much it *mattered*. But she'd gone way too far …

They stared at each other for a moment, both in disbelief.

"No point stopping then, is there?" he said at last. "At least I know where I stand."

Without another word, he went upstairs, and she could hear him bumping and banging around. After a while, he came back down with a suitcase, rucksack and hold-all, which he placed next to the front door.

"So, you're really going?"

"Yeah. Well, you don't want me here, do you? You've made it plain what you think of me."

In her heart, she knew what she wanted to say – what she *should* say. But she found she couldn't; another voice, deep inside, urging her not to give in. Otherwise, she might find herself in tears, begging him to stay, which was the last thing she wanted – to be weak and needy when *he* was the one in the wrong.…

So, when she finally managed to speak, she agreed with him. Yes, she said, matter-of-factly – he was probably right. Things hadn't been great for a while - so perhaps it was best to move on and make a clean break of it. Why carry on kidding themselves?

"Okay." His voice was flat and hollow. "I'll get 'van loaded up, and I'll be off first thing. No point wasting time."

"I'll give you a hand."

"It's alright…there's no need."

"I'd like to. It's the least I can do."

He took the case and the rucksack, while she took the hold-all, and they went out to the van. There was plenty of room next to his tools, which he kept in there most of the time.

"What about the bike?" she asked. "Will you come back for it?"

"No – I should be able to fit it in."

It would be a tight squeeze, but he'd probably manage it – the van was spacious enough.

"Will you go to Pete's?"

"Most likely – for 'time being, any-rode." He smiled sadly. "But that's not for you to worry about – is it, love?"

He seemed so drained of life – every bit of spark gone from his eyes, voice, the way he held himself. She watched helplessly as he got the bags on to the van, knowing she could stop this – and *yet*…The whole thing was surreal. It didn't happen to *them*!

"Will you manage?" he asked her. "For money, I mean."

"I'll be fine."

"Because I can sort something out to go in 'bank each month…"

"No thanks, Phil, honestly. You'll have to pay keep to Jackie, after all. And there's still what's left from the bungalow – we'll have to arrange to split that between us…"

"No, love, that's yours. You'll need it, being on your own. Don't forget, if you run short, let me know." Sighing heavily, he shut the van door. "I think that's everything – I'll get 'bike on tomorrow."

"Okay."

Without another word, they went inside and she headed up to bed. She thought he might go to the spare room, but he stayed on the sofa. Unsurprisingly, she didn't get close to falling asleep; and every so often, her heart broke as she thought she heard a stifled sob from downstairs. Again, that instinct to go to him, so they could at least *try* to make things right, battling against that stern voice telling her to be strong. *Don't. Just don't!*

It would be an understatement to say it felt horrible – knowing that she'd crushed someone – *anyone* – like that; let alone the man she loved. But the fact remained, he'd hurt and disappointed her, more than she could ever have imagined; and worst still, tried to dismiss how she felt!

Get off my case. He'd said it before; usually if she'd had a go at him for something trivial – and on reflection, he might have been right. Nothing like grief to put things in perspective… But this wasn't a stupid row over ruined dinners or a smashed vase; this was real, raw pain. Did he come close to understanding what she'd felt at losing Dot? She'd never known anything so intense – not even with Andy.

He'd been so quick to deny any ill-feeling towards her mum – but if she was really so "off-beam", why couldn't he look her in the eye? And if she *was* right – well, if he'd just admitted it, they may have stood a fighting chance…Then another thought crossed her mind. *I couldn't…*, he'd started to say; *I can't*…What was he trying to tell her? Was he anxious? Depressed? Since losing the business, she suspected he might be – and knew only too well what that could do. It made sense to think it might lead him to panic, then withdraw, then imagine others judging him. She would ask him in the morning and see what came of it. It had to be worth a try.

But by the time she woke up, he'd gone. No goodbyes; no last chances. No nothing. Just gone.

Chapter Twenty-three

Work helped, at first – it did her good occupy her mind. Each night she'd go home and wonder if he'd be there, finally ready to talk things through – but as the days went on, it looked less and less likely. Perhaps she should call? she'd wonder; then think again. No; let him ring *you*.

One Friday – two weeks to the day since Phil had gone – she got to work slightly later than usual. For a while now, she'd done a breakfast run on a Friday morning – something she'd gradually taken over from Carol, who was always pushed for time. While Kay didn't mind this, it occasionally annoyed her that no-one else took a turn. Today was no exception; and perhaps it was petty and trivial, but it irked her to find them sat there, waiting for her to arrive and take their orders. Wouldn't dream of starting a list themselves…

"So, what time's breakfast?" Hal Richmond piped up. All in jest, of course, but it riled her even more. "Come on, Kay, get your act together! We're starving here!"

"You know what, Hal," she snapped, "there's nothing to stop *you* getting off your arse and doing it, for a change. Just saying."

"Hey, steady on," Hal said, "I was only kidding…"

"Yeah, well, I've got enough on my mind, right now, without worrying about your stomach!"

"Look, Kay, I didn't mean any harm – and I know you've been through it with your mum and dad, but you seemed to be doing so well.…"

"It's not about Mum and Dad," she found herself saying. "If you must know, Phil's left me."

Hal's face dropped. "Kay – I'm so sorry – I had no idea anything was wrong."

"Well," she said, "you do now."

She managed to hold back the tears until she reached the Ladies', where she locked herself in a cubicle and sobbed as though she'd never stop. Oh God, oh God – what would she do? What more could life throw at her? Now she'd told someone, said it out loud, she knew this was for real – no more kidding herself that he might come back. Phil had gone for good – like they all had – and she was completely, utterly alone.

"Kay?" Carol's voice. "I won't ask if you're alright, because I know you're not. But come out, lovely – so I can help."

Her eyes still streaming, Kay unlocked the door and almost fell into Carol's arms.

"Come on, missus," Carol said gently. "Let's get you a cuppa, and you can tell me what's going on."

As they sat in the canteen, Carol listened quietly, as Kay poured out the whole, sorry story.

"I don't know, Carol – maybe it's my own fault. Perhaps I'm too independent, but I can't change who I am. And if he thinks that means he can just opt out whenever he feels like, then – I guess we're not on the same page, after all."

"Or it might be the stress of the last few years, catching up with you both," Carol pointed out. "Have you thought of that?"

"All the time…I keep telling myself it's just a blip, but when I think of it, I can't make sense of it all. I miss him so much, yet I feel so let down, I'm not sure I even *want* to put things right. It'll always be there, eating away – unless he's straight with me."

"I really hope you work things out – because you and Phil are the most solid couple I know. And look - you're not in the right frame of mind for seeing clients, just now. I notice there's a few cancellations, so why not take today off, and a few days next week? Just to sort yourself out and look after *you*."

A few days. That was all she thought she needed. But alone, with time on her hands, she began to dwell – not just on Phil, but everything; and the only conclusion she could come to was that it was *her* fault. *All* of it – right back to being at school. No wonder Mrs. Evans had sent her to the doctor – she *did* need fixing, after all!

She was due back in work the following Thursday, and had got herself up, dressed and ready to go, before realising she couldn't face seeing or speaking to anyone. She'd barely slept or eaten since Phil had gone, so was weak and exhausted – and when she did manage to get some sleep, her last thought before dropping off was, invariably, that she hoped not to see the next day. Knowing the family history, this concerned her; and after a week or so, as it showed no sign of easing off, she paid a visit to her GP. As well as increasing the dosage of anti-depressants she'd been on since losing Dot, he signed her off for a fortnight.

The problem was, a fortnight soon became a month - then another month. As each day passed, her despair deepened, as it looked less and less likely that Phil would return. She'd been warned about the side-effects of the increase in her meds; and while she knew it would help in the long run, her depression spiralled out of control as she struggled to adjust.

At times, her thoughts went beyond a wish to pass quietly in her sleep, as she'd start to make actual plans of how, and when, she might try to end her life. One evening, she'd reached the point of getting pills lined up in front of her, only stopping herself when she remembered her mum's devastation over Bob. If she went ahead, Phil would be left with the fallout; and whatever had gone wrong, she couldn't put him through that.

But also, there was a feeling, deep down, that this really wasn't her time, and there was more for her to do. What or when this was, she had no idea – but the thought of it, however tiny, kept her hanging on.

Chapter Twenty-four

Six weeks had passed before she knew it - and at the start of May, there was a call from Carol.

"I feel terrible having to say this…" she began.

Kay knew at once what it was about. In a few weeks she'd reach her trigger-point to get a written warning for time off sick.

"It's fine, honestly – I know the drill."

"Look," Carol said, "I don't feel right about giving a warning – talk about kicking someone when they're down! So, I'm going to arrange a meeting to discuss treating this as a one-off and getting an exemption. Your record's been spot-on until now."

It sounded ideal – except for one snag.

"Of course," she added, "the report would have to go to Martin. He'd have the final say. But we'll put as much info in it as we can. It'll be fine."

Kay's heart sank. She'd known Carol's boss, Martin McGee, for years; he'd been a mate of her first boyfriend, Simon. Both the same – spoilt, selfish Mummy's boys – the main reason she and Simon didn't last. They'd only gone out for a few weeks, then they didn't so much split up as fizzle out. Simon hadn't seemed to care, at first – but, thanks to Martin and his egging-on, he grew jealous and resentful, especially after Kay had met Phil. All water under the bridge, of now, and these days she got on well enough with Martin; but there was "getting on", and there was trust...

"Look," she said, "I hope you know how much I appreciate what you're trying to do. But it might be best to leave it. I'll take the warning on the chin."

Carol sighed. "Martin?"

"Need you ask?"

"Now, I know you've got your doubts, Kay, but I've always found him very fair."

"Maybe – but he was so nasty when I split up with Simon, then when I started seeing Phil. I've never forgotten it."

"I can understand that. But it *was* a good while ago. I know that doesn't make it any less hurtful, but he's grown up since then – and I doubt he's even in touch with Simon Shaw."

"I know.... and it's good that it's an option, but...I just don't like the idea of him knowing all my business. Sorry, Carol – you must think I'm so ungrateful."

"Not at all! I'm just concerned, Kay – because if you get the warning, that might make it harder if things...well, if things go any further."

"I know what you mean – but let's hope they won't, and that I'll be back, just as soon as these meds kick in."

"Well, there's a couple of weeks to go yet, anyway. Can you keep it in mind? Then if you do have a change of heart, just let me know?"

"I will. But I doubt it."

On the face of it, Carol was right. So much had changed, these past twenty-odd years, and both Simon and Martin were married with families. But were they *really* any different? What Carol didn't know was that Martin made disparaging comments behind her back, about her being "too soft" with her staff. If he disagreed with the exemption report, he might well make things hard for her. Carol had been so good to Kay, so she wouldn't have her putting her neck on the line. And then the thought of him knowing the ins-and-outs of her life…

Perhaps she could just bite the bullet and go back - the easiest way all-round to avoid the warning. By now, the increase in meds was finally starting to help, and the side-effects had thankfully worn off – but she was still far from ready to face people. Some days were better than others; but then, on what she'd thought had been a good day, the tears would come from nowhere.

In some ways, it was as if Phil had died, too. The difference was, she could change this. All she had to do was pick up the phone…But that was like admitting she was wrong, which maybe she was, for how she'd spoken to him - but not for being upset in the first place. She still felt she deserved an explanation – and if this wasn't forthcoming, they'd be back to square-one. Then, there was the chance was all too late, and he wouldn't want to know...the longer it went on, the more likely that seemed.

Each time the landline rang, there was that brief hope it might be him, followed by bitter disappointment when it turned out to be a cold-call. Knowing and accepting that he wouldn't get in touch, she unplugged the phone, switched off her mobile and ignored the doorbell when it rang, avoiding going out whenever she could. When the written warning duly arrived in the post, she tore it savagely to bits and flung it in the bin.

Another week passed – well, she guessed a week, but had lost all track of time – and one morning the doorbell rang, loudly, getting more persistent the more she refused to answer. Then she was aware of someone shouting her through the letterbox.

"Mrs. Wainwright? Katie? Are you there?"

She looked through the window and was horrified to see a police-car. Phil...

"What is it...what's happened to him?" she almost sobbed as she opened the door.

There were two policemen, one young and tall, the other balding and middle-aged.

"Him?" the older one said. "No, love, we're here to check you're okay. Your friend was concerned."

As it turned out, Jen had tried many times to ring, and had eventually called round – naturally thinking the worst when she saw the lights were on but got no reply.

"I'm so sorry to have wasted your time," Kay said mortified.

Not to worry, the policeman said, best to be safe - adding that she had a good friend, there. She should probably ring her, to put her mind at rest...As soon as they'd gone, she called Jen without delay.

"You gave us quite the scare, missus," Jen said. "Lisa was worried too. You're not on your own, you know."

And it was at this point that Kay realised enough was enough – she had to pull herself from the brink. Get back to work, keep her friends close, or they, too, might slip through her fingers.

Chapter Twenty-five

Thinking back to when Andy died, no-one could have prepared her for how that felt. She'd only got through it by trying to turn things around and, hard as it was, looking for any kind of positive. While this was a different situation – different kind of grief – there was no reason she couldn't learn to cope in a similar way. Perhaps it was what you chose to focus on that mattered most.

So, instead of dwelling on how much she missed Phil, she could think of all that was good about being single. As much as she loved him, he had his failings, like anyone; and while she could never forget the best in him, it wouldn't harm to remember his faults a little more. It started with the smaller things. For instance, if she missed the cup of tea he'd bring her each morning, she'd counter it by remembering his untidiness. Think of a pro; match it with a con. Deep down, this didn't rest easy with her – but what could she do? The other choice was to keep pining away for her old life....

During these times, she reflected often on that conversation with Dot, on the eve of the wedding. She'd never agree with her Mum's idea that some folks were "better" than others – but perhaps, after all, she had a point. Dot had compared her with Bob – and the more she thought about it, she and Phil were, indeed, Bob and Viv in reverse. Quiet, sensitive Bob, with his loud, tough but good-hearted wife...Kay was six when Bob died and had fond memories of them both.

Viv was warm, fun and great with kids; and because she and Bob had none of their own, she made a fuss of Kay and Andy, much the same as Phil with the twins. Bob was reserved, but still kind, watching indulgently as Viv ran around with them.

"Mad, if you ask me," he smiled, winking at Viv.

"Watch it, lad!" she laughed. "Or I'll have your guts for garters!"

Kay and Andy giggled, while Dot glowered at Viv.

"Guts for garters!" Andy shrieked.

"What's 'garters', Uncle Bob?" Kay asked.

"Now, that's enough, both of you!" Dot said sternly. "Leave Uncle Bob alone!"

Then, without warning, these two lovely people disappeared from their lives. Not long before this, her grandad died. The memory was vague, as were all her recollections of Howie; a weak, shadowy figure, who seemed always unwell. It was a while before they next saw Bob - and when they did, he was pale, solemn, and alone.

"Where's Auntie Viv?" Andy asked.

"Shut up, Andrew!" Dot snapped. "Stop being nosy!"

"Don't be too hard on him, sis," was all Bob said. "He's not to know."

That was the last time they saw him. The tears started soon after; hard to say how long it lasted, but it felt like it would never stop. No-one would tell her why, and she soon began to ask herself if, somehow, *she* was to blame for her mum being so upset. A couple of weeks later, it was Irene, not Dot, who picked them up from school. Their mum and dad had to go somewhere, she said, so she would be giving them their tea that evening; they were there for two or three hours but, again, it seemed like no end was in sight. The longer it went on, the more Kay wondered if this was because of whatever she'd done wrong – or if something bad had happened....

When George and Irene finally took them home, they found their parents dressed in black, sitting glumly on the couch.

"What's wrong, Mum?" Kay asked, as Dot started crying again and Frank held her, silently.

"Oh, Frank – what will I do without him?"

While Frank got up to make a drink, Kay and Andy cuddled up to Dot, trying to comfort her. Kay had worked out by now that this was all to do with Bob. She remembered the relief that it *wasn't* her fault, after all - and the sadness at knowing that she'd never see Bob or Viv again.

"It's all *her* fault!" Dot said furiously, as Frank brought in the tea. "That bloody Viv! We lose Dad, and the first thing she does is walk out the door! But what else do you expect? Family like that – jailbird father – wouldn't know the right thing to do if it hit them in the face! And the nerve of her, turning up today..."

"Well," Frank pointed out, "I suppose they *were* still married..."

"No, Frank, don't you dare stick up for her! She ended that marriage the minute she left him! Honestly, Frank, these people – they don't think like us…"

Almost word for word, the same thing she said about Phil. Of course, no-one deserved to be looked down on; it wasn't Phil's fault – or Viv's – how they'd grown up. But while she thought her mum could have shown more compassion, Kay could now see, at least in part, what she was driving at. Your upbringing did affect how you saw life, and – as she'd said to Carol – if it was going to work, you had to be on the same page.

She guessed it all came down to whether you'd had loving parents. If you'd never experienced that bond, how could you understand your partner's grief when one of them passed away? Viv hadn't had the easiest start; her dad was in and out of prison most of the time. In some ways, her childhood was worse than Phil's; his kindly, down-to-earth grandparents were poles apart from the McIlroys.

Viv had worked for Dot's Aunt Olive, who ran a florist's shop in Wavertree. Bob, when home on leave, would sometimes pop in to see his aunt, and Viv would flirt with him; he was too shy to make a move at first, but her teasing gradually brought him out. He surprised everyone when, at 33, he married this lively girl, some fourteen years his junior. Soon after, he decided to get the job ashore. Dot, convinced Viv had forced him into it, maintained that this was the start of her brother's decline; he'd have been okay, she said, if he'd only stayed at sea.

June, meanwhile, got on fine with her sister-in-law – who, after Bob's death, confided in her that it was he, not her, who had ended things. Depressed and grief stricken, he'd told Viv to go because he was "no good to her like this." Dot refused to believe it. "And in any case," she remarked, "she didn't have to *do* it!" Poor Viv. So hurtful, to be pushed away like that, then blamed for the tragic events that followed.

And yet, could Viv *truly* have understood what Bob was going through? For a start, there was the whole thing about men bottling up their feelings; and as Bob was deep and intensely private, his instinct would be to go into his own head. But also, perhaps Viv wouldn't have had the same attachment to her own father, as Bob had to Howie. To give Phil his due, he'd been more than patient; but there were still things he didn't quite "get", especially when it came to mothers.... No-one could blame him. It wasn't wrong - just different.

And while a *few* differences were good, there had to be some common ground. Perhaps, then, she'd made the right decision. The more she focused on this thought, the better she began to feel. There would be the wobbly moments of doubt, as expected, but she soon got into the habit of shooting them down in flames.

They were wrong for each other. She had to believe that; or else the grief would keep coming back to the fore, and she couldn't afford to let that happen.

As her mood began to lift, she gradually got some normality back. She switched her phone on, met up with her friends — started to eat and sleep properly, at long last. After a while, she felt strong enough to give work a try, and asked the doctor for a final note, with a view to a phased return from mid-October.

Days before she was due to go back, she tripped over a loose paving stone on her way from the shops, falling flat on her face, and heavily on her right arm. For obvious reasons, she'd hoped never to set foot in A and E again, but having a bad feeling, went reluctantly to get it seen to. After a four-hour wait, they took an X-Ray that confirmed her worst fears: a fracture to her right elbow. They considered operating, before deciding the best bet was to keep it in a sling and rest it when she could, except for physio, which they'd be in touch to arrange. And work was out of the question; she'd need a note for at least six weeks.

"This does make things a bit tricky," Carol said that night on the phone. "If we could *only* have avoided the written warning… although you're not too late to appeal it, you know. And we could still look at exemption."

"No, Carol…"

"Even if your job's on the line? Sorry to be so blunt, Kay, but I don't want things turning out badly. As it stands, the warning's been issued — and you know what comes next. They might be lenient if they knew the full story — but you don't want that."

"Look, I know it seems like I'm cutting off my nose to spite my face. But let's see how I go on with my arm – hopefully I'll get back before anything's decided."

"Okay." Carol sighed. "I just hope it won't be too late…but leave it with me. Let's keep an open mind."

But in her heart, Kay knew what was coming. *Dead woman walking*, she said to herself; and when she got called in for a "chat" the following month, she was almost used to the idea.

****

That night, she knew she wouldn't sleep. It was warm, sticky, and humid, and as she tossed and turned, her mind still racing, she felt more and more uncomfortable. After a few hours of re-positioning herself and fluffing up the pillows, she admitted defeat. Switching on the bedside lamp and Smooth FM[xx], she sat up and began to look at Jen's books.

She'd heard of some of the before – particularly "The Secret[xxi]", which Jen believed in passionately. Kay would always have her doubts, but Jen was so wise; there had to be *something* in it. As expected, it was almost relentlessly upbeat. But what did liked was the idea that, if you set your mind to it, you had it in you to achieve whatever you wanted.

Believing was the first thing. Then, to make it work, you had to emphasise your strengths, not your failings, and make the most of what you *could* do. In her own case, she'd lost so much – but what she did still have was a good starting place. A house she owned outright; some money in the bank; not a fortune but, for the moment, it would keep the wolf from the door. The other thing she now had in abundance was *time*. She'd been juggling so much, these last years. Every so often, it had crossed her mind to learn a new skill, a language, something just for *her*, but the very thought of it exhausted her.

She had no regrets about her years at the office, but perhaps she'd let herself get too cosy – and this might be the push she needed to challenge herself. So, tomorrow, the first step towards her fresh start would be a major clear-out; get rid of anything she didn't want or need – and as she did this, decide what she might want to do next. A sudden calm came over her as she realised that whatever this was, it would work out; she'd make it. With that in mind, she felt her whole body start to relax. Maybe she *would* get some sleep, after all.

Part Two: Taking off

Chapter Twenty-six

The book was better than Rachel had expected; although, in fairness, she hadn't expected much at all. Self-published – nothing wrong with that, of course; everyone had to start somewhere. But when Jill described it as a Liverpool-based family saga, she'd guessed it would be full of tired old clichés, and was pleasantly surprised to find it intelligent and well-written. The story was driven by the characters and their struggles; the setting played its part but was secondary to this, and while the poverty was certainly important, it was never exaggerated. You could easily place these people in comfortable, modern surroundings, and their issues would be the same.

Starting in the 30s and ending in the 80s, it spanned three generations of a Liverpool-Irish family. Part One focused on Pat Whelan, arriving in Liverpool in 1938 with pregnant wife Kathleen (Kitty) and their daughters, from their village in Donegal. They settle in court housing off Scotland Road; Pat can only find casual work on the docks, often struggling to get hired each day, while Kitty increasingly becomes the breadwinner, cleaning shops and selling fruit from a handcart. She returns to work soon after the birth of their son, Michael – and tragically, when the baby is just months old, dies suddenly from a stroke. What follows, inevitably, is Pat's torment and grief as he struggles to raise his family alone.

Something of a firebrand, Pat's hot-headedness gets him in trouble at work, and is why he's so often laid off. Yet he was perhaps the most loveable male character that Rach had come across in a while – warm, generous, with much sensitivity behind a rough demeanour. He adores Kitty - and her death leaves him a broken man.

Part Two began in 1960 – the eve of slum clearance. There is a sense of change in the air, and a mixed reception to this – while some, like the Whelans, believe it can't come soon enough, others prefer to tolerate appalling conditions for the sake of staying together. At a dance one night, young Mick, now aged 21, meets posh, Protestant Sylvia Roberts, who lives off Penny Lane with her strict, Welsh grandmother and timid, downtrodden mum. Their courtship is kept secret. Sylvie's controlling gran hates the idea of her having a boyfriend at all, let alone a Catholic, and Mick is a typical jack-the-lad - everything Gran is bound to detest.

When Mick is called up for National Service, he and Sylvie write to each other, using her friend Cath's address as a care-of, and she plans their wedding while he's away. On his return, she announces to her horrified gran and bewildered mum that she's getting married – and promptly walks out before they can say a word. They live with Pat for a while after the wedding, until Sylvie falls pregnant and they move to Speke; ideal for Mick, who now works at Ford's.

Rach sympathised with this young couple yet found she couldn't quite warm to them as she'd done with Pat and Kitty. Mick is a decent enough young man, but loud and a bit full of himself. Sylvie shows strength of character in standing up to her gran but is neurotic and more than a little buttoned-up. Which all made sense, Rach thought– with that kind of background, she was bound to be repressed. As for Mick, it was quite believable that he might be spoilt. His older sisters adore him, and he's the centre of his dad's world - even more so for not having a mum. Despite the focus being on Mick and Sylvie, it was Pat who still stood out for Rach. There was much emphasis on the bond between father and son, and the warm welcome Pat gives his new daughter-in-law.

Fast-forward to the 80s for Part Three. This could easily have been a carbon-copy of "Boys from the Blackstuff[xxii]"; but, as with the Depression years, the social issues, though ever-present, would never completely take over. If anything, life has improved for the Whelans, who now have their own home in Mossley Hill. Mick has been promoted to foreman at Ford's, while Sylvie works part-time as a school secretary. They have four children: twins Paul and Tony, in their early 20s; Christina (Chrissi), 17; and Claire, the baby at 16.

Sylvie's favourite by far is Claire, whilst despairing of tomboyish Chrissi. Their relationship (never great) has deteriorated in recent years, especially since the death of Chrissi's beloved grandad. Pat's dementia and subsequent passing, when she was fourteen, marked the beginning of a rebellion against Sylvie, who she feels showed no understanding of her grief. Sylvie, meanwhile, sees Claire as her only ally in a house full of men – and in this she includes Chrissi, who resists her mother's attempts to "girlify" her. Sylvie builds up an image in her mind of her youngest as polite and "good" - when in fact she is a manipulative, spoilt "princess". She and Chrissi are sworn enemies; and Sylvie, unable to consider that her favourite could be wrong, frequently accuses Chrissi of being a bully.

When Claire falls pregnant, Sylvie is forced to face reality. Once the baby is born, Claire takes no responsibility, leaving her mum to do everything as she's off galivanting with her friends. Sylvie becomes exhausted - putting a strain on her relationship with Mick, who does little to help around the house. Tension escalates between them; but she finds an unlikely ally in Chrissi, who calls out her father for his sexism. Despite their long-standing conflict, Chrissi joins forces with her mother in caring for her nephew. The novel ended with Sylvie's regret for how she has misunderstood – and sometimes mistreated – her older daughter over the years.

The more she read, the more Rach could imagine it as a play; could picture the set, how it would look, perhaps who might play the parts… which, of course, was exactly what Jill wanted! She often brought home offerings from members of her writers' group, hoping it would trigger something off for her to put pen to paper again. And the thought *had* crossed her mind…But no – that wasn't happening. It had meant so much to her, for so many years; but Rach was done with writing.

Chapter Twenty-seven

Kay had been fully prepared to dislike Stuart Snowe. Of course, she'd always reserve judgement; but with his dour demeanour and crisp, clipped speech, her early impressions were of someone brittle and cold.

Stuart was the Head at the primary school in West Derby where Kay worked part-time as a classroom assistant. Following her dismissal, she'd had just six months unemployed before finding the job advertised online. She decided to go for it on the off-chance, not building her hopes up too much – apart from her sick record, her lack of experience would likely go against her. But she'd had a good interview, deciding it best to be completely upfront; and as it turned out, they were impressed with her honesty. It was a pleasant surprise when she got a call offering her the post and asking if she could start in January.

After so many years at the same office, it was nerve-wracking; but she soon found her feet and settled in well. The class she was assisting in was Set 2 of Year 4 (second-year Juniors, in "old money"). While a few of the kids could be cheeky, most were loveable and easy to engage with; and she hit it off straightaway with the teacher, Jill Duncan.

In her 40s and originally from Edinburgh, Jill had come to Liverpool years ago to study, and had met her long-term partner on the course. She'd retained a soft Scottish lilt, and her reserved but kindly manner was not unlike Kay's own. The other thing they shared was their love of books. For some time now, Jill had hosted a reading group – a small gathering of five or six, including a couple of the teachers. Kay was more than welcome to join, she said.

It was something she'd often thought about. She'd once enquired about a book club at one of the libraries, but her gut feeling was to give it a miss – the guy who ran it seemed off-hand and rather unwelcoming. This would hopefully be different – Jill was lovely, and the other teachers who went seemed friendly enough. It would be a chance to get to know them if nothing else. They met once a month at Jill's flat on Hadassah Grove – a charming, almost olde-worlde little street off bohemian Lark Lane, just minutes from Kay's beloved Sefton Park. The flat was quirky, eccentric, and full of colour; much like Jill's partner, Rachel.

Kay had met Rach on a couple of occasions, only briefly. Somehow, they put her in mind of the girls from Fleetwood Mac; restrained, elegant Jill with her short blonde hair and tailored suits; flamboyant Rach in her beaded, flowing dresses, long crimped hair a vibrant shade of magenta, somewhere between hippie and punk. It was hard to form an impression over such a short space of time, but her manner was warm and open; and from what Jill had said, she was so giving of herself that she often got hurt by those less generous in spirit. Jill was clearly the calm, placid one, who protected her more extrovert, but fragile other-half.

There was a noticeable atmosphere at school between Jill and another teacher, Geoff Dent. It turned out Geoff had once been a good friend until, after a disagreement, he and his cronies had bullied Rachael online. Kay knew that Rach was a local playwright. Not a big name on the scale of someone like Willy Russell or Jimmy McGovern – most of her work was in fringe theatre, although she'd also written for TV - most notably, some episodes of an adaptation of "Hard Times".

Rach's most recent play – four years ago now – was about a battered wife. Kay vaguely remembered a review in the Echo. Geoff, who seemed to have turned against women after his divorce, took offence at this being, in his eyes, yet another portrayal of female-as-victim. He picked an argument about it on Facebook; before long, the trolls had joined in and the whole thing got ridiculously out of hand.

It ended with both Rach and Jill closing down their Facebook accounts. The saddest part was that Rach, although still very much involved in the theatre, had stopped writing altogether. Jill kept trying, without success, to convince her that it was silly to let one (bitter, screwed-up) person ruin something that meant so much. Understandably, she found it hard to forgive Geoff – she kept things civil and professional, but nothing more.

Until their falling-out, Geoff had been a regular member of Jill's book group, along with Ella Bancroft and Bryan Groom. More recently – and to Bryan and Ella's annoyance – Stuart had also started to attend. ("Can't you just tell him it's cancelled?" Ella had suggested to Jill. "I know there's no real harm in him, but bloody hell! Hard work isn't in it!"). But whatever their opinion of Stuart, at least they could tolerate him. No-one could bear Geoff; partly for his attitude to women, mostly for how he'd treated Rach.

Thankfully, Kay never had reason to speak to Geoff. As for Stuart, he *was* a strange cookie – hard to read, gave nothing away. His manner was an odd mix of timid and austere; there was much sniggering from the kids at his attempts to sound jolly and avuncular, reminding Kay of deadly-serious Mr. Fairbrother's morning call in "Hi-di-Hi". Her first meeting with him was not at her interview, as she might have expected, but a few days after she started, when he popped into class for a word with Jill, nodding curtly when Jill introduced her. How rude, Kay thought – he was her boss, after all.…

"I wouldn't take it to heart," Jill said. "That's just Stu. I don't think he even knows he's doing it."

"Then perhaps someone should tell him," Kay replied, drily. "And if he keeps looking at me like something the cat dragged in, it might be me!"

Jill laughed. "To be fair, I've known Stu for years, and he's painfully shy. Not that I'm making excuses – I honestly think he just doesn't know what to say."

Of course, Kay understood that – and while she'd never condone rudeness, she tried to give him the benefit of the doubt. But then, if he really *was* that shy, how did he get to become Head? The jury was out; she'd make up her mind when – *if* – she got to know him better.

As it happened, that opportunity came, not at school, but at the book group. She hadn't realised Stu would be going and groaned inwardly when he arrived. Again, just an abrupt nod in her direction. Great start, she thought.

For all his reticence, Stu spoke plentifully and quite eloquently throughout the evening. While Jill encouraged him to engage, Bryan and Ella didn't try too hard to hide their disdain. Despite her own reservations, Kay felt a little sorry for him, as well as slightly uncomfortable; she didn't like the idea of someone being ganged up on, whatever their faults. Because she'd only just joined, she hadn't had a chance to read the book so couldn't contribute much to the discussion. Still, she enjoyed listening, and the time passed quickly by. Happily, next month's choice was one she loved – Joanne Harris' "Chocolat[xxiii]"– and no doubt by then she'd have found her feet and have more to say.

To round off, Jill asked if anyone had brought their own work. The group, she explained, doubled up as book club and writer's workshop, as some of them wrote poetry. Great idea, Kay said; longing to tell them how, after 27 years, *she* was writing again…. As no-one wanted to read this time, they finished earlier than expected. Jill asked her about getting home. She'd be fine, she said – she'd get a bus to the Rocket from Aigburth Vale.

"Are you sure? It's a bit lonely round the Vale at night. I'll come with you…or if someone can drop you off…?"

"I'm going that way," Stu said.

"No, honestly," Kay began. "I'd hate to put you out…"

"Nonsense. I go through the Rocket anyway. It's no problem."

"And I'd feel happier if he took you," Jill added.

"Well, that settles it," Stu said, with the faint glimmer of a smile.

Kay followed him to his car, not looking forward to the inevitable awkwardness of the journey. Still, it was kind of him – and she appreciated it on this frosty night. To her relief, the conversation flowed better than anticipated. While you'd certainly never describe him as "gushing", Stu was less severe and much more pleasant than she'd first thought. Looking at him more closely, she could see he wasn't a bad looking man – somewhere in his 60's, probably handsome in his day. Tall, slim, greyish-ginger hair and an elegant face.

It turned out Stu was amongst those who brought his own work along for feedback – he mainly wrote poetry and had self-published a volume a few years ago. Before she knew it, she found herself telling him about her own book. It hadn't felt right before, in front of everyone; but somehow, her gut instinct was to trust this man who, with all his funny, closed-off ways, she couldn't dislike. He looked surprised – not in a bad way – and again, there was that almost-but-not-quite smile.

"That's wonderful," he said; the most animated she'd heard him. "Well done you!".

Chapter Twenty-eight

From then on, Stu became a firm friend. Before long, she'd told Jill about her writing, then the rest of the group, which included two other members - Anna and Kim, who'd worked with Jill in her early teaching days. They all gave her plenty of support, and some useful feedback, much of it positive – there were just a couple of parts she could tighten up a little. It was Stu who helped the most, proof-reading and editing the final draft, and he also suggested the title, "Turbulence". Once it was all finished, he asked her what she planned to do with it.

In truth, she hadn't thought too much about that. The thing that drove her to write, above all, was the love and enjoyment of it. If she could make some money, then all well and good – but she had to stay realistic, being well aware how hard it was to be accepted by a publisher. It wouldn't stop her trying, but the chances were slim. Stu agreed that traditional publishing perhaps wasn't the best route to start with; in fact, he said, it wasn't just hard for new writers, but nigh-on impossible. For him, self-publishing was a foot in the door. If you did well enough with it, there was always the chance, however small, that to something bigger. Admittedly, he hadn't known of many who'd gone on to make a fortune, but it did happen. It was worth thinking about.

It made sense. She'd put so much into her book that it seemed such a waste for it to languish in a drawer. She wanted it to be read and (hopefully) enjoyed; and if just one person got something from it, it would be a job well done. The downside, of course, was that to get anywhere at all with it, she'd really have to put herself out there – not something that came naturally – but Stu said he'd give her all the help she needed, and they worked together on setting up a blog, and various other ways to promote it. She managed to sell thirty copies in three months; nothing to write home about, some might say, but she was more than pleased.

The thing that lifted her spirits the most was how her friends and family got behind her – not only buying copies but recommending it to others, in the hope that they too would spread the word. Perhaps it *was* only thirty – but little by little, she was getting it outside her immediate circle. Through word-of-mouth, sales slowly but steadily increased until, another few months on, it had reached a hundred – not bad, Stu said, considering many sold nothing at all. She got good feedback and some decent reviews, with some readers commenting that it gave them hope of getting through their worst times. The whole point of what she'd set out to do!

Above all, she'd got back part of her life she'd thought had gone for ever - and that alone meant everything.

The idea had come to her just days after being finished up. Waking early next morning for that fresh start she'd promised herself, she began her long-overdue clear-out. Over the weekend, she bagged most of her old clothes, to be taken to the charity shops, and on the Monday, her next job was to tackle the mountain of paperwork that was stuffed into the chest of drawers. She started early, throwing herself into the task in the hope it would take her mind off what day it was - Phil's 50th.

It didn't take long to get through it all – she worked quickly, pausing only when she reached the bottom left-hand drawer. She'd left this deliberately to the end, because it contained a box of her parents' old letters and documents, which she'd found while clearing the bungalow. At that time, she'd been in no state of mind to contemplate opening it, so she'd brought it straight home, shut it away and never looked at it since. And didn't have to now, she reminded herself – there was no pressure; but she'd have to face it one day. Perhaps now was as good a time as any.

The most upsetting thing was Andy's funeral bill and cuttings from the Echo obituaries, but she'd prepared for that. A photo of a very young Bob in the navy; Dot and June as children, well-dressed, happy. Kay smiled to herself, guessing it was during their time in Woolton; at least *one* part of her mum's life was carefree. Then a bundle of older, yellowing papers – amongst them the death certificates for both sets of grandparents.

It was those on her dad's side that fascinated her. She knew so much of Dot's family history, so little of Frank's. She remembered nothing of Nin, or her grandad Joe; and, of course, her grandmother Mary-Ellen had died years before she was born. Because Frank was so young, his memories of her were hazy. The one thing clear was that she was worked extremely hard to hold her family together in the Depression; and now, with just this fraying bit of paper to go on, Kay tried to create an image in her mind.

"Mary-Ann Cooney (nee O'Neill). Date and Place of Death: Great Homer Street, Liverpool, 24th November, 1936. Present at Death: John Sheehan, Margaret Maloney." (Names that meant nothing to Kay). "Occupation: Street trader, housewife. Wife of Joseph Denis Cooney, Dock Labourer. Born: 29th June, 1906."

Barely 30; not at home, but on "Greaty", as Frank called it, famous for its many shops and barrow-women; as a "street-trader", Mary-Ann had probably collapsed and died at work. John and Margaret were likely passers-by who'd stopped to help.

"Cause of Death: 1. Stroke; 2. Enlarged heart; 3. General debility."

It was this last one that seemed the crux of everything: weakness, poor health, exhaustion. There were no pictures of Mary-Ann, so Kay had no idea of what she looked like; but imagined her as closer to 60 than 30; haggard, careworn, thin. Tough times: and as Frank often remarked, who the hell would want to go back to *that*? Poor Frank. To lose his mum and then, not so long afterwards, to have gone through what he did on that farm…No wonder he'd run away. Always so calm and level-headed, yet he must have carried around such pain…perhaps, at the end, he was finally letting go of anger that was pent up for years.

Drying her eyes, Kay continued to work through the bundle. Her parents' marriage lines. A photo of both families, early 70s, gathered at St. Barnabas Church, Mossley Hill – Andy's Christening. Then a thick notebook, in which she recognised her own handwriting, and realised immediately what it was – part of a book she'd started writing, a year or so before Andy's death.

Seeing it again was quite a surprise. When Frank and Dot had moved to the bungalow, she guessed they'd got rid of anything that wasn't needed. But somehow, her notebook survived, caught up amongst all the old documents they'd decided to keep hold of. Part of another life, long gone.... As she read through it, her naivete was all-too obvious. She could see now that it was "preachy"; too much "tell" and not enough "show". Yet, there were some good ideas. It had a decent storyline, with a few well-developed characters. Some needed more work than others – but still, the potential was there. Later that evening, once her clear-out was finished, she sat down to look at it properly, and before long, found herself jotting down some notes.

Chapter Twenty-nine

The book, started when she was 17, was inspired at least in part by "Brookside[xxiv]". The main characters were a couple – Mick and Sylvie Whelan – based loosely on Bobby and Sheila Grant. The main difference was Sylvie's well-heeled, Protestant background, as opposed to working-class, Catholic Sheila. Mick, meanwhile, is more easy-going, less belligerent than Bobby, but still has more than a touch of chauvinism; a staunch trade-unionist, his leftist principles fall sadly short when it comes to gender.

Like the Grants, the Whelans have a rebellious teenage daughter, Chrissi – fiercely intelligent with feminist views that clash often with her father's traditionalism. She also argues bitterly with her mother, and her spoilt younger sister Claire. Their sons, Paul and Tony, are very different twins. Compared with the girls, they are somewhat in the background. Paul is loud but kind-hearted, while Tony is quiet, intellectual and gay, although this is never revealed to the family (Mick, unsurprisingly, is homophobic).

There were also notes on what would have been the first part of the novel, set in 1960, when Mick and Sylvie meet and fall in love. It had got as far as him proposing, shortly before leaving for National Service. Sylvie's anxious Mum and formidable Welsh grandmother were to be based on Dot's descriptions of Gladys and Dilys. Like Frank, Mick had lost his mother at an early age; his father, Pat, a good-hearted Irishman, welcomes

Sylvie warmly to the family, in sharp contrast to her Gran's cold disapproval.

They meet at a dance; she: posh, shy, uptight, virginal; he: loud, tough, cocky, jack-the-lad. Despite the similarities in their backgrounds, this couple were nothing like Frank and Dot. Of course, it would be easy to make comparisons with herself and Phil, but this idea had been born way before they'd met. It was never "their" story; nor would she want it to be.

For a start, Mick (unlike Phil) is far less of a rebel than he'd like to believe. His Teddy Boy image is all about fitting in, not kicking back, ending abruptly with his National Service. Besides this, Mick has known nothing but love and acceptance. He has never been looked down upon or ridiculed; and despite growing up in poverty, without a mother, has enjoyed a happy, carefree childhood as the doted-on youngest.

Sylvie had also spent much of her life with just one parent, but in vastly different circumstances. Her father walked out when she was 5, tearing apart her already fragile mother who, not being able to manage, had little choice but to move in with Gran. It is a cold, austere household compared with Mick's, yet Sylvie too is over-indulged; like Pat, her mother had tried – perhaps too hard – to compensate.

As Kay developed the characters for her new version, she found she'd made Mick and Sylvie less likeable than in the original. The more she thought about it, this fitted in with the storyline, especially their treatment of Chrissi. While it made sense for them to have a daughter like Claire, who would be Chrissi's main influence?

Her grandad, of course. In the early draft, it was touched upon that Chrissi had a strong bond with Pat and had struggled when he died - and her mother's lack of empathy had led to resentment. Kay decided to explore this further. Pat - previously a minor character - would need to play a bigger role, so there had to be more scenes based around Mick's home life, not just his courtship of Sylvie.

Originally, the early chapters revolved around dancehalls and cafes. The couple first meet at the (pre-Beatles) Cavern, and their dates are frequently at the Kardomah (which both Dot and June talked of fondly). These places would still feature, but the main setting now would be Scottie Road and the docks, where Mick works with his dad before the army and Ford's. The relationship between father and son would be more of a focus, with more insight into Pat's background, especially his suffering after losing his wife.

Just like the first-time round, Kay began at the end. Re-writing the later sections wasn't hard at all, because of course she'd lived through the 80s, and could vividly recreate the music, fashion, and political climate of the time. The early parts could be trickier. 1960 might as well have been another world – at least in areas like Scottie. Slum clearance was still a few years away, and the poorer districts of "old" Liverpool were much as they'd been for decades. To get an insight into what life was like, she looked at some old photos on local history sites.

1934: a group of children gathered in a court off Silvester Street - where Frank was born. The family only moved to Nin's in 1936; Kay wasn't sure which court they'd lived in, but any of the toddlers could have been her dad. None of them looked happy; the surroundings were dark and dismal, the houses dilapidated. 1946: a drawn, painfully thin young woman with her little girl, surrounded by rubble in her backyard in Canterbury Street, off Islington. 1954: another woman with a baby, outside another crumbling home in nearby Soho Square, as she chatted to MP "Battling" Bessie Braddock. Tired and worn, yet tough and determined – just how Kay imagined her grandmother. Someone commenting on the site had posted a YouTub[xxv]e link, which turned out to be just what she was looking for: a documentary filmed in inner-city Liverpool, circa 1959[xxvi].

Just over a decade before Kay was born – it might have been a century. Families huddled together in the same bed; water dripping into a bucket from a hole in the ceiling. Constantly, the women are seen scrubbing their steps or windows, or at the washhouse where, amidst the heat and toil, there seems plenty of chat. It is made clear that, as hard as this is, it is better than what went before. Many heartrending tales of sickness and early death, although not without humour, too. The film would end on a positive note, with children in a schoolyard – a symbol of hope with their laughter and song.

If nothing else, it put her own problems in perspective. Not for the first time, she felt guilt for her depression. She had enough to eat and a nice home; and whatever she'd dealt with these past few years, it didn't compare with the sheer drudgery of these women's lives. But, as Jen often said, a person's problems were real for *them*; and money would never be a cure for grief.

All true, of course, but it didn't harm, either – and just imagine coping with sick parents, bereavement, marital breakdown, in those cramped, cold, damp houses, with little cash to spare and no labour-saving devices. More than anything, it made her feel that bit closer to her dad. She'd always thought of Dot's life as more difficult…. If only Frank had opened up more; but then, would anyone have really *listened*?

Feeling guilty was easy – but how would that change what had been and gone? She'd had this conversation with herself many a time. So, instead of wasting precious time on it, she could do something positive to honour Frank's memory. What better than dedicating her book to him, and making it a tribute to his family?

Once she'd decided on this, the path was clearer. The novel would now be in three parts, beginning in the late 30s at the time of Mick's birth. She'd also work on the characters of Pat and his wife - loosely based on how Kay envisaged Joe and Mary-Ann.

Her initial idea for Pat was that he'd be rather quiet. But as she developed him, it somehow seemed right for him to be more of an extrovert – a "man-mountain", in character as well as stature. Rough-hewn and rugged, yet unafraid to wear his heart on his sleeve, and woe betide anyone who laughed. No-one would dare, of course – his size and hot Irish temper see to that. Yet, for all his toughness, he is gentle with his children and, of course, his beloved Kitty. A reserved but resilient lady, Kitty had Frank's stoicism and was based on how Kay envisaged Mary-Ann (as well as the women in the film and photos); but there was also something of Dot, in her fear of others' opinions.

Little detail would be given as to why they'd come to Liverpool, apart from the mention of a recent altercation back in Ireland, at the farm where Pat had worked. The voyage is rough (hence Stu's suggestion for the title), seeming to forewarn the challenging times to come. On arrival they look for lodgings in the south of the city – Edge Hill, Dingle, Wavertree - but find the rents too high, even in the poorer streets. With no other option, they move to a slum district between Scottie and nearby Islington - somewhere like Canterbury Street or Soho Square.

They struggle through the first months, constantly regretting their decision. Pat often finds himself on the side-lines while other men are picked for work on the docks. This is, at least in part, due to his fiery nature. He refuses to "play the game" and is unable to keep his mouth shut when things aren't right – his main strength, but also his downfall. Simultaneously, Kitty's new job at TJ's gives a new lease of life, whilst ruining her health. She makes some wonderful friendships and looks forward each day to the chats and laughter; but with house, children and fruit stall, the work sadly proves too much for her. Pat's fears are confirmed when she collapses one day at the shop; to make it worse, her death comes just after a row. Kay then went on to explore how hard it would be for a man in that position, at that time – not only dealing with the grief but having nowhere to go with it.

She worked night and day on the book. It was wonderful to have got writing back, and once she'd started, she truly wondered if she'd ever stop. There was less time to spare once she'd started work at the school, but she still managed a few hours each night. The more she did, the faster the ideas came flooding in. She was on a roll, loving every minute; and while she knew there'd be no money in it, she truly didn't care. Life had a purpose once more. It was all good.

Chapter Thirty

Rach's mother, Beatrice – a brisk, no-nonsense ward sister – often told her she needed a thicker skin. All well-meant, of course; despite their vastly different natures, they were always close. But Bea worried for her younger daughter who – like her dad, Morris – seemed so easily overwhelmed

Her parents had met whilst working at the same hospital, as Morris completed his final year of med school. He was a warm, engaging man, much-loved by his patients; ebullient, exuberant, yet it took little to bring him low. He relied on his wife to keep him grounded – as did Rach and her sister Becky. It had terrified them when, five years ago, Bea was diagnosed with breast cancer, but thankfully it all came good in the end.

Rach started work on "Parole" just a few months before her mother was taken ill, and it was put on hold until she'd fully recovered. The title was partly inspired by a Mike Leigh play, "Hard Labour[xxvii]", about a downtrodden woman suffering the "life-sentence" of a loveless marriage. The protagonist, Ruth, was likewise trapped for many years; the main difference being that her husband claims to love her ("I wouldn't do hit you if I didn't care.") When he beats her so badly that he almost kills her, the shock of what he's done causes a fatal heart attack.; and Ruth's ordeal is finally over. The play dealt with the complexities of Ruth's emotions, as she grieves whilst simultaneously celebrating her new-found freedom.

Once finished, it was performed at Impetus – the small, left-wing fringe theatre which Rach had helped to set up and run since the early 90s, specialising in work from local writers, often with socialist or feminist themes. Rach knew "Parole" was hard-hitting and wouldn't be to everybody's taste; she'd been prepared for mixed reviews, but nothing like the response she got, especially from someone she and Jill considered a friend.

In retrospect, perhaps she should have expected it from Geoff, who was bitter after a nasty divorce in which he got little access to his children. He argued – quite rightly – that it wasn't only women who suffered in life; but was too quick to assume that "the feminists" wouldn't understand this. Men had no choice but to "put up and shut up", he said, shooting down in flames Jill's suggestion that patriarchy, not feminism, might be to blame. They debated the subject on several occasions, until Jill, in her under-stated way, quietly closed it down.

Rach hadn't realised that Geoff had planned to watch the play. It had been quite a shock to go on Facebook and find a rant from him, posted to her timeline – how he was "disappointed, but not entirely surprised" that she'd written "such sexist, misandrist drivel." Flustered and distressed, she made the mistake of trying to reason with him; with hindsight, she'd have been best to take Jill's approach, with something polite but dismissive to nip it in the bud. But, at that point, she had no idea of the extremity of his feeling. She was genuinely upset to think she'd offended him, and anxious to put it right. So, she began by saying she hadn't meant it to come across that way – then to explain that she'd tried to be fair in her portrayal of the characters. For instance, Ruth's brother was a kind man who helped her rebuild her life.

But this had no sway with Geoff. If Rach *really* had a balanced view, he said, she'd have written a play where the *man* was the victim – now that *would* be radical. Everyone laughed at men who were abused, he added – yet the stats showed it happened as much, if not more than, the other way around. Rach (fool that she was!) tried to convince him. She saw his point, she said – although she doubted it happened more *often* to men than women. Not that this made it any less important, of course, and there was still a long way to go. But these days, there was certainly more awareness than there'd been in the past – and hopefully, more understanding. Awareness? Geoff sneered - all well and good, but what he'd like to see was real, practical *support*. He still pressed her on why her main character wasn't male, so she was completely honest. She'd known women who'd been victims, but no men; and her work was based on these women's experiences. More feminist bullshit, he retorted; if Rach *truly* cared about battered men, she'd *learn* about them.

It seemed she could do or say little that was right. Geoff had the idea fixed in his mind that she was against all men, against *him*, and nothing would convince him otherwise – and would twist everything she said to prove this point. Ironically, the more he went on, the more "rad-fem" she felt. For some men, a woman was always in the wrong. Did they all think like this, deep down…? Don't go there, she told herself; this is what he wants. For you to feel like that, *say* that, so you'll fall into his trap…So, she tried a different approach.

"Fair enough, Geoff – guilty as charged. But let's say I'd done what you wanted. Would it really make you feel any better?"

No response. As things went quiet for a few days, she thought that might be an end to it. But then he started up again – this time joined by trolls. There were three of them, all from an online men's forum that Geoff had joined. Officially, this group dealt with genuine issues – mental health, fatherhood, wellness. In reality, it was little more than a platform for misogyny. The problem was, they argued, that women had too much to say, these days – and it didn't make them happy, because deep down, they wanted to be controlled. They used Rach's play as a case in point – "I mean, if she's so desperate to get out, why didn't she do it years ago?" She could have explained to them the impact of abuse on self-esteem but didn't waste her breath. She hoped that by completely blanking them, she'd make them give up and lose interest – but it only got worse.

The language grew cruder, the tone more threatening, as the comments became homophobic, and they ridiculed her profile picture of herself and Jill. So far, so predictable, and in any other circumstance she might even have laughed at them. But, as she continued not to rise to it, one of them warned her to stop ignoring them - otherwise they might just try and find out where she lived. Then, if that wasn't enough, things took an anti-Semitic turn.

They made much of the link between Jewishness and feminism, arguing that women like Rach were "spoilt princesses" who knew nothing of real oppression. Of course, Rach knew that she'd been lucky – but she'd always understood this, even as a child, often asking herself why others couldn't have the kind of life she had.

She'd had a wonderful childhood, but her parents had worked damned hard for it, and would never have got where they were without her grandparents' sacrifices. This was especially true for Morris, who'd grown up in relative poverty in Liverpool's "old" Jewish quarter around Low Hill, the son of a tailor. His parents had scrimped to get their boys through university, also dealing with the threat of persecution reaching the UK. Morris, the youngest of two, was born at the height of the Holocaust, not long before the family shortened their surname from Rosenbloom to the uber-English "Rose". Growing up, Rach got upset when she imagined a different outcome to the war.

As the abuse got more extreme, Geoff seemed to fade into the background; perhaps feeling guilty at what he'd started, or maybe sitting back to enjoy his handiwork. Either way, Rach's next dilemma was whether to tell Jill, who'd already commented that she wasn't herself, and was starting to worry that she'd done something wrong. This was the last thing she wanted – but at the same time, was concerned that Jill would still have to face Geoff each day in work…

"Look, Rach," Jill said that evening. "Whatever it is, please just *tell* me."

"Honestly, Jill, I'm fine – it's just…really, love, I don't want to bother you. It'll all blow over - something and nothing."

"*Rach!*"

"You're not letting this go, are you? Well, just to warn you, it might make things awkward."

"I don't care. I'll cross that bridge when I come to it."

"Okay. So – I'm guessing you've not seen Facebook[xxviii]?"

"No – not for ages. You know me. I was never its greatest fan."

"And Geoff's not said anything to you?"

"*Geoff?*" Jill looked surprised. "To be honest, I hardly speak to him, these days. I've backed off a wee bit since he's started banging on about women – just easier to stay at arm's length. But hang on – why would this be to do with Geoff?"

"Here – take a look."

Rach passed her phone to Jill, who read the whole thing with no comment until reaching the end.

"Jesus Christ, Geoff!" she muttered. "What the fuck have you gotten yourself into? I just wish you'd said something sooner, Rach. I hate the idea of you going through this on your own."

"I just didn't want to make things hard for you at work," Rach said tearfully. "And I kept telling myself, maybe he'll see sense – but in the end, I think it went further than he'd ever intended."

"Yeah, but *he* started it all off – and then to sit back like that and let it happen! I could swing for him! I'll be having words tomorrow – he could get in a lot of trouble for this."

"No, Jill, please! I just want it to stop, that's all. You know, I'm just wondering, if he's so unhappy, did his head get turned by that awful group…?"

"Maybe so – but it's no excuse. He's a grown man! Look – I won't say anything if you don't want me to. But I'm not speaking to him again unless I need to; and if he asks why, I'll have to be upfront."

"That's fair enough. I was going to block him on Facebook, but now I'm thinking of coming off it altogether."

"Good – I'd hoped you'd say that. I am, too."

And so, it all blew over – but when Rach next tried to write, she just couldn't do it. Perhaps she *did* need a thicker skin; but all she knew was that the passion, the joy in it, were gone. Jill pleaded with her to keep going, not to let them win, but it wasn't that simple. Without the love, there was simply nothing to give. She still taught part-time and kept up her work with the Impetus Youth Group; her pleasure in nurturing others' talent remained as strong as ever. Just not her own.

Until this book. You never know, she thought. Maybe.

Chapter Thirty-one

They had "Bake Off" recorded from the night before, but Rach would catch up with it another time, she said; she had "a few bits to do."

"Marking?" Jill asked.

"No, just…a project."

"Sounds intriguing!"

"Look – if I tell you, I don't want you getting your hopes up. I'm writing something."

"Oh, Rach! That's amazing!"

"*Jill…!*"

"I know… I know. I don't mean to jump the gun. But you know how I feel." Jill sighed. "And seeing *him* every day, having to be polite, when I could punch his lights out!"

"Don't let him get to you, my love. It was *my* choice – and I didn't have to listen to them, did I?"

"Maybe – but as you said, it's not that easy. I do understand that." She paused. "So – can I ask what it is?"

"Well – that novel you asked me to look at…"

"Kay's book?"

"Yeah. I think it could work on the stage."

"That's what I'd thought, too," Jill smiled "And I guessed you might say the same."

"I see. More than a little devious, Ms. Duncan, you must admit!"

"Worked a treat, though!"

"Hmm…seriously though, Jill, I mean it about not getting ahead of ourselves. It's early days – it might all come to nothing."

"But even if it does – you're doing what you love again."

"Well, it's not easy, after all this time away from it. When I read what I've written, a lot of it sounds – I don't know, *clumsy*. Plus, we don't know what your friend will say."

"To be honest, I reckon Kay would love it. Do you want me to ask her?"

"When I'm getting somewhere with it, maybe…But not yet."

As planned, Jill put on "Bake Off[xxix]", but gave up half-way through, too excited to concentrate. She couldn't help it. If it didn't work out, that was fine; at least Rach was *interested* again, and that in itself was enough. She insisted she was fine, happier without writing, but Jill wasn't fooled, and had pleaded with her to give it another go. This was partly due to her own guilt; although Rach was adamant she didn't want it taken further, Jill still felt she could have done more. She hated working with Geoff, having to be pleasant while knowing he'd got away with it – all because Rach was trying to make *her* life easier.

Unbeknownst to Rach, Jill did have words with him the following day. She'd started off by keeping her distance, and he soon picked up on things being wrong.

"Look," he said, "I don't know if Rachel's mentioned anything – but I think there may have been a misunderstanding."

"No," Jill replied, briskly. "No misunderstanding. I read it – and yes, she *is* upset."

Geoff's face fell – he'd obviously been expecting to fob her off. "Oh! I'm sorry to hear that. It wasn't personal– I was just debating. And I've nothing against Rach. She's a lovely person."

"Well, you maybe should have told your pals that, when they started bullying her…But let's leave things where they are, eh? The damage is done."

She said nothing to Stu at first – it all came out a year or so down the line, and he said that if only he'd known, he would have backed her to the hilt. Jill didn't doubt this; for all his reserve, but he was no pushover. In fact, he said, it still wasn't too late, if she wanted to raise something now…As much as it galled her, she had to say no – Rach wanted a line drawn under it, and they'd need to respect her wishes. Things soon settled down – but Rach was never quite the same, and each time Jill tried to broach the subject, it ended in a row.

"Look, Jill," she said at last. "I know you mean well, but you don't get it. I doubt you ever will."

For a few days they barely spoke, until she arrived home one evening to find Rach in tears. "Oh, love," she sighed. "You can't go on like this."

"I know," Rach sobbed, "and I'm sorry I took it out on you. I was acting like a spoilt brat."

"We all have bad days," Jill said gently. "It's allowed, you know. But I need to ask, Rach – when you said I'd never get it...?"

"I didn't mean that how it sounded...it's just, all that stuff about denying the Holocaust. I had a great-uncle who died– Nanna's brother. We all know of *someone*. Poor Nanna was heartbroken, and so frightened of it coming here. She was always a bag of nerves. That's why Dad is – why *I* am!" She teared up again. "But it was wrong of me to assume you wouldn't understand. We've all got our shit to deal with."

"Yeah - but nothing like the Holocaust. I just hope I didn't sound dismissive."

"No – you just want me to be happy. And I will be once the dust settles."

As time went on, Rach did get her spark back – but not writing. She still couldn't feel it. But now...perhaps it would all come to nothing. That wasn't the point. The *desire* had returned; and who knew where that could lead next?

Chapter Thirty-two

Jen's first impressions of Stu were not the best. She wasn't alone in this, of course – and while Kay had seen the kind, genuine side, there were few who got that far. Combined with his reserve was a directness which seemed blunt, even harsh, without warmth or humour to soften the blow. To those who knew no better, he was lacking in emotion and empathy; a contradiction when you read his poetry or saw his paintings. He was as talented an artist as he was a writer and had taught A-Level Design before getting his Headship. The finer feelings were clearly there; he spoke little of his childhood, but she somehow guessed it hadn't been great.

Jen had only met him once, briefly, a month or so before the book went online; she'd called while Stu was still round at Kay's, helping with her blog. As always, there was nothing beyond the trademark brusque nod.

"I can see how supportive he is," Jen said later. "But he does have a very cold way about him."

"In all fairness, I honestly don't think he realises."

"Then maybe someone should let him know?"

Kay laughed. "I said the same to Jill when I first met him – almost word for word! She introduced us, and he barely acknowledged me! I was fuming."

"I'll bet you were!"

"His heart's in the right place. Look at all the help he's giving me– I'd have no idea where to start! Still, I know he could work on his manner – you're not the first to notice."

Everything Jen had said was spot on – she couldn't disagree. Besides, it was unrealistic to expect all your friends to get along. They weren't *obliged* to like each other! Yet, there was still that slight disappointment, that Jen hadn't got to see the nicer side...Why did it bother her?

Not long after this, school finished for Easter. Kay took a trip to Devon to visit Auntie June. The internet connection was dead-slow-and-stop. She didn't waste time trying, making the most of the peace and quiet, and catching up once she was home. Amongst her messages was an email from Stu. She found herself smiling, all at once realising he'd been on her mind for most of her time away; and *this* was why it mattered.

"Hi, Kay - hope your break was good. If you'd like to get together later this week, I've got some more ideas for the blog. Let me know what you think."

What she thought, was that he believed in her. That he understood, not just her passion for writing, but her need for privacy and, at times, solitude; and that he wanted this book to happen for her, almost as much as she did herself. Perhaps *this* was what she'd meant, about being on the same page...

Jill, Bryan and Ella had all commented on how she'd brought out the best in him. He'd softened, they said, since his friendship with Kay, remarking how much he thought of her.

But – assuming there was a chance of him feeling how she did – would it honestly work? On the face of it, unlikely. For a start, could *everyone* be wrong? It wasn't just Jen who was less than enamoured, and she had to ask herself if there was something she'd missed, or didn't *want* to see? But then, the whole point about Stu was that he gave away so little – of course they had a different view of him, because he was more himself with her than he was with them. This showed his trust in her – surely a good thing?

Then there was the age gap. Not that this mattered now – but twenty-odd years down the line... But hang on – talk about jumping the gun! Who was to say he'd be interested – or even free, for that matter? He'd never mentioned anyone, but being so private person, no-one could know for certain. She'd always been so focused on the future, preparing for every eventuality. Had it really done any good? Some things had a habit of knocking you sideways, no matter how "ready" you believed you were.

There was one more thing. What she felt for Stu was calm, collected, almost *rational*. No butterflies...a world apart from what she'd had with Phil. But what else could she expect, when Stu was as different from Phil as anyone could possibly be? All she knew was that when she thought of him, which was often, it brought a quiet happiness; gentle, understated perhaps, but happiness, nonetheless.

Chapter Thirty-three

Once Rach had a clear plan in mind, she began to look at the structure the play would follow. Acts One and Two would be done though flashbacks; Three would start with Pat's funeral, then jump forward a few years to show the impact of his loss.

After a slow start, it was like she'd never been away. She'd expected to be rusty – but once the idea had taken root, everything fell quickly into place, and she began to work at high speed, as she always had. It was hard to believe how easily, effortlessly, she had got back into it. The desire *hadn't* gone, after all – crushed underfoot, maybe, but still very much alive! Jill was ecstatic, of course. Rach knew how guilty she felt, which was typical – an earthquake could happen in Outer Mongolia, and Jill would find a way to make it *her* fault!

She still hadn't mentioned it to Kay – Rach didn't feel the time was right. At the back of her mind was still the fear she'd hate it, and any animosity this might cause. If the whole Geoff episode had taught her anything, it was that you could never predict how someone was going to react. She was prepared for disappointment- but, for the moment, wasn't quite ready for her bubble to burst. Not just yet, anyway.

****

"Has Stu told you his news?" Jill asked Kay during the kids' break.

"About retiring? Yeah – he due did mention it."

"Looks like it's all set for the end of the year. And…. you might as well know, Kay – I've put in for the Headship."

"Good for you!"

"Thanks – and look, I'm sorry I never said anything earlier. The interview was yesterday, and I didn't want to tempt fate by telling people."

"Don't worry - I'd be just the same. Although for what it's worth, I think you'll have walked it."

Jill laughed. "Not so sure about that – but thanks for the vote of confidence."

I mean it, Jill – it's what you deserve."

All the while, as Kay kept her tone light, her heart was sinking fast. The end of the year – they'd not long returned from October half-term and were now on the countdown to Christmas. She'd cope, of course – things had changed constantly at the office, especially in recent times, and she'd always just got on and adapted. Jill would make a fantastic Head; it would be lovely to have her as a boss, and although they'd no longer work beside each other, they'd still be able to have lunch and catch up. The main worry was who'd replace her in the classroom - and that it might end up being Geoff Dent.

But as it turned out, Geoff had just got a new job in Formby, nearer where he lived, due to start next month. Thank God, Jill said. Bad enough working together - but, if she was lucky enough to get the job, the one thing she dreaded was being his line manager. Whatever happened with the interview, it was a huge relief all-round that he'd be gone.

As for Stu…They'd stay in touch, that went without saying, but it would be hard, not seeing him every day – unless things moved on between them. As she realised how much she'd miss him, it seemed to hit home just what he meant to her. She'd told no-one how she felt, hoping he might pick up on it…but so far, nothing. Too shy (she hoped!) - or (more likely…) not interested? One thing for sure, she couldn't carry on like *this* – waiting and wondering – and that meant putting her fears aside and finding the chance to speak to him. A huge risk, she knew, but one she'd just have to take.

Jill, as expected, passed the interview with flying colours. Once she'd got the news, Stu settled on the first Friday in December as his leaving date, giving just over a month to work his notice, and show Jill the main aspects of the job; although, as he said, she'd find her own ways as she went along.

Two new teachers would start in the new year, to take over Jill and Geoff's classes. In the meantime, Kay and Pam (Geoff's classroom assistant) would have to step up and take some of the lessons on their own – Jill would be there to help when she could, and the other staff would split the marking between them. Kay was nervous at first, but soon got into her stride.

"Knew you would," Jill smiled. "I've every faith in you."

Once she'd bedded in her new role, she planned to get Kay and Pam onto higher level teaching assistant courses, so they could mark when needed, and take their own classes without support. Then who knows, she said – the next step might be teacher training. She had a few more ideas up her sleeve for staff development but would take it bit by bit over the next year.

It all felt very positive – and despite her apprehension, Kay not only took on board the changes, but began to really look forward to what was to come. If only it could all happen, and yet Stu could still somehow be there…She still hadn't found the right moment to talk to him; he'd been so busy, showing Jill the ropes, and school wasn't the place anyway, of course; she'd have to try and get her chance away from work, perhaps after he'd left, although her main worry was leaving it too long, and them starting to drift apart.

As his last day drew nearer, he was adamant he wouldn't have a leaving-do – once he'd gone, he'd arrange a night out with just Kay, Jill and Rach. It turned out he'd known Rach for years before he'd ever worked with Jill, and they had several friends in common. "Quite the social butterfly, is Old Frosty!" Ella had once mocked. The others had laughed – while Kay observed, not for the first time, that Ella was nowhere near as nice as she'd first thought.

"Look," she said to Stu. "I know you don't want a fuss, but I'm taking you for a meal when you finish. Apart from anything, I wanted to say thanks properly, for all your help with the book."

"Nonsense!" he blustered. "You did all the hard work – I just gave a few words of advice."

"It was more than that, Stu. I'd never have done it without you!"

"Of course you would. Don't underestimate yourself. And as for the meal – that would be lovely, although I'm not too sure about letting you pay." That almost-smile. "But somehow, I've a feeling I don't get a choice in the matter…"

She booked a table at an Italian she knew was his favourite. When it came around, the following Friday, Stu's last day at the school was a low-key and unremarkable as he'd hoped for. Although it was how he wanted things, Kay couldn't help feeling a little sad for him – and glad she was taking him out, however it went.

It was a pleasant enough evening. The food was good, the conversation flowed, but the restaurant was noisy; and despite being away from work, she still couldn't find her moment. Afterwards, they headed over to Dale Street for a drink in the Ship and Mitre, where Stu was a regular – he liked his real ale. Being a Friday, the pub was as busy as expected, but Kay managed to find a cosy corner while Stu went to the bar. He returned with a bitter for himself and, for her, a tall glass of something red that smelt of cough-mix. "Cherry beer. See what you think."

She took a sip. It wasn't terrible, but there was no mistaking that background taste of linctus.

"They do all sorts, here – peach, raspberry, chocolate." He clinked his glass. "Cheers – and thanks for tonight."

"You're more than welcome – here's to a long and happy retirement!" Another sip – perhaps it could grow on her. "So – have you made any plans?"

"Well – perhaps a long-overdue trip to Canada to see my brother. We speak a lot, but I've not seen him in five years."

Kay had never heard him mention a brother – assuming his only family was a sister he visited in Cambridge. Such a private, private man…it hit her just how little she knew about him. But that might change if – hopefully *when*…. she took a deep breath.

"Listen, Stu, I've been meaning to speak to you. I need…to ask something." He looked at her quizzically. "It's just…I feel…"

Then, suddenly, a shrill voice – more than a little irritating. "*Hi! Thought* you'd be in here!"

She looked up and recognised Dom Lyttle, who'd been on a night out for Rach's birthday a few months back. Along with a group of his close friends, he'd once been part of the youth group at Impetus. Stu had also been there that night, and Kay had noticed then that he seemed to know Dom quite well; she'd wondered if perhaps he'd taught him in the past, or maybe been involved in some way with the theatre?

She'd only met him once, but her gut feeling was not to trust Dom. Twenty-something, mid-height and slender, he seemed to delight in taking cheap shots at those around him; most annoyingly, he had a habit of speaking to his friends in his own secret "code". Jill wasn't over-keen, either; Kay had said nothing about her own misgivings, but Jill had once confided that Rach saw Dom as "misunderstood"; and while this might be true, it could just as easily be an excuse for being a gobshite.

"Well!" Stu exclaimed – surprisingly animated. "I'd never have expected to find *you* in here!"

"I *know*! Fish out of water!" Dom looked around him with smug disdain. Bloody hell – he *really* thought he was something! But Stu – to Kay's disappointment – seemed to find it amusing.

"I'm not stopping long," Dom went on. "Just guessed you'd come in here after your meal. I'm meeting the girls in a bit – we're doing a pub crawl. You guys coming along?"

"Not for me, thanks," Kay said – she could think of nothing worse. Hopefully, he'd move on soon, and she could pick up where she left off…But, to her dismay, Stu was more than keen to join them. "Of course," he smiled; he'd smiled more these past few minutes than in the whole time Kay had known him. So – that was *her* plan up in smoke!

"Are you sure, Kay?" Stu asked her.

"No, honestly. Lots to do tomorrow – early start…."

"That's a shame. Maybe next time. One for the road?"

"Okay…"

As the two of them went off to the bar, she couldn't suppress a sigh – such a frustrating end to the night. Perhaps she should have spoken up earlier, instead of faffing around. Oh well…finishing her drink, which had now become cloyingly sweet, she watched Stu and Dom as they waited to get served. Stu seemed like a different man – relaxed, warm, animated. How she wished he'd be with…Ah! Of course!

It was *so* obvious. Why the hell hadn't she seen it? Most likely they all knew, and assumed she'd worked it out, too – like anyone with an ounce of common sense would have done! It no doubt explained why he gave nothing away; even in this day and age, people could be judgemental, and he couldn't be blamed for protecting himself. What she saw now was the "real" Stu. She'd been right that he wasn't the "cold fish" people imagined - but this side of him would never be for *her*.

Whatever she thought of Dom, she was glad he'd turned up. He'd done her a favour; otherwise, imagine the embarrassment, and how completely ridiculous she'd feel. Thankfully, she'd been spared *that*. All in all, it could have been much worse; and she'd have no-one but herself to blame. My God, she thought; you stupid, *stupid* woman.

Part Three: Flying

Chapter Thirty-four

Still groggy from a rather heavy night, Sean made another coffee, lit a cigarette, and began to read Rachel Rose's play.

He was here, in London, for the next few weeks as he worked on a stage-adaptation of a little-remembered series from the early 80s, set during the 1830 Swing Riots. Thankfully, he wasn't playing the lead role – a man, at one point in the story, brutally beats his young son. Not that Sean wasn't up for a challenge - but the guy was a hero, not a villain, and this was the problem.... No doubt, there were ways to justify it – different times, different standards, the effects of grinding poverty on family life – but it didn't sit right, somehow.

Pat Whelan, on the other hand, would never dream of harming his wife or kids. The father-son relationship was one of the things to celebrate about this book (and Rachel's script, of course); and as for Pat, Sean had played his type many times before; as Rach had said, it had his name on it.

They'd first become friends when they worked together on "Hard Times"; Rach had written two of the episodes, and Sean had played tragic Stephen Blackpool, who was just the sort of hard-done-by, but honourable workingman he'd come to specialise in. To begin with, though, he'd had his doubts about Pat. He'd been thinking for a while that he needed to broaden his horizons, perhaps by playing completely against type. For this reason, he'd felt a bit "so-so" when she'd first approached him – but, for her sake, he wanted to give it a go.

She was such a talented writer, as well as a good mate, and that bullying incident was awful – he'd really felt for her. It was good to see her writing again; such a loss if she'd given up for good. He also liked that she was giving a chance to new actors, who at one time or another had been part of her youth group. Rach was such a great mentor; and, like Sean, the theatre was her first love. As with most of her projects with Impetus, this play was her "baby", and she'd be directing as well as writing the script.

"Hard Times" was perhaps the best-known TV show he'd done, and the only one where he'd played a major part. It could have led to so much more. But he always returned to the stage, and more than anything, enjoyed the smaller, low-key productions that kept him close to his roots. While he'd never complain about making money (who would!) it wasn't what drove him. "Of course, we don't all have that *luxury*," his ex, Susie, had bitterly remarked. Jealous, although she'd vehemently deny it; the cause of so many of their rows.

Sean's house, on the Antrim coast, in a beautiful setting near the Giant's Causeway, had been built for him by his father, Gerry. For Suzie (whose parents gave her diddly-squat), this meant he'd had it all on a plate. Never occurred to her that it was *normal* to look out for your kids; or that *her* folks might be the weird ones… Gerry, a stonemason, had done the same for all three sons, to give them a "leg up", as he called it; like so many of his generation, he'd had a tough start, and wanted better for his own. Born and bred in a small, red-brick terrace off the Lower Falls, Gerry's own Da was in the same line of work; a solid trade, but there were ten kids crammed into that wee house, and life was a constant struggle - always "first up, best dressed."

It was completely different for Sean and his brothers, who'd grown up in Belfast's affluent south suburbs; despite the Troubles, it was a fun-filled, carefree childhood. Gerry was a big-hearted, jolly personality, as was Sean's mother, Sadie, and his many aunts and uncles. At weekends, they'd take turns to host family parties – where, in the Irish tradition, everyone was asked to do a "turn". The kids would play in the bedrooms amongst the coats, hoping to keep out of the way; not that it ever worked! Sean, back then, was rather a quiet boy, who didn't actively seek the limelight, and had to be encouraged to do his party-piece. But once up there, he found he really loved performing. It was this that had got him into drama at school, then Uni – and it all led on from there. His brothers, Jim and Kieran, had followed Gerry into the building trade; but not once had any of them criticized him for choosing a different path, and they'd given nothing but support.

Although Sean had never known poverty, his parents' and grandparents' stories had left a marked impression on him. He enjoyed nothing more than to put the world to rights over a pint (or, better still, a whisky!) or two, but wondered at times if his left-leaning views were at odds with his love of the finer things – good food and wine, holidays, clothes. "Champagne socialist" was another of Susie's jibes; but then, as Rach said, why feel guilty for making the best of your life? It was surely about *everyone* having that chance….

This apartment, in "gentrified" Shoreditch, reflected his tastes. Perhaps not the cheapest option, but more than worth it. Oak flooring throughout, sleek black kitchen and bathroom, the lounge furnished opulently with leather sofas and a gorgeous, Persian rug. Sean lived here for much of the time, returning to the house in Ireland for holidays and long-weekends.

But his love of the good life would always come second to his passion for acting. When a play was adapted from a novel, he always read the book before looking at the script, maybe more than once, to get a proper feel for the character, and bring out all the author intended – so easily lost in translation. And as for *this* book – like Rach, he'd expected to hate it, and was pleasantly surprised to be proved wrong. By the time he reached the end he felt quite sorry to have finished it, and certain he'd take on the role.

Before calling Rach, he had a peek – not for the first time – at the photo of the author. Red-haired, pretty; creamy skin and rose-gold curls. And those blue-green eyes, full of the humour and compassion so apparent in her work… Without further ado, he reached for the phone.

"Rach? How are you? I finished the script, and yeah – I'd love to do it. And can you let Katie know how much I enjoyed the book? Really warm-hearted – generous in spirit."

Chapter Thirty-five

"Some good news," Jill said. "Rach spoke to Sean McNulty. He's keen to take the part – and he loved the book!"

"The one who was in 'Hard Times'?"

"That's it – Stephen Blackpool." Jill smiled. "You look taken aback!"

"A bit!" Kay laughed. "It's all happening so quickly. Not that I'm complaining!"

The truth was, she was more than a little overwhelmed. The book had done much better than expected – and now, to have her idea adapted for the stage! A small, low-budget production, but still way beyond she anything she'd ever imagined.

As for Sean McNulty – he wasn't a huge name, but she'd seen him in "Hard Times", and knew he'd had acclaim for his portrayal of the luckless Stephen. It was a few years back now, but as she recalled, she'd been quite a fan! Of course, she was pleased – how could she *not* be? To think he'd read the book and seemed to enjoy it...just being kind, perhaps, but even so – having someone like him on board would certainly do no harm, and possibly bring her that bit closer to being taken on by a publisher. Exciting times, but scary – there was always that old fear of it blowing up in her face.

The trouble was, when she let it go, it had a habit of coming back to bite her on the backside. Take the whole debacle with

Stu; even now – almost a year down the line – she cringed at the thought of how close she'd come to humiliating herself. Staying in touch had been hard at first. The easiest way to move on would be to cut all ties, but she couldn't be that cruel; he'd been so good to her, and had become, in his matter-of-fact way, one of her dearest friends. And after all, it wasn't *his* fault – he didn't *ask* her to fall for him!

That night at the Ship and Mitre, he returned from the bar with Dom and she got up quickly to leave.

"Sorry," she muttered. "Just suddenly not feeling so good. Maybe something I've eaten…"

"You do look a bit pale," Stu said, worriedly. "Will you be okay getting home?"

"Yeah…fine…"

"Because I really think it might be best to call a taxi…"

"No, Stu, please don't worry – I'll get one outside. Enjoy the rest of the night. I'll be in touch."

With that, she grabbed her jacket and fled, jumping straight into a cab as she reached the rank in nearby Whitechapel. She berated herself for her pure stupidity, throughout the journey home and for many weeks to come.

How silly, how *arrogant*, to think he could feel the same! In hindsight, she could see she'd read far too much into the help he'd given and the interest in her work. No doubt he enjoyed her company and appreciated how she accepted his quiet ways without judgement. But nothing more; nothing less.

Thinking about it, she'd never really had a platonic friendship with a man. There were guys she'd got on well with at the office, but they only ever socialised as part of the wider group; and it was such a female environment, with women outnumbering men by at least three-to-one. She thought the world of Jen's partner Jonathan and had seen Col as the brother-in-law she'd once hoped Pete would be. But Stu was the only one who'd been *her* friend first. Perhaps this was why she'd called it so wrong... As time went on, she realised it wasn't just Stu's feelings she'd misread.; she'd been right to question the lack of "butterflies." Unless you counted Simon Shaw, there'd been no-one but Phil, and this was her problem. She could only guess that with Stu (or anyone else) it would feel totally different. But not *that* different....

Accepting this made it easier to deal with, but it would be a long time before she stopped feeling small and silly for not having even an *inkling* that Stu might be gay. For a good while, she kept in touch only through WhatsApp. She wasn't well, she said, when he suggested meeting; after feeling ill that night at the bar, it turned out to be a nasty virus which proved hard to shake off.

"I hope it wasn't the beer," Stu remarked.

"No, no," she said quickly. "Just a bit rundown. Probably best to keep things quiet till I'm on the mend."

She hated lying like this, and knew that eventually, she'd have to put on her "big girl pants" and face him.

"Didn't realise you'd been poorly," Jill said one lunchtime. Kay looked at her quizzically. "Stu told me about the virus…"

"Ah!" She hoped she didn't sound flustered. "Yeah - it was no biggie. I'm fine now."

"Well – that's good. I'll tell Stu. He'll be glad to see you."

No getting out of it, then. But while she'd always feel slightly foolish for getting it so wrong, at least he'd never find out; and as she'd confided in no-one, there was no chance of it being let slip. Gradually, the friendship fell back into place, with no damage done. It worried her, though, that the more she moved on, Phil seemed to be back on her mind.

If she'd learnt nothing else, it was to be more honest with herself, and admit life was better with a man. She smiled at this thought, imagining Lisa's reaction – her feminist card would be well and truly revoked! But seriously, this wasn't about being needy. She managed fine on her own, was perfectly content – but she was 46, not 86, and "content" just wasn't enough. If it didn't happen, she'd live with it; but if it did, she wouldn't complain! The right one was out there, she was sure.

Chapter Thirty-six

Not long after Stu's departure, and once Jill was settled into her new role, she and Rach invited Kay over for dinner; she'd cooked for them a few times now, and they were keen to return the favour. After an Asian-inspired, vegan feast of Thai sweetcorn fritters, Keralan cauliflower curry and a home-made coconut ice-cream, Rach asked if she'd look over a script she'd been working on. The first thing she'd written in a while, she said, and she'd be interested in Kay's opinion.

She instantly recognised her own book, adapted into a three-act play. In the opening scene, set in 1981, a 14-year-old Chris makes tea for her grandad, and listens, fascinated, to his memories of Kitty, which were shown through flashbacks. Next came Mick and Sylvie's story, told in a similar format, as Mick reminisces with his father – now in a home, and just starting to show signs of senility – about National Service, marriage to Sylvie, slum-clearance and their move to Speke. The last act began with Pat's funeral in 1982, before jumping forward two years to Chrissi's rebellious late-teens and her-ongoing feud with her mother and sister.

As she finished reading, Kay was aware of Rach and Jill, nervously awaiting her reaction. Quietly, she handed the script back to Rach, who took her silence as disapproval.

"I hope I haven't done the wrong thing. The idea came to me as soon as I read it. I've not done anything in such a long time, and

I just thought... look, if you don't want me to do it, I completely understand. The main thing is, it's got me thinking about writing again, and that's..."

"Stop worrying!" Kay laughed. "I *love* it!"

Jill laughed. "Told you."

Of course, it wouldn't be a big production. Impetus wasn't that sort of place; it was all about promoting new talent and getting them a foot in the door. But before anyone got their hopes up, Rach would need to sit down and speak to the artistic director, Adele Sparks.

Adele had been as upset as Jill when Rach stopped writing; Rach had done so much for the theatre, she said, often calling her its "beating heart." But, at the same time, she'd have to consider if the play was suitable, and there was a chance it may not be. Impetus had always specialised in hard-hitting topics, and this was...well, this was a rather gentle story of an everyday family. For Rach, this was what left-wing theatre was all about; but for Adele's, it might be just a little too "safe".

Luckily, Adele was on board straightaway, and more than pleased at Rach's change of heart. Their only problem was that the main theatre was pretty much booked up, so they decided to use the studio, which was perfect for smaller projects. At the end of July, after six months of planning and getting together a budget, Rach told Kay that they had a date in mind. They were looking at the last week of November, over three nights from Thursday to Saturday.

Rach had asked Louise Atherton if she'd consider playing Kitty. They'd worked together many a time, and Lou had played Ruth, the battered wife in the ill-fated "Parole". Allan Cowley (also in "Parole" as Ruth's protective brother) would be Mick in middle-age, with his real-life partner, Angie James, as older Sylvie. Dennis Potts – another longstanding friend – would play Pat as an elderly man; with his shock of pure white hair, he was often picked for roles much older than his 66 years.

The younger parts were given to promising members (past and present) of Rach's youth group, most of whom were still finding their feet. Mick and Sylvie in their courting days would be played by Ben Randalls (easily the most talented of them all), and Jade Hughes, a close pal of Dom Lyttle; while Jade's best friend, Chloe Green, would play Chrissi. Dom also had a part, as quiet, elusive Tony, with Mark O'Brien as his brash twin Paul.

Tony only appeared twice and blended into the background; a bone of contention with Dom, who saw himself as a favourite, and had expected a much bigger role. To appease him, Rach ended up writing an extra scene, where Tony would come out to Paul, expecting the worst kind of reaction, only to be completely taken aback by his brother's support.

"You don't mind, do you?" Jill asked Kay. "She's been stressing over it – you know what she's like.!"

"Honestly," Kay smiled, "the three of us are as bad as each other – not happy unless we're worrying! It's fine – in fact, it's a great idea."

"I was sure you'd be cool with it, but she asked me to run it by you. She wanted to stay as close as she could to the story."

"Yeah, but at the end of the day, Jill, this is *her* project – and if she wants to put her own stamp on it, she's got every right. If I wasn't keen on that, I'd never have agreed."

"That's what I said – although I must admit, I do wish she wouldn't pander so much to Dom."

"Well, that did cross my mind too – but then, she knows him much better than I do, so who am I to judge?"

"You're too polite by half – but I can tell you're not a fan, either."

"I'd hoped it wasn't that obvious. Let's hope Stu hasn't picked up on it. I'd hate to upset him."

"Not as far as I'm aware – although I've told him what *I* think, and he's taken it on the chin. Deep down, I reckon he knows what Dom's like, but still – no fool like an old fool, eh?"

Kay nodded, but said no more; months later, it all still felt a little too near the bone.

And now, Sean McNulty.

"You're right," she said to Jill. "I *am* taken aback…just a surprise, that's all."

"Well," Jill said, finishing her coffee, "he and Rach are good friends. And Sean's been very quiet these past few years. Since his dad died – I think he had a bit of a breakdown, to be honest. There was a year where he didn't work at all."

Poor bloke – he'd had a rough time. Come to think of it, Kay hadn't heard of him being in anything on TV since "Hard Times". His father had died shortly after this, and when he finally sorted his head out and got back on the radar, he'd stuck with what he loved most – the theatre. Perhaps, Kay thought, she was building it up too much. The guy was only human – nothing to be scared of; and yet, she couldn't get rid of the feeling that it was all a step too far.

Maybe "scared" was the wrong word – but certainly unsettled. At the back of her mind was the thought that it could lead to their paths crossing, and she believed firmly that you should never meet your heroes.

Not that she could even call Sean a "hero". She didn't *do* heroes, in the way of idolising someone and hanging on to their every word. As a teenager, she'd loved all the New Romantics – Visage, Ultravox, Spandau Ballet, Duran Duran – but had hated the idea of screaming and crying at concerts or calling herself "Durannie number…" (as Mel and her cronies had done). Even at 14, it had all seemed a bit pathetic.

Nonetheless, she had her favourites, and a few years back could probably have counted Sean McNulty amongst them. It didn't have to be the "big" names – she was always drawn by the types of characters they played and how they portrayed them (although it didn't hurt if they were a bit of alright, too!). She'd seen Sean in an Irish show they'd brought over to the UK in the late 80s, then in a few supporting parts in British period-dramas, before his biggest role to date – Stephen Blackpool.

Kay had read "Hard Time^{xxx}s" as a teenager. Although she loved Dickens, and enjoyed gritty realism, it was never a favourite. A harsh, grim tale, lacking the joyousness of his other works – although, in fairness, this was just what he'd intended, so the book had done its job. She recalled Stephen Blackpool as a sad, put-upon man who, at just 40, is known as "Old Stephen". Worn-out from working at the mill and caring for his gin-soak wife, he can never be with the woman he truly loves. A man of quiet dignity – but dashing? Sexy?

Yet, in Sean McNulty's hands, Old Stephen became an unlikely heartthrob. Of course, this was at least in part due to the actor's dark, rugged good looks, and the accent – for this role, faintly Lancashire (not broad, as in the book), but still with that slight hint of a brogue. Besides this, he gave an intensity to the character; tired, lonely, but with the suggestion of inner-strength and determination. In the novel, there was an illustration with the title "Stephen Blackpool in Despair", which Sean had brought vividly to life. In his squalid house, paralytic wife sprawled across the bed, he sat, head in hands, looking desolate, brooding – and rather hot! The ratings increased, mainly because the viewers were rooting for Stephen, hoping he'd escape his marriage and finally find happiness; and of course, were heartbroken when he met with a sticky end.

Kay tried to remember if he'd won an award for the role, and looked on Google – no, although he had been nominated. There were various articles, mostly dating back to 2010 when the series was shown, about how he drew admiration from women who (like herself) preferred a down-to-earth, honest-to-goodness man over the manicured, manscaped metrosexual. Some described him as warm and friendly, but others mentioned various online altercations, especially on Twitter. How true this was, she had no idea – but somehow, she guessed he wouldn't suffer fools gladly. And this was what worried her, were she to meet him – that she'd say the wrong thing, make a fool of herself, and get the rough end of his tongue. It was something which, with any luck, she'd manage to avoid.

Chapter Thirty-seven

In early November, Rach got in touch to let her know rehearsals would start on the 7th – three weeks before the play was due to open. And then, the question she'd dreaded. On the Saturday before this, the cast were getting together for a drink at Hope Street Hotel - and did she want to join them? An outright no would sound churlish– and she hated herself for feeling this way. She felt so ungrateful; anyone else would be lapping this up, and here was she…

"I'm not sure, Rach. But thanks for asking."

"You'll be fine," Jill said at work the next day. "I know it probably all feels quite daunting, but they're a good bunch – and you know a few of them anyway."

"It's just…" How to say it, without sounding as silly as she felt. "You know how I am in big groups. I've always been the same."

Get a grip, she chided herself – it's just a drink! A couple of hours if that. All this fuss, over a bloody drink….! But the harder she was on herself, the more depressed she began to feel.

"You don't do yourself any favours," Jen said later, on the phone. "The way you beat yourself up. I mean, would you speak like that to me ?"

"Of course not."

"And yet you do it so readily to yourself. It hardly seems fair."

"It's just, the more I listen to myself, the more ridiculous I sound. I'm forty-bloody-six, for Christ's sake! It shouldn't even be an issue."

"You mean this Sean What's-his-face being there?"

"Yeah – pathetic, isn't it?"

"Well, it could be intimidating - although, is he really that well-known? Can't say I've heard of him myself."

"Remember "Hard Times"? Stephen Blackpool."

"Ah, yes – I do now. Very nice! Lucky you. Can you take a plus-one?"

They laughed. "Oh, Jen – it just worries me. When I googled him, it said he's always having set-to's on Twitter[xxxi]."

"But that's Twitter for you – all sorts of trolls."

"I guess that's true. Look what happened to Rach. But – and I feel so daft saying this – I really liked him in "Hard Times". And if he was off with me…." She sighed. "So, there it is."

"I see where you're coming from. But at the end of the day, he's just doing his job, like the rest of them. And remember – they've asked you because *you* wrote that book – and that's what they're doing there, after all. There's no show without Punch!"

On the Saturday evening, Sean met up with Rach and Jill a few hours ahead of the rest of the group. He'd arrived in Liverpool two days earlier and checked in at the dockside apartment which would be his home for the next three weeks. He'd paid upfront on his card, which had pretty much wiped him out, but what the hell – you got what you paid for. He'd get a one-off payment for doing the show, and he was sub-letting his apartment to a friend of his, Tom Milner, a fellow actor who was working in London for a week during the time Sean was away.

It always worked out in the end. He had several credit cards, but because he always made the minimum payments, there was never any issue. Except for that one time, after Gerry's death, when he'd lost track and got himself in a tight spot, but his brother Jim has helped him out. Now he didn't have Da, Jim was the one solid presence in Sean's life that he knew he could count on. Never let him down.

The day before, Rach and Jill had taken him on the City Tour Bus, which they'd picked up by the Anglican cathedral, stopping off at by Mathew Street - lovely to see, although in truth he preferred the bohemian atmosphere of Hope Street and the Georgian Quarter. Then he'd looked around the Philharmonic Hall and had a drink in the art-deco bar across the road, where he'd already met some of the cast. Today, they'd had an early-doors meal at the London Carriage Works, before moving across to the bright, modern bar with its plush leather sofas.

"So, anyway," he said to Rach, "you were saying you'd asked Katie along?"

"Yeah - although somehow, I don't think she'll make it. She didn't sound too sure at all."

"Shame...."

"Well," Jill added, "you never know. But Kay doesn't like big groups, and that might put her off."

"And most likely a bit scared of you, too," Rach added mischievously.

"Me? I'm a pussycat!"

"Well, I don't think Dom would agree! You had a right go at him, yesterday."

"The guy was winding me up. Total gobshite. He was lucky I didn't deck him one! I was sorely tempted – but then," he grinned, "House Mouse might beat me up!"

"House Mouse?"

"Stu. Think about it – if he ever married Dom and took his surname..."

"You're terrible, Muriel!xxxii"

"Terrible, but true. Strange combo, them two. And there's something with Dom that doesn't add up.... I mean, the way he is with them girls – that's a wee harem he has there!"

"No way! They've known each other since they we're kids - they're just really close mates."

"But the face on him when I was talking to Chloe! She's a lovely girl. Too good for *him*!"

"And too young for *you*, McNulty, so behave!"

"No, Christ, I don't mean *that* – and as if she'd look at me!"

"I could be wrong, but I think she might just have a tiny crush."

Sean laughed. "I'm old enough to be her Da!"

"And don't forget," Rach smirked, "you're playing her grandad!"

"You're pushing your luck, now, missus!"

"Seriously Sean," Jill said, "just take care. She's a nice girl, as you say – I'd hate to see her hurt."

"Okay - I still think it's ridiculous, but I'll watch what I'm doing. But back to Katie. You don't think she'll show up?"

"I hope she does - but knowing Kay, I think she'll find all this a bit much.... oh, hang on..." Jill glanced towards the door, and as Sean looked over, he saw a group of girls enter the bar, followed by a tall, red-haired woman, alone. "I stand corrected. Looks like she's had a change of heart."

Chapter Thirty-eight

Keeping in mind Jen's advice, Kay had gone along casually dressed – jeans, flats, a loose, multi-coloured blouse and matching jewellery; nothing over-the-top. She didn't feel too bad – quite relaxed - until she the first person she saw was Dom Lyttle, at the table nearest the door with Jade and Chloe. Jill and Rach stood close to the bar, deep in conversation with a tall guy she recognised as Sean. Should she wait till they spotted her, or just bite the bullet and join them? But before she could give it another thought, Dom was hugging her.

"How are *you*, hon?" he trilled. "*Great* to see you!"

"And you," she lied. "Did Stu not fancy coming along?"

"Not his scene, babes. You've met the girls, haven't you?"

"Just the once. Rach's birthday."

"That's right," Chloe nodded. "The meal at Ego."

"Yeah," Kay smiled. "Then the drink at the Fly in the Loaf. Brought back memories of when it was Kirkland's – we'd start off there before the Casa."

"*Really?*" Dom pulled a face. "You don't strike *me* as a clubber!"

"Any reason why?" she asked, unable to hide her irritation.

"Oh, you know," he smirked. "Not exactly the *type*, are you?"

She took a deep breath and let it go – it wasn't worth the hassle. Still, her annoyance must have been obvious, as an awkward silence ensued.

"So," Jade said at last, "have you met Sean yet?"

"How could she?" Dom snapped, before Kay had the chance to reply. "She's only just walked through the door!"

"Oh, alright, smart-arse!" Jade shot back. "She might know him through Rach, for all you know!"

"Well, that's *me* told! So, Kay - *have* you had the pleasure of the lovely Mr. Mc?"

"Not yet, no."

"You're not missing much."

"Ignore him, Kay," Chloe said. "Sean's great. Dom's just pissed because he called him a gobshite."

"Takes one to know one," Dom scowled. "But you see, Kay, our Chloe won't admit it, but she's got a bit of a thing for old Sean the Sheep. Haven't you, babes?"

"As if. He's my dad's age!" Chloe laughed, but Kay could sense her discomfort, and wished Dom would lay off. Of the two, Jade seemed the more self-assured and able to deal with Dom's crap; whereas Chloe seemed gentle, dreamy, maybe a touch naïve. Dark and slender, she reminded Kay a little of Jen at that age. It would be interesting to see what she made of Crissi;

perhaps not the obvious choice, but Rach knew what she was doing.

"So what?" Dom said. "Stu's got 10 years on *my* dad, but that didn't stop me!"

"Yeah," Jade chipped in, "but you're a freak!"

(Nice one, Kay thought)

"You must admit, Chlo," Dom continued, "you're always on about him – how *lovely* he is..."

"Well, he *is* – in a father-figure sort of way."

"In a dirty-old-git sort of way...oh, hello – look what the cat's dragged over."

Kay looked around to see Rach and Jill heading over towards them, with Sean in tow.

Dressed in black jeans and black t-shirt, Sean seemed even taller than Kay had expected. He had enough five-o'clock-shadow that, if left just a day or so more, would become a small beard. Tattoos – not covered in them, like Phil - just a couple on each arm. The typical "dark Irish" look; deep blue eyes, combined with blackish-brown, shoulder-length hair, tied up in a man-bun.

He smiled at the two girls. "Hi Jade. Hello, Chloe, love." A kind, fatherly wink; Chloe blushed – perhaps she did have a soft-spot... He nodded at Dom, who glowered back.

"So pleased you got here," Rach said to Kay. "We were hoping you would."

"Aw, good to see you, too." Then, "Hiya," coolly, to Sean.

He shook her hand. "Great to meet you at last, Katie," he said warmly. "Heard loads about you – and I really loved the book!"

"Ah…thanks…" For one awful moment, she was about to call him "Stephen", but luckily stopped herself in time.

"Sean wanted a chat with you," Jill said. "So, we thought we'd leave you to it. We can catch up later."

"See you in a bit," Rach added; and off they went, only for Kay to find that Dom and the girls had moved on too.

Shit. She never thought she'd end up on the spot like this – and for once, almost wished Dom had stuck around! Heart pounding, she found herself staring at the floor.

"So, I've loads to ask you," Sean said. "And not sure what anyone's told you – but, for the record, I don't bite!"

As her cheeks flushed, she imagined how ignorant he'd think her – or, even worse, a daft little girl, for not being able to take things in her stride. And he'd be right.

"I'm sorry. It's just a bit…new to me, all this…"

Sean smiled. "Don't apologise! To be honest, Rach mentioned you were a wee bit nervous – and you've still taken the plunge and come along. I think that's brave."

"Well, thanks…that's kind."

"Not at all! It's true – and I'll tell you this, we've all been there, at one time or another. But don't forget, you're the important one here – there'd be no play without the book, after all."

Slowly, Kay could feel herself start to relax. "My friend said exactly the same."

"Sounds like a wise woman. Anyway, you're doing grand – better than you think. I mean, you seemed to be getting on okay with your man over there…" He looked across towards Dom, who had moved his posse to the other side of the bar.

"I've known Dom for a while," she said. "And the girls, too."

"Pals of yours, are they?"

"Well…Chloe and Jade are lovely, but Dom's a bit full-on for me, I'm afraid."

"That's a polite way of putting it! And then there's Stu, hardly says a word. Strange man."

"To be honest," she said, "Stu's one of my closest friends."

"Ach!" Sean grimaced. "Sorry about that. Note to self, McNulty. Think twice before sticking your feet in your big trap!"

Then both burst out laughing, and Kay felt a weight off her mind. All that fretting, yet here they were, and *he* was the one who'd made the blunder…They laughed for some time – the sort of laughter that went on and on, the more you tried to stop it; and trying to be serious would just set off a fresh explosion.

"I know Stu doesn't give a great impression," she said, wiping her eyes once they'd finally calmed down. "But he's a very clever man. You can have a really good conversation with him."

"Well, I'll have to take your word for that one." Sean grinned. "Did you ever see the episode of "Father Ted", when Father Stone comes to stay?"

"Oh, don't – you'll start me giggling again, and I'll feel terrible! Stu means well, you know. It was him who encouraged me to publish the book."

"Well, fair play to him for that. Perhaps I've misjudged him.... Anyway – before I dig myself in any deeper, I'll get the drinks in."

He got up to the bar, returning a few minutes later with a bottle of Prosecco, a plate of nuts and some other delicious-looking canapes.

"What do I owe you?"

"Don't be so daft! Besides, I've some making up to do, after insulting your pal."

"Well, Stu doesn't always help himself – I've told him as much myself."

"Am I off the hook, then?"

"Hmm," she smiled, "the jury's out on that."

Chapter Thirty-nine

Funny how the nights you'd dreaded turned out to be the best. She felt ashamed of the picture she'd created of Sean in her mind. He'd turned out to be warm, funny, generous to a fault – and yes, she admitted, more than a little attractive.

Somehow, he seemed younger than she'd expected; but then she realised this was because she remembered him as careworn "Old Stephen". In real life, he'd pass for early 40s at most, although she knew he was 51. In good shape, and very rugged, which of course she loved in a man. She liked his almost-beard, and although not over-keen on man-buns, it suited him rather well…. And she couldn't help but notice, appreciatively, a nice coating of thick dark hair on his forearms – and a bit which just peeped out above the neckline of his top...

Stop it. Had she really learned *nothing* about reading too much into things? Knowing she was nervous, he was just trying to put her at ease. Nothing more…. But still – it was a great evening, and she'd always enjoy the memory.

Next morning, she slept in a little later than planned, and was woken by a beep from her phone. Still bleary-eyed, she saw a text from a number she didn't recognise. She groaned when she read it: "Hello, chuck! Well, I think u can say u pulled there! McNulty's tongue was hanging out all nite!"

Irritated, she texted back, "Is this Dom?" Nothing for a bit – then a cartoon of a leprechaun with a rooster, and the caption,

"I'm so Irish, even my cock's green!" She ignored it – with any luck, he'd get bored in a while.

Jen was due round for Sunday lunch As Kay was somewhat behind schedule, she got a quick shower and grabbed a bowl of cereal, before tidying and getting a chicken ready for the oven. Her phone kept beeping as she pottered about, but she was determined not to rise to it – while wondering, as she so often did, what Stu could possibly be thinking.

"I knew you'd be fine," Jen said later. "And what was Sean like?"

"Really nice. Very friendly."

"I've got to ask - is he as good-looking in the flesh as he is on-screen?"

"Hmm," Kay smiled, "yeah – I suppose."

"Listen to you!" Jen laughed. "After all that worrying, so matter-of-fact!"

The phone beeped again. Kay sighed. "Dom. He collared me when I got there last night."

"And now he thinks he's your new bestie?"

"He keeps sending these jokes. They might be funny if I liked him! I've ignored them, but he won't take the hint." Another beep. "See what I mean?"

As she went into the kitchen to get the coffees, she took a glance at the texts. Sure enough, one was from Dom, which she deleted. The other was from a different number – again, one she didn't know: "Hi, Katie, it's Sean. I asked Jill for your number – hope that's ok? Enjoyed our chat last night. Hoping we can meet again - would love to do ferry trip. Be great if you could join me. Take care. S." She switched the phone off – plenty of time to reply once Jen had gone – before taking the tray back through to the lounge.

"As I thought - another stupid joke."

"Well, they can't be that bad. Because *something's* put a smile on your face!"

"That's the 10th time you've looked at your phone," Rach teased, as Sean checked again for Kay's reply. "Do I detect a soft-spot?"

"Maybe a bit…Well, alright, maybe a lot! Thing is, though, I could be wasting my time. She might be with someone?"

"No," Jill said, "she's separated. But look, Sean, she's had quite a rough time. I'd be upset if I heard you'd let her down."

"Well, that's me told!" Sean winked. "Your woman's a tough cookie, Rach."

They'd met for Sunday dinner at Keith's Wine Bar on Lark Lane, and a few hours later were on their third bottle of red. Keith's was a quirky wee place, a throwback to the 60s, while Lark Lane itself reminded Sean of a tiny, condensed version of

New York's Bleeker Street. Rach had asked about his chat with Katie – and for much of the afternoon he'd talked of little else. As he'd guessed from her writing, she was wise and compassionate. They'd both been through the same with their fathers, so she completely understood; it was the first time he'd really opened up about it to anyone, outside family. And when he compared that with Susie, who'd showed no support, and treated his grief as a massive inconvenience…

Keeping in mind Jill's warning, he'd take things slowly – if at all. He'd still had nothing back from her, and was on the verge of giving up when, right on cue: "Hi Sean. Of course I don't mind. Yes, lovely night and good to meet you too. Ferry trip sounds good. Know you'll be busy, so let me know when best. Speak soon. K."

Chapter Forty

The date was arranged for the following Saturday. They met at the Albert Dock, outside the Tate, and for a brief second, she didn't recognise him – his hair loose this time and wearing a red flat cap and large shades. Again, the time flew by. They started off with a look around the Liverpool Life Museum – then lunch at the Pump House before the ferry. Despite the cold, it was a sunny day, and beyond Wirral they could easily make out Snowdonia. Afterwards, they headed back through the Dock to Liverpool One, before jumping a cab back to the hotel bar, where they got the same table as before; all the time talking, laughing, about anything and everything.

As the wine flowed, Kay found herself talking at length about Andy; not just losing him, but people's attitudes. Sean was saddened to learn of the neighbours' unkindness, and what she'd been through at school.

"Thing is," she said, "everyone tells you, that's just kids, but you meet these toxic bloody people all the time. Like Dom, for instance. I think it's just *in* them. I suppose it bothers me less, these days – I seem to be able to weed them out, then give them a wide berth. But I was clueless, back then. Sometimes I could kick myself, for not standing up to them sooner."

"Yeah," Sean pointed out, "but you could only go with what you knew. Remember, there was just no-one to back you up. I mean, I had Jim to look out for me. Like at school, when one of the hard cases had a go at me and my pal for joining the drama group – and there was Jimmy, straightaway, only had to look at him and the guy backed off. But, without him, I dread to think what might have happened – I was a quiet wee soul, back then."

"I doubt that, somehow!"

"Aye, I was, so – well, the quietest of the three of us, at least. Jim was the tough one, Kieran was the funny, cheeky one – and in the middle there was me, head in a book all the time."

Kay smiled. "Sounds just like me."

"Some lads have that knocked out of them. We were so lucky with Da... I've so much to thank him for. It was him who got me into acting." He chuckled. "We'd all have to do our party-piece at get-togethers. It's a real Irish thing."

"Sounds like my cousins in Glasgow. We had some great times with them. Uncle Tommy had a fantastic voice."

"And did you kids all hide out upstairs?"

"Sure did!"

"Well," Sean went on, "they'd always find us, and get us to have a go. Jim would grumble, but just do it – Kie loved all the fuss. Then Da would say to me, 'c'mon, son, your turn.' But I was never so keen. 'Well, we can't force you,' he said. 'But what's the worst that could happen?' So, I'd get up there, and after a few times, I thought, I could really get into this! That was Da - never put the pressure on, just encouraged..." He swallowed hard.

"Anyway - looks like they're ready for closing. It's gone way too quick again. Do you fancy a stroll?"

They walked along Hope Street towards Paddy's Wigwam, where they climbed the steps, looking out across the length of the street to the Anglican.

"Not so sure what I make of this," Sean said. "The other one's gorgeous – I looked around it last week. You can see it took years to build, all that detail, and... are you alright, Katie? You look far away."

In the distance, Kay had caught sight of a passing plane and, as always, became engrossed.

"Sorry," she said, "I was just thinking of Andy. He was so into planes, and whenever I see one, I just...."

"I know – you think you're getting there, then boom! Back to square one."

"They were such a huge thing for him. I'm just so sorry he never got to fly – and feel awful because I don't like it. Do you think I'm being daft?"

"No - I think you're amazing." And he held her close, kissing her softly, deeply, again and again.

Chapter Forty-one

Mostly, it was the good days Phil found hardest. To get that bit closer to feeling happy – then remember he was coming home, not to Kay, but to Pete and Jac.

Of course, if they'd just got on a bit better, it might have been easier. How they'd managed to last this long, Christ only knew – they argued all the time, over pretty much everything. Money, bills, housework – and then the daft stuff, like what to watch on telly, or who would answer the door. Tonight, it was the fish and chips that Jackie had just brought in. Pete opened the bags, face tripping him.

"Fuck's sake, Jac, I said no peas! D'you never listen?"

"Four fish, two splits!" she snapped. "That's what I told you I were getting! You said that were fine – then wait till I'm back for t' start moaning! Well, if you're not happy, next time *you* can get off your arse. There's your answer!"

Phil sighed. Would they *ever* give it a rest? He knew he should really be thinking of getting his own place, but where to start? He'd never been good with bills and the like – Kay had always sorted that side of things. Thank God *one* of them had their head screwed on! Col had offered to put him up, but he had enough going on at the moment – his wife, Yvonne, had terminal breast cancer, and had just been given weeks; maybe even days. Poor bloke was in bits. Phil and Robbo tried to help as best they could, but there was little they could do but just *be* there. Maybe, after the worst happened, he'd give it some thought – as much to be around for Col, as to get away from Pete…

"Beer?" Pete asked him.

"Aye, alright – if you're having one."

"Well, go on!" Pete barked at Jackie. "Get a shift on!"

"You're bloody joking, Pete! I've just got in from 'chippy!"

"And *we've* just got in from work!" Pete snarled. "While *you've* been sat on your fat arse all day!"

"Now, knock it off, our Kid," Phil warned. "No need!"

"Yeah, no need, Pete," Michelle piped up. "So shut your cake-hole!" Then, to Jackie, "I wouldn't put up with it, sis. I'd have kicked him out years ago, 'way he speaks to you!"

"Well, too bad it's *my* house, eh? So, c'mon, Jac - what's 'hold-up?"

Jackie grabbed the remote and switched over to ITV – "Granada Reports[xxxiii]". "You'll just have for t' hang on - I'm watching this."

"Y'know what," Phil said, exasperated, "it'll be cold, at this rate. *I'll* get 'em. You want your heads knocking together, you two!"

"No, you don't!" Pete growled. "*She's* doing it!"

"And who's *she?*" Jackie shot back. "'Cat's mother?"

Without a word, Michelle got up, fetched the beers, almost throwing Pete's at him. "There. Now shut it!"

"Aw, I didn't mean for you to go, babes," Jackie said. "It's just *him*!"

"I know, sis – I just went for t' stop him going on."

"Well, good," Pete smirked. "'Bout time you did your bit – you're round here often enough."

Michelle glared at him, while Jackie sighed.

"Now, just get off her case, you! You know she's run ragged, looking after Mum."

Pete laughed derisively. "Your bloody mother! That's all I get out of you two! More like, you get 'kids for t' do it, while you both sit there, watching 'Loose Women'!"

"So, we can't have a break, now?"

"I know, Chell – bloody men!!"

"D'you mind?" Phil said, irritated. "I'm sat here, y'know!"

"Sorry, PJ, I didn't mean you. *He* just does my head in!"

She looked over at Pete, who scowled at them as he lit up, the ash dropping into his food. He didn't seem to care.

It was just so sad. There was Col and Yvonne – still in that tiny flat in Earlestown, both on a minimum wage; he was a caretaker, she was a cleaner. It was a constant struggle to make ends meet, but they were happy – loved each other to bits – and were now about to lose it all. Then there was Pete and Jac – lovely home, never short of cash...kids, grandkids...hated each other's guts.

The sadness hit you as you walked through the door. It was a shame, as the house was fantastic – to give Pete his due, he'd put some work into it. Not to Phil's taste, mind, and certainly not Kay's; the lounge had a flowery carpet, and the wallpaper was candy-striped with borders, making the room seem smaller than it was. The shelves were stuffed with porcelain dolls that Jac collected, and the windows had frilly curtains. Still, old-fashioned as it was, it had the best of everything; including a plush, red suite; although Pete's armchair had been ruined by fag stains, much to Jac's annoyance.

Mostly, though, it was Pete who kicked off the rows – many a time, Phil had got on to him about the way he spoke to her. Try having some respect, he'd tell him. "Why?" Pete sneered. "Fat lot of good it did you!" They'd nearly come to blows.

As they ate in awkward silence, Phil looked idly at "Granada Reports". The presenter – not the usual one – was interviewing a punky-looking woman with bright pink hair. With her was a guy- an actor – who Phil remembered from a few years back.

"Look who it is, Chell," Jackie said. "It's that Irish bloke – Sean What-is-face."

"Oh yeah," Michelle cackled, "wouldn't kick *him* out of bed!"

"What were that thing he were in?"

"Oh, I know – "A Hard Life", I think it were called..."

"'Hard Times'," Phil said, as they both gawped at him, gob-struck.

"How d'you know that?" Jackie asked him.

He laughed. "Don't sound so shocked, Jac – I'm not thick!"

"Aw, I didn't mean that – just didn't think it were your thing."

"Well, it weren't, really – but Kay liked it."

"And you watched it with her?" Michelle smiled. "Weren't you good?"

"Bloody soft, more like," Pete muttered. Phil glowered at him.

He turned his attention back to the programme. The guy – Sean McNulty – was talking about a play he was doing.

"And you were saying that in some ways you prefer the theatre to TV?" the presenter asked.

"Absolutely," Sean said. "And to be honest, I really enjoy the smaller projects – like what I'm working on with Rach."

"Ah, yes." The presenter turned her attention back to the pink-haired woman. "So, Rachel, this is something of a come-back for you, too.?"

"Yeah - I'd not written in a while. I suppose – well, life takes over, sometimes, doesn't it? But it's good to be back on track – and to be working with Sean again."

"So, tell me a bit more about the play."

She'd got the idea from a book, she said, by a local self-published author who was a friend of her partner. It followed a Scouse family through the decades, starting with an Irish immigrant who is tragically widowed, less than a year after their arrival in Liverpool. Phil was only half-listening – until they mentioned the writer's name....

Katie Cooney. A housing-officer for years; lost her brother at a young age - suddenly – and had dedicated the book to her late father, who'd had vascular dementia. The early part of the story was set in the north-end slums (where Frank grew up) and there was a couple who sounded a bit like Frank and Dot. Posh, Protestant girl; Catholic lad from the wrong side of town.

Phil knew Kay had written when she was young, way before they'd met, but she was never keen to take it up again; as this woman, Rachel, had rightly said, life *did* get in the way. But now, she'd gone out there and made it happen for herself; and it had to be good, for this Rachael to be putting it on the stage. He was pleased for her – could be prouder; but at the same time, sad that she'd had to leave him to do it. Had he really held her back that much...?

By now, the presenter was asking McNulty about his character, whose wife dies early in the story. He described him as salt-of-the earth, and his wife as a "grafter – a real tough woman." "But in some ways," he added, "I think it's her downfall. She takes on way too much." The presenter smiled, remarking that most women were guilty of that, as Rachael nodded in agreement.

"Well," McNulty added, "Katie's been there herself, she won't mind me saying."

Phil felt a sudden anger; this guy seemed to know a hell of a lot about his wife.

"It's amazing how she's turned things around," McNulty went on; and all at once, his face seemed to light up. "She's a lovely woman – one of the nicest people you could meet."

Phil knew that look; the one *he'd* had when saw Kay for the first time.

"Careful, PJ," Michelle said. "You're spilling your drink in your dinner!"

"Shit!" He looked down at the fish and chips, now a sodden mess. "Never mind – I weren't that hungry."

"Well, in that case, give it here!" Pete got up, grabbed the plate from him, and began to wolf down the food.

"Bloody hell, Pete!" Michelle said in disgust. "They've got beer on 'em!"

"*He* won't care!" Jackie sneered. "He'll eat owt, him…aw PJ, love, you don't look well! Are you okay?"

How did he feel? Hard to put into words – but the one thing for sure, it was pretty far from "okay."

Chapter Forty-two

Jen had also watched Sean's interview and rang Kay straight afterwards. "Hello, dark-horse – didn't say a word, did you?"

"Ah – "Granada Reports"?"

"Yeah – you don't half play your cards close to your chest, missus!"

"Well – I wasn't sure they'd mention it…"

"I meant Sean! He's mad on you!"

"But that's actors - they wear their hearts on their sleeve."

"No, Kay – I could see it in him."

"Alright – so maybe we *have* been out a few times…"

"I *knew* it!" Jen laughed. "Well, I'm made up for you – it's what you deserve."

"Thanks, Jen, but do me a favour? Don't tell anyone yet – I'm probably being silly, but I don't want to tempt fate."

Fingers crossed, Jen thought.

It had been so sad when Kay and Phil split up. Kay had tried to stay strong but was fooling no-one; and Phil would be lost without her. A loveable bear of a guy who, like many big, tough men, was as soft as anything underneath, and adored his wife.

To begin with, Jen was convinced they'd be able to sort it out, but as time went on, the less likely that seemed. On that afternoon at Cuthbert's, when Kay first lost her job, Jen had asked her if she might use this – and his 50th birthday – as an excuse to get it touch.

"So – are you going to call him?"

Kay shook her head, sadly. "I don't think so, Jen. He might have things planned – and if I ring it might ruin his day."

"*Make* his day, more like!"

"I can't, Jen. No contact for months, and now this has happened, well - how would it make me look?"

"Like you're missing him?"

"Or like I'm using him…. I mean, I can just imagine what Pete would have to say! He doesn't like me as it is!"

"But then, does Pete really like *anyone*?"

"No…and that probably includes himself. It's just…I can see what you're trying to do, Jen. But if Phil was coming back, he'd have done it by now."

"But you could both be saying the same thing – sitting there, waiting for the other one to pick up the phone…."

"Maybe…but then, he could have met someone else – and that's another blow I just don't need."

As Jen saw it, their only problem was that too much happened at once. The business failing, at the same time as Frank and Dot's decline in health; in other circumstances, Kay could have considered a career break, or even just reducing her hours – anything to take the pressure off. But as it was, there was no choice but to soldier on. She'd looked so ill, and Jen was more than a little concerned. It had upset her to see them arguing so much – they were two of the best people she knew. Both wounded souls, in their different ways, but always managed to help each other through; it was their strength.

Thinking back to when Dot died, Jen remembered getting the call as she was about to leave for work, and that it was Phil on Kay's phone; she was trying to get some sleep, he said, and was in no fit state to talk. When Jen went round that evening, it was heart-breaking to see her – not crying, just staring ahead in a daze. On TV there was a feature ("Granada Reports again") about Liverpool's old department stores – Owen Owen's, Lee's, Blackler's.

"I got lost once in Blackler's," Kay said, as if from nowhere. "Andy wasn't with us – I'm not sure why. Just for a few minutes, I couldn't see Mum – and I was so frightened. I've never been so scared, until this. And then, that time we had to go to Irene's for tea. I kept thinking, where's Mum? What if something's happened to her? Turned out she was at Uncle Bob's funeral. At least they're back together. That's something." The hint of a smile, which turned at once to terror – and Jen imagined that little girl in Blackler's, 40-odd years ago. "I don't think I can do this, Jen," she said flatly.

Phil stroked her hair. "It's early days yet, love. Give yourself time."

"That's right," Jen added, encouragingly. "It's all so raw at the moment."

Phil made mugs of strong tea and his signature dish of door-stop bacon butties, smothered with brown sauce. They looked as rough as Jen had expected but tasted amazing. Kay ate hers slowly and managed less than half.

"She's eaten nowt all day," Phil confided later, as he showed Jen out. "It's like she doesn't wanna be here. 'If I could go and be with her, I would,' she keeps saying."

"She doesn't mean it, Phil. She's not thinking straight."

"Hope you're right, love – 'cos I dunno what I'd do without her."

"You won't have to be," Jen said gently. "You'll make sure of that."

And right up to the funeral, that's what he did. He couldn't be faulted. So why, on the day it mattered more than ever…? There had to be more to it than met the eye.

In her heart of hearts, Jen still had that small hope that, whatever it was, they'd somehow manage to work things out. But, if it really wasn't to be, then Kay could do worse than Sean.

Chapter Forty-three

"You know," Sean said, "there's one thing I've never worked out. What the hell Zippy[xxxiv] was actually meant to be?"

"A frog, I think – though some reckon an alien…Then there's the whole thing with Bungle's pyjamas…"

"You mean, the way he walks round in the nip all day, and only gets dressed for bed? Yeah, could never get my head round that one!"

They'd met at Lark Lane on a brisk, chilly Saturday morning – a fortnight after their first date – and were walking through Sefton Park, around the Palm House and towards the lake.

"And remember Hamble from "Playschool[xxxv]"? Now she was one scary chick! Pure creeped me out!"

"One of my dolls looked a bit like Hamble. I liked her – but then I've always been for the underdog!"

"And you slept with a thing like that, at the end of your bed? Hamble - sister of Chucky[xxxvi]!"

"It gets worse. I had a clown, too – with an American accent! You pulled a string and it said, 'have a nice day.'"

"Jesus! I'm having nightmares already!"

"There's a photo of me and Andy here," Kay said, as they reached Peter Pan. "I'll have to dig it out."

"How about I take some now?"

He took two or three of her next to Peter, and a selfie of them both - in the exact spot where she'd stood with Andy. Then they continued their walk, passing by the Bandstand, the waterfalls, and alongside the Dell.

"Andy fell in there once," she remembered. "Mum was beside herself. Then this bloke walking by jumped in and grabbed him. Ended up soaked in mud – I don't think his wife was happy!"

"Kieran was always getting into scrapes. He fell head-first into a puddle once, and me and Jim ran over in a panic – it didn't look like he was moving. So, Jim turns him around, only to find him laughing his head off! We got a row off Ma for bringing him home dirty – well, I tell a lie – it was more Jim than me!"

By now they'd come full-circle and were back at the Palm House just as spots of rain began to appear. "Shame," he said. "Thought it might have held up…."

Along with Hope Street and Lark Lane, the park had become, for them, what Otterspool had been for her and Phil. Although Sean was busy with rehearsals, they met whenever they could, their days mostly ending at the hotel bar. But she was yet to be asked back to his apartment. It turned out he was the perfect, old-school gent; no bad thing, of course. But it had been way too long – more than two years – without a man…And she was more than ready.

Chapter Forty-four

Of course, he wanted her – what man wouldn't? So, what was holding him back?

Somehow, there was an innocence about her; not childlike - certainly not naïve. It was hard to put into words; but maybe, somewhere at the back of his mind, was the idea that she was just too pure; too good to touch.

He hoped he wasn't *that* regressive – but then, Suzie had accused him many times of being less right-on than he liked to believe. Did she have a point? "I don't know where you get this from, Suze," he'd say. "I do everything round here. And you know I've loads of pals who are women. More than guys, for that matter." This, she retorted, was just like racists who denied it with that old chestnut, 'but all my best friends are black…!'

But they'd grown up so differently, and this was at the heart of their problems. Perhaps what he liked in a woman – softness, nurturing – might seem at odds with his beliefs; but what Suzie didn't get was that a girl, brought up the same way, would probably seek out those traits in a guy. It all came down to what you were used to; and in his case, this was a family who had each other's backs. Because he found Suzie's matter-of-fact indifference hard to understand, she thought he was looking for a mother-figure; but while he adored both his parents, he'd always been that bit closer to his father.

He and Suzie were okay before Gerry's decline – which, when it came, was pretty rapid. Less than a year earlier, they'd thrown a surprise party for his 70th. Before opening the buffet, he'd stood up to thank his sons, talking proudly and at length about all they'd achieved, then rounded-off with the announcement they'd all been half-expecting – that after 55 years in the building trade, he was finally retiring.

Not before time, everyone said. Gerry had looked tired lately and had been getting some back pain. 70 was too old for such a physical job, and Sean was relieved that his father could see this for himself. But looking back, perhaps it was all too sudden. He might have been better with semi-retirement and winding down bit by bit. Within a few months, Sean had already noticed a change; and within two years, Alzheimer's was in full flow.

Sadie struggled at first to keep Gerry at home, until Jim, concerned for her health, convinced her he needed full-time care. He lasted three years after moving to a care home, and mostly kept in good spirits. In the end, he had no idea where he was, or who any of them where – yet somehow, he was still Da. The names and faces might be jumbled up, but the humour – the personality – remained. It was this that Sean clung onto.

There were some far worse than Gerry. At least Gerry was happy; and given what some of the others were going through, Sean could live with that. His mobility was good, and he was often up and about, "causing mayhem," the nurses said, with an indulgent smile. Mostly, he mistook Sadie for his Auntie Mary ("Auntie Mary had a canary," he teased); Jim for his father;

Kieran for his younger brother ("Wee Davey"), and Sean for his Uncle Vinnie. For Sean, this was all good – Da had been close to Uncle Vin and had often remarked on his middle son's likeness to him. It was the laughter that kept them going. Da was back to being a wee boy – lively, mischievous – and his "shenanigans," as Sadie called them, couldn't fail to bring a smile. What choice was there? They could dwell on why, of all people, it had to be Da – or they could make the best of things and see the funny side whenever they could.

And suddenly, he was gone. It had seemed to Sean as though maybe he'd go on forever like this; in his own world, perfectly content. Then one morning the nurse had gone to wake him, to find he'd slipped away peacefully in his sleep. The sort of ending they'd wanted for him, and inevitable it would be soon, but this made it no less devastating. Looking back, Sean realised he'd returned to work – and London – much too soon, and would have been better staying close to his family. Sadie had prepared for what was to come and handled it all with a quiet dignity. Jim and Kieran struggled, like Sean, but had their wives and children to rally round. In London, Sean looked to Suzie for the same kind of support and found it sadly lacking.

Feeling as he did, he was finding work draining, and had little energy left to socialise. He knew this wouldn't be forever – he just needed some quiet time while things were so raw. But Suzie kept on at him to go out, expecting life to carry on exactly as before. Eventually, he felt so worn-down that he agreed, reluctantly, to go with her to her friend Olivia's house party. As the night wore on, he got deep in conversation with a woman who'd also lost her father – after a few drinks his guard was down, and he found himself close to tears. Next morning, he got the silent treatment, until he finally asked Suze what was wrong. He'd embarrassed her, she said; they'd be lucky if they were invited to Liv's again.

"To be fair, babes," he pointed out, "I did try and tell you I wasn't up to going...."

Suzie rolled her eyes. "You used to be such a laugh– and overnight you've turned into this sad, middle-aged loser!"

"Ach, would you give us a break, Suze? Da's only been gone a month!"

"Yeah, and don't we know it!"

"Oh, right – all heart, eh?"

"Well, for Christ's sake, Sean, he'd been ill for four years! Surely you must've seen it coming?"

"He could have been like that for *twenty* years, and I'd still feel the same."

"Yeah, well you need to snap out of it – because I can't deal with much more of this shit!"

Eight years together, and only now was he seeing her true nature. He'd always known she could be sarky and cynical but had assumed this was just a front. She was so outgoing, funny, bubbly – and only later would he realise that he'd naively mistaken her extroversion for warmth. They'd met in the early

2000's, whilst working on a production of "Othello[xxxvii]". There were some great times, and they'd had a wild social life. All well and good, while it lasted, but once all that was stripped away and she was just left with *him*…It wasn't easy to accept, but deep inside he knew she didn't love him; probably never had.

About a fortnight after this, the bombshell came when she announced, matter-of-factly, that she was putting her acting career on hold and going alone on a year-long trip around the world, taking in India, China and Thailand before eventually reaching Australia. It was something she'd always planned to do – and now, as he was so difficult to be with, seemed the right time for them to be apart.

Sean was gobsmacked. He knew things weren't great, but he had no idea she'd go to this extreme. Apart from anything else, he was concerned for her safety. When he looked at it rationally, he knew plenty of others – male and female – who'd done it and been fine; but because of where his head was, he couldn't handle the thought of something happening to her. He tried to tell her how he felt; he understood she needed to do this, but did it have to be right *now*? Yes, she said – because that was the problem. She couldn't cope with the way he was; it wasn't what she'd signed up for. So, yes, it did have to be now; so she could get away *from him*.

Of course, he should have done exactly what she'd asked of him and let her go. Instead, he asked her to marry him – stupidly believing she might soften if she realised just how much he cared. Inevitably, the opposite happened, and she tore into him

– had he not listened to a word she'd said? - before packing and leaving for good. All gone…. like his Da.

After that, he didn't want to *feel* anymore – so he hit the bottle and the weed. Went on a bender that lasted a month, ending one morning when, to his horror, he awoke to find himself in a cell. He remembered nothing of how he'd got there, or what he'd done…To his relief, it turned out he'd been pulled in for being drunk and disorderly, and he was sent home with nothing more than a ticking-off. Luckily, no-one he knew was any the wiser; or so he thought. Before "Hard Times", nobody would have cared less, but now – well, he wouldn't exactly have called it a big deal, but there was a small item in one of the tabloids. It was enough. That night there was a call from Jim.

"Just so you know, Ma read about your antics. For Christ's sake, lad! What the fuck are you playing at? I know you miss Da, but you're not the only one!"

"I know, Jim. What can I say? The last thing I wanted was to upset Ma. And you're right – you're both getting on with it – but you've got Linda, and Kieran's got Jayne…"

"But it's not like you're on your own, Sean. What about wee Suzie?"

"No, Jimmy, not anymore." He realised he was crying. "She walked out a few weeks back – couldn't handle me being down."

"Aw, shit – that's tough. Doesn't excuse it, mind – but I'm sorry."

It was the wake-up call Sean had needed. He knew Gerry would be ashamed, and that was the worst thing. He took a three-month break from work, staying at the house in Ireland and spending most of the time with his family, to make things right with Jim and, of course, Sadie. Once he'd finally sorted his head out, he returned to London, and the theatre, which meant even more now; he was doing it for Da, to ensure all his support was not for nothing.

But he was never quite the same. That day, on the call to Jim, was the last time he'd cried. He'd felt so raw and exposed, and didn't want to be in that place again. So, he shut himself down, choking back his emotions and focusing on anything else, until they went away. In doing this, he'd grown tense, irritable, snapping at people and losing his temper more. Not how he wanted to be – but what could he do? It was either this, or being vulnerable – and just now, it was the lesser of two ills.

It was different on-stage. The characters became his outlet; no-one could judge his emotions if he was someone other than himself, instead praising his heartfelt performances. He brought something of his father to each role – and when required to show distress or anguish, he did it for real. As for women – since Suzie there'd been no-one serious, just meaningless flings.

But Katie – she, like the stage, was his safe place. He wasn't going to screw this up, so all the messing around would stop; and he'd bide his time. She was worth the wait.

Chapter Forty-five

The play opened the following week. Kay went with Jen on the Thursday evening; Rach met them briefly when they arrived but was behind the scenes for most of the time, and Jill had come with Stu the night before. A few rows in front Kay spotted Pam, her fellow teaching assistant – and was taken-aback to see who she was with.

"Well, that's a turn-up for the books. I thought she hated him."

"Who is he?" Jen asked.

"Geoff Dent. He was horrible to Rach a few years ago. With any luck, she won't realise he's here. Jill won't be happy – she thought Pam was a friend."

"Awkward! So, what happened between them?"

"Long story. It was all on Facebook – then the trolls got in on it, and…oh, here we go…I'll tell you later…," she tailed off, as the lights went down.

****

The opening scene is Mick and Sylvie's kitchen, circa 1981. In the background, a radio plays Soft Cell's "Tainted Love[xxxviii]". Chrissi, aged 14, puts the kettle on and sets out two mugs, singing loudly along. She clearly loves this band – indeed, she looks not unlike Marc Almond, with her smoky eyeliner, jet-black clothes and hair.

"Chrissi!" comes a female voice. "Keep the noise down. I'm sick of asking you!"

Chrissi rolls her eyes, ignores her, and carries on singing.

"Chrissi! I won't tell you again! Now, Paul's taking me shopping. While we're out, I need you to make lunch for your grandad."

"I know," Chrissi snaps. "I don't need to be told."

"Look, Chrissi, I'm not arguing. Just do as your told!"

Again, Chrissi ignores her.

"We're going now, babes." A male voice, this time – very scouse, more so than either Chrissi or her mother. "See you later."

"Bye, Paul."

As she hears the door slam shut, Chrissi resumes her song. At this point, Pat enters from the left of the stage – now aged 82, and despite walking with a stick, still sprightly.

"Jesus Christ – d'you call this music?" His tone is warm and laughing, not critical – and as she turns around, he winks to let her know that this, as always, is meant in fun.

"Quit your moaning, old-timer," she teases, leading him over to the table and helping him into his seat. "I know what comes next…well, in *my* day…like, 200 years ago…"

"Cheeky mare…I'll have your guts for garters!"

(Kay smiled, thinking of Bob and Viv).

Chrissi changes the station.

"Ah, thanks, love," Pat says, "you're a good girl."

The song playing now is "Sweet Sixteen[xxxix]", by the Fureys and Davey Arthur – which Kay had mentioned in the book after hearing it on the documentary. As Chrissi makes lunch, Pat listens quietly, his expression wistful.

"You okay, Pops?" she asks gently, placing before him a plate of sandwiches and a mug of tea.

"I'll be fine, darlin'," he sighs. "It's just – well, you know…"

"Are you thinking of Kitty?"

"As ever." He sips his tea. "D'you know, it's over 42 years since I lost her – your Da was just a few months old. Still feels like yesterday." He swallows, wiping his eyes.

"I know, Pops. And I love hearing about her."

"But you're just a wee girl – you must get pure sick of me going on about the past."

"Never. It makes me feel like I know her."

"She'd have loved you. You've both of us in you – her stubbornness, my temper."

Chrissi laughs. "Oh, Pops! You *never* get angry!"

"Ah, but I did, back then – I was a real hot-head. But that's not always a bad thing. Nothing wrong in standing up for yourself."

"That's what I tell Mum. She doesn't get it."

"We're two of a kind, right enough. But Kitty was different – quiet, but tough as they came. If she dug her heels in, there was nothing down for you! Mind you, she broke her heart crying when we first came over. Sure, the voyage was bad enough, with the girls being so ill. Once we got here, we thought that was the worst of it – but see that wee house off Soho Street? Bloody shocking…!'"

His voice fades, and at this point there is a change of scenery. Pat and Chrissi are still visible at the table, but now in the background – while at the forefront is the tiny, crumbling scullery of a 1930s slum house. Kitty, on her hands and knees, scrubs the floor vigorously, even ferociously, barely pausing for breath. Stout, ruddy-faced and a few months pregnant, her reddish-brown hair is tied back in a head-scarf, and she's dressed in a wrap-around apron. Pat (now played by Sean) enters the scene; he wears a threadbare vest and faded grey trousers.

"C'mon, love," he says to Kitty, his tone gentle but firm. "You've been at that all day." He helps her to her feet.

"I can manage," she says briskly. "I'm not made of glass!"

"Aye, but you can't be too careful." He looks around the room. "You've done a grand job. It's looking better already!"

They hear a crash of thunder. Rain comes through a hole in the ceiling; some of the plaster falls away, shattering onto Kitty's newly cleaned floor. Pat hugs her as she bursts into tears.

"Aw, come here. It's not the end of the world."

"I know," she sobs. "But what the hell have we come to, Pat? Look at it! This was meant to be a new start, but sure, I'd rather sleep rough, than in this godforsaken hole!"

"Look, I know it's not great, but it's just for a wee while. When I start getting work, we can find somewhere better."

"I hope so."

"We'll get there — and if we don't, at least we're all together."

She sighs despondently. "So, you think we might not?"

"Well....I won't lie, the job situation's not great. But it's worse back home, so we've nothing to lose — that's how I see it, and... Ah, Jesus, would you listen to that?!"

The neighbours can be heard screaming abuse.

"I'll kill you!" the husband roars.

"Go on, then!" the wife sneers. "I'm past caring. I hate your guts! I wish you were dead!"

"What a place," Kitty says, with another sigh. "But you're right. We're better-off than some."

He pulls her protectively closer, as the neighbour continues his rant; she winces as the first blows are struck, and the wife squeals like an injured cat.

"You okay, love?"

"Yeah - just brings back some bad memories."

In the book, Kay hadn't gone too much into Pat and Kitty's backgrounds – only that he was a farm labourer from a small village in Donegal. Rach had filled in the gaps, and in her back-story, Pat is one of nine sons from a dirt-poor family. Kitty, by contrast, is one of three daughters; her father is a skilled man – a blacksmith – and compared with Pat's widowed mother, relatively well-off. But he is also a violent, drunken bully, who is furious when Kitty leaves home to marry a man he thinks beneath him.

As the beating continues, Pat's face clouds with rage.

"Call themselves men!" he says bitterly. "I've a mind to get round there and kick the shite out of him!"

"No, Pat - it's not worth it. We've problems enough as it is, without you getting yourself hurt."

"No chance! Have you *seen* him? Wee runt that he is..."

"Trust me, if you interfere, it'll make things worse for the poor woman. I know that only too well."

"But it doesn't seem right, just sitting here, letting him away with it."

Kitty smiles. "You're one of the good ones. If only more were like you."

"I'm fucked if I can make sense of it. It was always drummed into us lads — never raise your hand to a woman. And at one time, I thought everyone was the same."

"Well - that fella next door's a breed apart, that's for sure. I know we can't go back, but I miss home. We might have had nothing, but we'd lovely neighbours — good people. But this place — it's another world."

"There'll be nice folk here too, love — a lot will be just like us, here because they're struggling. But I'll do me best — and if it doesn't work out, we could always think about a cheap passage to the States. There's worse we could do."

She brightens. "I like the sound of that. A fresh start. My school friend, Mary — her family went to New York. They did well."

"A lot of Irish there end up in the polis."

"That's what Mary's father did. I could just see you on the beat!"

"Aye," he chuckles, "and first in line would be the likes of our pal next door! They wouldn't last five minutes! Now, come on, lovely, let's get to our beds — you'll be wiped out."

As he leads her off-stage, the scenery changes again; once more, Chrissi and older Pat, in 1981, are back at the forefront.

"And for a while, I thought we were," Pat says sadly, as Chrissi makes a fresh pot of tea. "The work came in, and for a couple of months or so, we got by. Until I screwed up."

"Aw, Pops." Chris sits back down at the table. "So, what went wrong?"

"Well, there was this fella I worked with - Matty Breen. Shy lad – maybe a bit simple – reminded me of my wee brother Paul. I always looked after Paul, and I ended up doing the same for Matt. So, there was these two brothers who gave him a bad time. Always waited till me back was turned, but I'd the measure of them – and you know how much I hate bullies. One day I caught them at it, and I lost me rag – went to give them a hiding, but sure, I'd shot myself in the foot – what I didn't know at the time was that the gaffer was them lads' Da. And when he got wind of it, I stopped getting the work."

"But you still did the right thing, sticking up for Matty. I'd have done the same."

"I know you would, sweetheart," Pat smiles. "And don't get me wrong, I still think it's the best way. But if only I'd put me brain in gear, before lashing out…"

"Easier said than done, Pops."

"You've an old head on young shoulders," he chuckles. "So - the longer it went on, the harder it got for me and Kitty. She got a handcart to sell fruit and veg - it bothered me that she was over-doing it, being pregnant and all – but what could I do…?"

…. Back in 1938, and Pat and Kitty's tiny kitchen, where she stands washing dishes; now more obviously pregnant, looking tired and drained. Again, the sound of rain, pattering heavily at the window – there is now a bucket beneath the patch of damaged ceiling; despite Pat's attempts to mend it, water still seeps through. Pat comes in, drenched.

"Nothing doing?" Kitty asks him.

"No, love." He removes his shabby coat and cap, both dripping-wet, hanging them near the door – then stands behind his wife at the sink, his arms around her waist, lovingly kissing her neck.

"Away, now," she says. "I'm busy."

"Sure, I can do these…"

"No – leave it. I've nearly finished."

He looks at her. "You need to take things easier – you're worn-out. C'mon – sit down and I'll mash up some tea."

"For God's sake, Pat!" she snaps. "I've no time to be sitting, drinking tea with you! There's too much to do"

"So, let me help. I've time on my hands, after all."

She laughs. "I know you mean well, but you're a man – you've no clue!"

"Well, at least take a break for a wee minute?"

"No – once I'm done here, I'm taking the cart."

"But look at it! Can't you wait till it's dry?"

"It could be like this all day – and we need the money."

He bristles. "I'm doing me best…"

"I never said you weren't – but it doesn't change the fact we need the money! Still - I heard there's cleaning jobs at TJ Hughes. A woman was telling me at the wash house."

"But the baby's due next month – you don't want to overdo it."

She flings the plate down on the draining-board. "You dare tell me what to do!"

"Love, I'm sorry – that's not how I meant it."

"Good – because I'd enough of that with Da."

"Aw, c'mon – surely you know me better than that." (She nods, though still angry and tight-lipped). "And if you want that job," he continues, "it's up to you, but… can you not just see I'm worried about you? You take so much on."

"I think I'm the best judge of that."

"You never stop as it is…."

"Well, beggars can't be choosers. Look, Pat, I'm doing my best to help. I thought you'd be pleased."

"I am, love. But the truth is, I feel so bloody useless. It should be *me* doing all this, not you."

She softens. "I know…But at least let me think about it. If things pick up on the docks, I'll leave it – that's fair enough. Anyway - looks like the rain's easing off." She puts her shawl on. "I'll take the cart. See you later."

In the next scene, jumping forward several months, Kitty finishes at the washhouse, having gone straight after her shift at TJ Hughes, and has the clothes in a bundle, ready to carry home. By this time, she has given birth to Mickey; again, she looks drawn and pale, but is laughing with the other women.

"Look," one of them says, "your fella's come to walk you home."

Pat comes in, kisses his wife, and takes the bundle from her."

"Aw – isn't he good?" Another chimes in. "You've got him well-trained!"

Kitty, although tired, seems embarrassed, rather than glad of the help – and a little annoyed. As they walk, the scenery changes behind them, from the washhouse to the court off Soho Street. Pat carries the washing, his other arm around Kitty's shoulders. She has a bout of coughing.

"Still not shaken off that cold, have you, love?"

"I'll be fine. So – nothing doing again?"

"'fraid not – so, I thought I'd give you a hand."

"You don't have to." She sounds slightly irritated. "I don't know what them women'll say...."

"Does it matter?"

"I just don't want them thinking I can't look after my family – after all, it's me they'll judge, not you! Besides, won't your pals from the docks laugh if they saw you?"

He chuckles. "I'd bloody flatten them if they did!"

"You really don't care what anyone thinks, do you?"

"No," he grins broadly, "couldn't give a shit!"

They enter the house. In the kitchen, their daughters have started off a pan of stew – Maggie, the eldest, is holding two-month-old Mickey, who is chortling happily.

"Good girls," Pat says to them. "Now – you put out some dinner for Ma, and I'll take Mickey." He lifts the baby from his sister's arms. "It seems ages since the two of us laughed together," he remarks, as Kitty starts unloading the washing

"Well," she snaps wearily, "if I get a minute, I'll let you know."

"Aw, don't be like that. I know it's tough – but it doesn't mean we can't make the best of things."

"Look, Pat – I can't help thinking this is because you saw me laughing with them girls."

"No, love, that's not what I…"

"You men are all the same! It's fine for *you* to go to the pub with your pals, but you begrudge me a bit of fun, even if it's while I'm working myself into the ground!"

"Hang on – I don't begrudge you anything! I'm glad you've made friends. I just want *us* to have fun, too. Like we used to."

"Well, perhaps you should have thought of that before bringing us here and getting yourself into rows at work. It's good you've got principles – but just now, we need you out there, bringing the money in. Maybe then we'd have a fighting chance."

"And you think I'm not trying? The slightest thing and you're on at me – I'm getting sick of it!"

"*You're* sick of it?" She thunders. "Well, that makes two of us!"

Mickey, startled by the noise, begins to cry. Kitty snatches him from his father. "Look what you've done now!"

"Kitty - I'm so sorry – I didn't mean to raise my voice..."

"I don't want to hear it, Pat. Just leave me be."

She turns her back on him and leaves the room, hoping to quieten Mickey. The girls stay for a moment.

"She doesn't mean it, Da," Maggie says. "She's just tired."

"I know, love, but she's right."

"Oh, Da – you're doing your best. Will you be okay?"

"I'll be fine, darlin'. Now, you go and help Ma."

Once alone, in his frustration, Pat bangs his head against the wall. A bit of loose ceiling falls away.

"Jesus *fucking* Christ!"

Chapter Forty-six

"You alright?" Jen whispered to Kay.

"Yeah - just brings back a few memories."

One particular incident came to mind. A Saturday, when Frank had returned from a stay in hospital, and she'd spent most of the day at the bungalow. When it came time to go home, she made sure everything was ready for the carers' evening visit, leaving a flask of coffee to keep them going.

"Try not to keep getting up too much, Dad, if you can help it," she warned Frank.

"Well, Katie," Dot piped up, "you can't expect him to just sit doing nothing. Besides, his mobility's not *that* bad."

"Thanks, Mum," she'd snapped. "I'm trying to make sure he doesn't end up back in hospital! I wonder why I bother, sometimes..." She sighed. "Anyway - I'm off. Be careful, Dad."

It was after 7 when she got home, to find that Phil had ordered a Chinese – she'd had a long day, he said, and they both needed a lift. As they sat down to eat, it seemed as though, for the first time since Frank's illness, they might get some quality time; until the phone rang.

"Just leave it," Phil said. "At least till you've finished, any-rode."

"I can't," she said; he shook his head sadly as she took the call.

"Katie? It's Dad – he's fallen already!" A sob in her Mum's voice. "Can you come back?"

"I had a feeling this would happen," Kay sighed. "What was he doing? I'd let everything ready for the carers."

"He needed the loo... Then he decided to make a cuppa."

"But I'd left that flask..."

"I know, but that was coffee. We wanted tea."

"Oh, for God's sake – the carers could have done it, if he'd only waited! So – have you pulled the cord for the lifeline?"

"Oh, yes..."

"And did they say how long the paramedics would be?"

"They weren't long at all...less than half an hour."

"Hang on – they've already been?"

"Well, yes..."

"And he's alright? No broken bones?"

"No... but we still want our cup of tea – and I'm worried he'll fall again."

"Look, the carers should be due any minute – they'll sort it out."

"Oh, they've just gone."

"Without making a drink? That's poor. I'll be having words."

"No! Don't, Katie!"

"Why not, Mum?"

"Well," Dot said sheepishly, "I knew when I told you, you'd end up coming back, so..."

"...you said you didn't need them? Oh, *Mum*!"

"Don't snap at me, Katie – it's not *my* fault he's like this!"

She could hear Frank shouting irascibly in the background.

"She'll be here soon, Frank.... You see what I mean?"

"I know – but look, Mum, Phil's ordered a take-away – and it's the first chance in ages to have a relaxed night together...."

"Oh! Okay, then. You enjoy your meal. Don't worry about us."

It did for her every time. She looked at her plate – the food was already going cold and looking less appetising. She saw the tension in Phil's face, felt it in her neck and shoulders. She'd hoped that after they'd eaten, they'd curl up with a glass of wine and a film; maybe get an early night...but now it was the last thing she felt like doing.

"To be honest, Mum, I don't think that relaxed evening's happening now. So, alright – I'll come. Tell Dad not to worry."

"Bloody hell," Phil said, once she'd ended the call, "you've been there all day!"

"I know, Phil," she shot back, "but what can I do?"

"Look, there's no need for t' bite me head off, love! Any-rode– give us a minute. I'll get 'van ready."

"No - you've had a drink."

"Only one..."

"Still, I'd rather not chance it. I'll call a cab."

"Fair enough. I'll come with you..."

"No - I'm best on my own."

She rang the taxi - ten minutes at most.

"Look, love," he said, "don't take this wrong – but why have carers, if she just sends 'em away and rings you?"

"It's not that simple, Phil. She's lonely…."

"Yeah - but you need *some* time out for yourself. I mean, you can't carry on like this. You're worn-out!"

"Alright - so, just say I leave them to it, and Dad has an accident? People can be so judgemental – and it's me they'd point the finger at."

"Hold on - who'd be pointing' 'finger?"

"Just *people*."

"So, you're running yourself ragged, for 'sake of folk you don't even know? Makes sense, does that!"

"Everything's so black-and-white with you. Typical man!"

"Here we go..."

"Well, it must inconvenience *you*, all this…." Her phone beeped. "Look, I've no time to argue. The taxi's here."

"Look, Kay, I'm just worried about you. Can you not see that?"

"I'll have to go. Just leave me be."

Funny how things turned out. She'd been so determined that, if the book was a tribute to Frank, her own stuff should be kept out of it….

As she'd written, she'd sympathised so much with over-worked, self-sacrificing Kitty, and had tried to portray her worry, guilt, and concern for others as something only a woman would understand. But now, watching her as she pushed her husband away, she felt a flash of annoyance -which she realised was at herself, for how unfair and, at times, self-righteous she'd been. Poor Pat. Poor Phil….

Chapter Forty-seven

"I'm not proud of myself," Pat says tearfully to Chrissi. "I went straight to the pub. She wants me out the way, I thought – so I'll wait a couple of hours, let her cool down.... but before I knew it, I was tanked up – can't say I remember getting home, just know I crashed out in the chair. To this day, I ask myself, why did I do it? Why didn't I just stay? Turned out, that was the last time I spoke to her."

"You weren't to know that, Pops."

"You're right – but it doesn't make me feel any better. Anyhow – by the time I woke up, she'd gone to work. Must have been at the back of nine – your aunts were at school, and your Da was with Mrs. Brennan. She always minded him, in case I got hired for the day. But that morning, I was too hungover to stand in line, and besides, I knew it was pointless. Fresh start tomorrow, I thought – I'd see if anything was doing at the south docks, where the gaffer didn't know me...Next thing, there's a knock at the door. A couple of girls from the shop. They told me Kitty had collapsed, and to go to the Infirmary." He swallows hard. "So, I rushed over there, and they took me in a room. A massive stroke they said – even if she survived, she'd never be the same. She lasted a week...never woke up. Telling your aunts was the hardest – and getting them through the funeral...."

.... Inside the church, Pat stands with his sobbing daughters, a protective arm around each of them. His face works furiously as he fights back tears but, determined to be strong for his children, he won't allow himself to cry. The priest, Father Byrne, says a few words about Kitty – her strength, courage, devotion to family. Then a prayer - "O, lamb of God, you, who take away the sins of the world..." - before they prepare to leave for the interment. Pat makes his way to the front to bear the coffin. Three of his friends from the docks help him; and as he takes the weight on his shoulder, he briefly closes his eyes. The intense pain is etched across his face – but still no tears.

The next scene is in the tiny parlour. In the corner nearest the kitchen, the women (mostly neighbours, and some of Kitty's workmates), cluster around Maggie and Maureen. The elderly, be-shawled Mrs. Brennan has looked after Mickey during the funeral, and still holds him now, every so often passing him to her friend, Mrs. Connolly. Pat, meanwhile, sits in silence with his three pals, who offer their support through glances of unspoken, male understanding. They are joined by Father Byrne, whose attempts at conversation fall flat; while Pat is polite to him, it's clear he's in no mood for small-talk....

.... As Kay watched, she remembered Andy's funeral; Dot in the living-room, with all the females (apart from herself) gathered around. In the front-room, Kay sat with Frank, along with George, Ray, Tommy and Stevie, who tried to chat with her – but, just like Pat, she had no stomach for it. What she wanted was to be quietly with her father – poor Frank, the strength sapped from him, looking so completely lost. The worry, the concern, seemed all for Dot; and somehow, it felt there would be no way that Frank could be a part of it....

….. Father Byrne takes his leave. "Thanks for asking me back here, Patrick," he says, shaking his hand. "Look after yourselves."

"Thanks, Father," Pat manages a smile.

Then his work-pals get up to go. "Take care, lad. And if you need anything…."

"…. Remember, girl," Mrs. Brennan is saying to Maggie, who nods earnestly, "it's *your* job to take over where your Mam left off. You'll need to come out of school – you'll have enough to do." Pat glances over imploringly at his neighbour, who doesn't notice. She still has Mickey in her arms. "And *this* little one – no Mam to look after him…"

"Aye," Mrs. Connolly agrees, "poor soul…"

"Thanks for everything, Mrs. Brennan," Pat says, politely but firmly, taking Mickey from her. "It was good of you to mind him for us. But the girls are tired. It's been a hard day."

"Oh! I see!" she looks slightly put-out. "Well, she sniffs, "I'll be going, then. And don't forget, Mags – if you need a hand, give us a knock."

Then she goes, followed by Mrs. Connolly and the other women, who all hug Maggie and Maureen on their way out. Once everyone has left, Maggie begins to gather the crockery.

"Leave that, darlin'," Pat says. "I'll do it later. You need your beds."

Maggie puts down the plates. "But Mrs. Brennan said..."

"Take no notice – she means well, but she's hasn't a clue!" Maggie smiles, as Pat continues. "All this talk of you coming out of school – however much we struggle, I'll not have that! I know it doesn't feel like it just now, but we wanted a chance of a better life for you. And if Mrs. Brennan thinks I'm keeping you at home, like a skivvy, she can think again! We'll pull together, like always." She nods. "Anyway, you girls go and get some sleep." He kisses them goodnight.

"You'll still be here tomorrow?" Maureen asks tearfully.

"Of course, love. I'm going nowhere."

Once alone, Pat – still holding Mickey – takes down a photo from the mantlepiece and, with another sigh, sits down. Himself and Kitty on their wedding day; he looks at it for a moment, smiling warmly at the memory. Then, all at once, great sobs rack his body, his face twisted in agony. Not wanting the girls to hear, he makes no sound – as though the howls, the screams, trapped inside, are physically hurting, tearing him to shreds.

Then, as the scene fades, a haunting instrumental of "She Walked Through the Fair[xl]" would bring the first act to a close.

Chapter Forty-eight

Phil had thought, more than once, about going to see the play. Although he'd never been there, he knew where the theatre was, and that it had started the night before. It wasn't on for long, so if he did decide to go, he'd need to get a shift on. But there was a good chance that Kay would be there – and although part of him (*all* of him!) hoped for this, he had no idea of how she'd react. His gut feeling was to keep away.

Of course, he knew Kay hadn't meant what she'd said that night – and that he should have slept on it before packing his bags. She'd been at the end of her tether, and he couldn't blame her. But it brought so much back to him; stuff he hadn't thought about for years...

His first crush, at the age of 8, was Danny Cooper's mum. Danny had joined the school not long after Phil and Pete – and like them, was straightaway a sitting target, for very different reasons. A small, fragile lad, he was easily startled, and it took little to make him cry. On top of that, he was "posh", having moved to the estate from the middle-class suburb of Windle. From all accounts, they'd been a comfortably-off family who'd hit hard times; his mum was on her own, perhaps widowed, more likely divorced, and she over-protected her boy, who was all she had.

The usual cat-calling soon became full-on, physical bullying. When Phil caught Wayne Watkins and his mates trying to put

Danny in the bin, he was straight in there, pulling Danny free, and thumping Watkins, who burst into tears on cue. Their form teacher, Mrs. Crick, was over in seconds.

"Whatever's the matter?"

"It's Philip Wainwright, Miss," Watkins snivelled. "He just punched me in 'nose!"

"Oh, did he, now? We'll see about *that*!"

And, as happened so often, he was dragged off to the Head, Mr. Jackson (better-known as "Jake"), who gave him the cane – and a lecture about bullying!! Usually, he managed to keep any tears at bay, but this time was a struggle. It wasn't so much the cane that upset him – it was how he'd tried in vain to tell Jake that it was Watkins, not him, who was the bully, and Jake immediately shut him down. Hastily drying his eyes before Watkins and his gang got a chance to see, he turned into the corridor, where he found Danny waiting for him with Pete.

"Thanks for sticking up for me," he said anxiously, as Phil approached. "And sorry I got you into trouble."

"Weren't your fault, lad. It were that fucker." He smiled at the memory; even then, his language was choice.

Danny looked at Phil's hands. "Are you okay?"

"I'll live. You?"

Danny shook his head, beginning to cry. "I hate it here. I wish I could go home."

"Missing your mates?"

"Yeah..."

"Same here."

"You're not from round here, then?"

"Only moved a few months back. We lived with Nan and Gramps before then. Don't 'alf miss 'em."

"Like I miss my dad," Danny said, tearing up again. "And my old school. Mum keeps asking if I've made new friends. I have to lie to stop her worrying."

"I'd do 'same, if mine gave a fuck." He smirked, and Danny managed a faint smile. "Any-rode - hang round with us, if you like."

Danny looked nervously at Pete, who was staring sullenly at the ground. "Will your brother not mind?"

"Don't mind, do you, our Kid?"

No answer. Phil rolled his eyes. "Don't fret over him. He'll be fine."

They may have had little in common, but Phil came to see Danny in the way he'd later see Col and Robbo. Much as he loved his brother, it was hard work (like now!) being with no-one but him, day-in, day-out. It had been different at their old school, where they'd had a good gang of mates, and Pete, as quiet as he was, had just mucked in and got along. Phil had tried to give the new place a chance, but they'd felt like outsiders from day one. They dealt with it in their different ways. Pete completely withdrew; while Phil, for all his bravado, cared more than he let on. Whereas Pete could play happily alone for hours, Phil had always done best being around others. With Danny, he felt he'd got back a bit of himself, and the life he'd been used to; while Danny, in turn, had someone to look out for him. An unlikely friendship, but it worked all-round.

For all his shyness, Danny had a great sense of humour, and would laugh heartily at Phil's outrageous comments and foul language, while adding the occasional quip of his own. Needless to say, Mrs. Crick thought Phil was a bad influence on Danny, who'd been a "sensible boy" until then, she said – and tried, with no success, to separate them. As time went on, Danny came out of his shell, and even Pete began to relax. As for Phil, he started to lose that angry, defiant stance he'd developed since joining the school, and grow back into the happy-go-luck kid he'd once been.

Before long. Danny had invited them back for tea. His mother, Wendy, was like no-one Phil had met before – youngish (probably about 30), with long blonde hair, very pretty. But it wasn't just that – she was kind and generous, so different to their own mum... hard to put into words, really, but when they were around her, everything just seemed *right.*

He'd dreaded their first visit, knowing how scruffy they were, and guessing that, like the teachers, she'd look down on them. Instead, she was smiling and welcoming. She cooked meals like fish fingers, chips and peas, or sausage and mash with onion gravy. Simple, ordinary things but, compared with the crap they got at home, it tasted amazing – like their Nan's dinners had done. To follow, there'd be all types of pies and crumbles – apple, gooseberry, rhubarb, cherry – either with ice-cream, or thick, yellow custard. As they ate, she'd ask them about themselves. Pete, as always, said little, but Phil told her all about their grandparents, and their old school. As he talked, she smiled and nodded, properly listening; as if she really cared.

Wednesday became their regular night to go round – the highlight of their week. No matter how bad things were, they had that to look forward to. At first, they stuck to the Wednesdays, but after a while they'd start to turn up, unannounced – until, eventually, it was pretty much every night. Looking back, they were cheeky buggers, but they hadn't meant to play on her. It was just so nice there, and so awful at home. Could anyone have blamed them?

But deep-down, there was always that fear that all this would end, and they'd outwear their welcome. Mostly, Wendy was as patient as always – but every so often, there'd be just a sign, however small, that she was getting pissed-off. Like the time she'd asked them not to come the next evening, as she was taking Danny to his nan and grandad's. They'd turned up anyway, claiming they'd "forgotten", but really hoping they'd be asked along.

"Look, Philip," she sighed, "you can't stay. We're going out soon. I did tell you."

She didn't raise her voice, but the annoyance was plain to see.

"I... I'm sorry," he muttered, mortified. His usual bluster had left him; it was the first time she'd been anything less than friendly, and it hurt to the core.

They'd left it a few days before their next visit, anxious of what kind of reception they'd get, but she was back to her old self, and things returned to normal. Even so, they'd learnt it wasn't a good idea to push your luck, and went round a little less often than before. It seemed to have the effect he'd hoped for. "Not seen you boys for a few days," she'd smile. Every so often, she'd ask them about Pauline – perhaps she had her suspicions that things weren't right. He kept it vague; but all the while, he'd have this pipe-dream that she'd take them in.

Then one day, during the summer holidays, Pauline took them shopping at the Co-op[xli]. Why she'd done this, Phil wasn't sure – she normally just sent them to the corner shop – but whatever the reason, she wasn't happy, and had dragged them on the bus, her face tripping her. As they stood in line, Phil spotted Wendy, a couple in front of them; she mightn't have seen them if he hadn't shouted her. She turned around and smiled.

"Hi," she said to Pauline. "I'm Wendy."

Pauline looked at her as if she had two heads. "You what?"

"Danny's mum."

"Danny who?"

"Philip and Peter's friend?" she said, her face dropping a little. "They come to ours for their dinner."

All at once, Phil wished he hadn't let on. He felt ashamed that Pauline knew nothing about where they went for tea. Of course, *he* knew why they didn't tell her (why waste their breath?) - but Wendy might think they were hard-faced sods, turning up there all the time, and not even mentioning her to their mum.

It got worse. Pauline smirked. "Oh aye," she said flippantly; and that was it. No "thanks for feeding my kids", or even a "nice to meet you." Wendy's face fell even more, and Phil knew in his heart that their days were numbered. She looked, in turns, confused, hurt, then finally angry, as she realised she was being made a mug of. Often, looking back on this, he wondered what he'd really expected? Perhaps that she'd see instantly what Pauline was like – and that things might change for the better…

The trouble was that Pauline, to the outside world, seemed okay. She could go for weeks without stepping over the door, but when she did, she made an effort – and neatly dressed, with a bit of make-up, she wasn't a bad-looking woman, small, slender (a "little dot", as Grandad called her), quite pretty, with long, curly dark hair. Phil saw now that Wendy hadn't come close to guessing their situation, but (rightly) saw Pauline as sullen and rude.

As Wendy got served, Pete helped himself to a bag of crisps from the end of the counter. "Fuck's sake!" Pauline snapped. "I'll have for't pay for them, now!"

"Well," Wendy said, as she put away the last of her shopping. "Bye, then." Pauline ignored her.

"Bye," Phil called, as she walked away. "See you tomorrow." She didn't reply.

When they arrived the following evening, they were turned away. Dan was going to his nan's again, Wendy said – a last minute thing. The same happened the next night, and the one after that, until she finally came out with it: "Look, boys, I'm not saying this to be unkind. Once a week is fine, but you can't keep turning up all the time."

"But it's not …!" he began.

"It is, Philip," she said firmly. "You know that – and it's got to stop. You've got a home of your own, after all."

"Here's your hat, what's your hurry?" he said bitterly – a phrase he'd picked up from Grandad.

Wendy sighed. "Now, come on – I didn't say that."

"No," sobbing, "but that's what you meant!" Then, before he could stop himself, "You're all 'fuckin' same! And *you* can fuck off, an' all!" he lashed out at poor Danny (he'd never forgive himself for that), who'd just joined his mother in the hall, and burst into tears.

What had he done? Wendy sadly shook her head. "I think you've said enough, young man. Now just go."

"But I didn't mean…I'm sorry," Phil said desperately to Danny; but from the look on Wendy's face, he knew there'd be no going back. He'd lost the best mate he'd ever had and would just have to live with it.

"C'mon," he muttered to Pete, who'd spent the whole time staring at the floor – and as they slunk away, they could hear Wendy consoling her son, telling him he "could do better" than friends like that. It had hurt for a while, and he'd felt like shit for taking it out on Dan; but it gradually faded from his mind. Or so he thought.

"Perhaps I *could* do better than you." It didn't matter if Kay had meant it or not – *he* knew it was true. At the back of his mind was always a fear that it was too good to last; and, like Wendy, she'd end up seeing it for herself. And it wasn't just what she said, but how she'd looked. Disappointed – in herself, as much as him, for expecting too much.

For a good while, he thought he'd got lucky – and that she'd decided, for whatever reason, to let it go. In bed, on the night of the funeral, he'd told her that he knew he'd let her down, and how sorry he was – and although sleepy, she murmured something in reply. Next morning, it was like nothing had happened, and things got back to normal – well, as normal as they *could* be. Perhaps she'd found it in herself to forgive him – in which case he'd just be glad of it, and make sure it never happened again. But it turned out she'd just blocked it from her mind, and it all came back out of the blue. In desperation, he'd come up with that excuse about his nerves, but she'd never buy it, not with his brass-neck. "Nothing phases you," she'd tell him; so why would this?

For all their differences, he'd never disliked Dot. It was true that she'd annoyed him, especially in the early days, when nothing he could do was right. But with all her faults, she thought the world of Kay. They had in common, at least – and there was no doubting that the woman had been through the mill. In later years, it frustrated him that she seemed to lean on Kay for everything. He knew at times that Kay thought he was unfair – but just as she saw it as her job to look after her parents, it was *his* job to look after *her*. It was the least he could do. She'd done so much for him; turned his life around. He'd been wild before they'd met – booze, dope.... He'd be lying if he'd said they weren't good days, but he couldn't have kept on like that forever – and after marriage to Kay, he'd been amazed at how quickly he'd settled down.

He'd have done anything for her if he could. And no – he didn't hate Dot; but even if he had, he'd have gladly pushed that aside, and read her eulogy. If he'd only known how.

Chapter Forty-nine

This was the problem. He'd never learned to read properly and couldn't find the courage to tell Kay – or anyone. At first, when things were so tense with Dot, it just didn't feel right – he was already treading on thin ice, so why make it worse? Perhaps one day…. But there was no rush. As the years passed, he often thought of it; but, as with most things, the longer he left it, the harder it got. Mostly he was able to wing it, so that in the end, it was easier to say nothing.

He could read a bit; could recognise some words. But anything long or complicated – forget it; and as for sentences – no chance. He worked out a lot of things from memory, or from signs, which of course he relied on for driving or biking. He was okay on place names, recognising them from the signposts or maps. There were many words which he knew in his head but wouldn't have a clue how they looked. Writing was even worse. When it came to birthday, anniversary, or Christmas cards for Kay, he had to play the "hopeless male" and ask for Jackie's help.

The thing was, when he was out there grafting, it didn't matter – he put in long hours, and Kay didn't expect much more. But when the work dried up, there was nowhere to hide. Suddenly, he had all this time on his hands, while she had none – and just helping was no longer enough.

When it came to cooking – if she'd only had time to show him, instead of writing it down… They'd always shopped together, but it was Kay who'd thought about what they'd needed – and he was happy to push the trolley! Going alone was a different matter. "Didn't you look at the list?" she'd ask, as he brought back the wrong thing yet again. She tried to see the funny side at first, joking that it was like Jack and the Beanstalk, but eventually got exasperated.

He often thought back to the time he'd messed up with the beef. He could recognise what it was, of course – it was working out the different cuts that was the problem. Had he stopped to think, he'd have known that the cheaper the cut, the more likely it was, as he could make out the prices just fine – but, as usual, he panicked and blundered in. The more wound-up he got, everything became a mist in his head until, in the end, he picked up the first thing to hand, hoping for the best. Kay was upset at the waste of money - rightly so, as they'd been struggling at the time. He'd been on the verge of telling her that night, as he'd been so often before; but something always got in the way.

And then the funeral. He'd been so glad that Jen was there to take over – relieved, but ashamed. He knew folk might be judging him, and thought he heard someone whisper "Unbelievable!", although he couldn't be 100 percent sure. Because of this, he'd felt awkward, almost an outsider, as they left the chapel; and at the pub, as they clustered around Kay at the table (there for her because *he* wasn't!), he'd just backed away to the bar. He hated himself for it, but panic had set in again. If he joined them, he could do one of two things; act like nothing had happened, or tell them the truth, and at that moment, he couldn't face either. Perhaps he'd tell her that night, he thought; but when they got home, she was wiped-out and needed her bed. Next day, when she seemed to have moved on, he'd thought, least said, soonest mended...

On the night of the row, he'd wept silently, knowing he'd run out of choices. Be honest or lose her – it was that simple. At around 6.30, he'd gone into the bedroom, where she tossed restlessly in her sleep. "Kay," he said softly. She stirred slightly, mumbled something in her dream. "Kay," he said again – and if she'd woken in that moment, he'd have probably told her everything. Instead, she turned on her side, settling into a deeper, restful sleep. "Kay, love…," once more. Nothing.

He kissed her, realising then that the time would *never* be right. He had to go, get himself sorted; only then, maybe, there'd be a chance to win her back. It was this hope that had kept him going these last couple of years, as he'd worked on solving his problem, once and for all. But now, it looked like he may have lost her for good – and he had only himself to blame.

Chapter Fifty

The second act, like the first, opened with music – "Three Steps to Heaven[xlii]" and "Cathy's Clown[xliii]"- this time playing in the background at the care-home where Mick visits his father. "Brings back some memories, this," he says with a smile.

Pat nods, but it's unclear how much he's taken in. Just six months on from the chat in the kitchen with his granddaughter, and it's clear his health has significantly declined. His short-term memory has all but disappeared; yet he has less trouble with events of years before, as Mick recalls the early 60's – meeting Sylvie, army life, and the family's move to Speke, again shown in flashbacks.

In Act 3, the mood has darkened considerably. Chris, alone in her bedroom, listens to the Cure as she looks at photos of her grandad – a recent one of them together, another as a young man. From downstairs, there is the hum of chatter from guests at Pat's wake. A knock at the door; Paul's voice.

"You alright, sis?"

"No."

"Can I come in?"

"No."

"Too bad." He enters, sitting on the edge of the bed – tall, sinewy, with closely cropped hair, he is tough-looking, but has a warm smile. He glances at the photos, sighing. "I know."

Chrissi turns down the music. "We've *all* lost him, Mum said, before. We're all upset. Not just *you*. But I never said it was."

"Well, you know what me Ma's like. But she should know it's different for you – he was your best mate."

"I just can't believe he's gone, Paul. I mean, I know he wasn't the same in the end – couldn't remember us. But if I could just have the old Pops back, one more time…"

"I know, kid – I'm the same. But I daren't say anything in front of me Ma."

"I sometimes think I hate her."

"Aw, you don't mean that. It's just 'cos you're upset."

"No, Paul, I do. Claire gets worked up over pathetic stuff, and Mum's all over her. It's like no-one else matters!"

"Paul! Chrissie!" comes a sharp voice.

Paul rolls his eyes. "We need to stick together on this," he says in an undertone, before calling back, "Alright, Ma. There in a bit."

"Well, hurry up. Your Auntie Maureen's going home soon."

"I'll be down in a bit – I've just said. But give us a minute, eh? I'm talking to Chris."

"Still moping, then?"

"Oh, come on – no need!"

"Look, Paul, this is much worse for your dad than anyone – after all, he's lost his *father!*"

"Yeah, but she's just a kid. Give her a break."

"Well, Claire's younger again, but …"

Chrissi breathes in sharply. "Leave it, Ma," Paul warns.

"Alright, then," Sylvie says huffily. "Fair enough, Chrissi – just stay in there and feel sorry for yourself. Never mind anyone else. Now, get a *move* on, Paul!"

"Will you be okay?" he asks Chrissi.

"No. But just go, Paul. Or you'll never hear the end of it."

Alone again, Chrissi turns up the music, which plays out as she gives way to her tears; then the jump forward to 1985, and her rebellious later teens.

■■■

"Brilliant!" Geoff Dent said. He and Pam had collared Kay on the way out and they stood chatting, somewhat awkwardly, in the foyer. "Rachael's done a cracking job." He sighed. "Look, Kay, you might have heard there was some unpleasantness between us a few years ago."

"A bit," Kay said quickly, "but that's none of my business."

"Well, I'm not sure how much they told you – but I feel dreadful about it." He looked sad – and Kay, despite herself, couldn't help but be a little sorry for him.

"Was that the troll guy?" Jen asked as he headed out.

"Yeah – awkward! I think he genuinely regrets what happened – but I've a feeling it's all too little, too late. He caused so much trouble at the time, and…oh, hello," as Sean approached, "…talking of trouble!"

"We meet at last," Sean said, shaking Jen's hand. "I've heard so much about you – all good, I hasten to add!"

"Likewise," Jen smiled.

"A few of them are going for a drink," he said to Kay. "But if you don't mind, hon, I think I'll pass. I'm pure wiped out!"

"Do you still want dropping off?" Jen asked her.

"Well…" Now Sean had joined them, perhaps they'd have a nightcap – just the two of them – maybe in his apartment….

But "See you tomorrow, babes," he said.

She tried to ignore the pang of disappointment. He was tired, and so was she – hadn't they just said so? He was giving his all to the role – *her* role – and she was more than glad. But bloody hell. Would she have to wait forever?!

Chapter Fifty-one

"So, how have things been?" Denise asked Phil. "It's been a while since you were last here. Eighteen months, at least."

"Bloody hell – it goes nowhere!"

"So," she repeated. "How have things been?"

He sighed heavily. "Up to now, not so bad. Still doing them classes you told me about. Not saying it's been easy, but I'm getting there."

Denise smiled. "Well, that sounds really positive."

"Yeah."

"But now? What's happened, Philip?" she asked gently. "What's brought you back to counselling?"

He shook his head. "Where to start? You couldn't make it up!"

Denise, of course, would know this was about Kay. On his last visit, she'd urged him to swallow his pride, get in touch and be upfront. Now, he'd have to admit he'd ignored her advice. He should never have come....

When the doctor had first sent him for counselling, he'd hated the idea, and was honest enough to tell her on the first session. "Dunno why I'm here in 'first place," he'd grumbled. "All I wanted were a pill!"

Denise, in turn, told him straight that he was hard work – a tough nut to crack. Still, the time passed quickly – and before he knew it, he'd opened up about the bad times in his childhood, as well as happier memories of his grandparents. "You see?" she said. "Not as bad as you thought!"

He'd expected her to be patronising, like his schoolteachers, but she'd turned out to be lovely; an ageing hippie, but none the worse for that – a bit like Jen, twenty years on. Slim, silver haired – probably a looker in her day! Her manner was kind, without being sickly-sweet, and she'd assured him that nothing he said would go any further. He soon felt able to tell her anything; and although he hadn't intended to mention reading or writing, he ended up blurting it out. To his embarrassment, he got tearful, but Denise didn't judge. She helped him find an Adult Literacy class – and suggested another trip to the doctor, in case there was an underlying cause.

He bristled. "Not sure I wanna know, to be fair."

"You're not alone in that. It's your choice – but you're more likely to get any support you need."

"Well," he muttered, "'spose it can't hurt..."

The doctor arranged some tests, which confirmed he was dyslexic – quite severely so – with mild-to-moderate ADHD. It certainly made sense, thinking back to his struggles at school. At first, he'd get what they were on about – but then the teacher would go off the point or move on to something else. He knew he was supposed to piece it all together and make sense of it, but by the time he'd tried to do this, he was already too far behind. As the teacher's voice droned on, he'd make a rubber ball from elastic bands, which he'd then unravel.

"Philip Wainwright, I won't tell you again. Now, stop fidgeting and *concentrate*!"

He gave up in the end. He was the first to admit he'd arsed around, especially once he'd got in with Col and Robbo; and as time went on, they turned up less and less, bunking off to hang out with the gang. The one subject he'd done well in was woodwork, but the teacher was that psycho, Richie Toale. When he eventually came to blows with Toale, he'd walked before he was pushed - and after that, gave no more thought to learning. He'd already found work, so there seemed little point.

It hadn't been easy, taking that first step and joining the reading class; but thankfully, it couldn't have been more different from school. The tutors were volunteers, all friendly, and there was no pressure, which helped a lot. Hard as it was, he'd learned a lot in the first few months, and what's more, was enjoying it. He never thought he'd see the day! There was still a long way to go, but at least he wasn't scared anymore. His plan was to get in touch with Kay when he'd gotten to where he wanted to be – without her ever being the wiser. Deep down, he knew she might well meet someone else, but told himself he'd cross that bridge when he came to it. He just hadn't banked on it being like *this*....

Denise glanced at the clock. "Look, Philip, I don't want to rush you – but we're halfway through the session now…"

"I know. I dunno what I'm doing here, love. I'm wasting your time."

"No – I don't believe that. You wouldn't have come back for no reason." She poured more water. "Let's try a different way. Tell me about your week."

"Well – not great, to be honest. Me best mate's missus passed away Monday."

"Oh, no – I'm sorry to hear that."

"Thanks, love – she were a good friend to me, too. She'd been ill a while, but just got told there were nowt they could do. She'd not long gone in a hospice, so we pretty much knew that were it. But, I dunno – as long as they're here, there's still hope – d'you get me?"

"I know just what you mean. After all, you do hear of people beating the odds."

"That's what Col said to Yvonne. Don't get me wrong, I reckon he knew deep down she wouldn't make it, but he never told *her* that."

"And how's he doing now? Silly question, I know."

"Really bad – not eating, not taking his meds – he's diabetic. Says there's no point – he only kept going for her. A bit like Kay when she lost her Mum … So, me and Robbo keep checking in with him – make sure he's not done owt daft."

"You must be shattered, with work and everything else?"

"Aye – but to be honest, I'm best keeping busy. Takes me mind off …other stuff."

"Other stuff?"

"Yeah." Another long pause. "You 'know, I thought I were getting there. Then Friday night, out the blue, it all goes tits-up."

"I see."

"Gets in from work. Our Kid and Jac were tearing a strip off each other, as usual, and her sister were there, putting in her two-pennorth. Does me head in, but what can you? Anyrode, Jac puts on "Granada Reports". I were only half watching it, half eating me tea. Next thing, they're on about a woman from Liverpool who just wrote a book. Turns out to be me missus."

"Oh! Well – I wasn't expecting that!"

"Me neither!" He grinned, despite himself. "And it sounds like she's doing really well. There were this fella on, talking about her. Looks like someone's got hold of it and put it on 'stage."

"Wow - that's impressive! It must be something special."

"I know! And don't get me wrong- I'm that pleased for her…"

"But…?"

"This actor bloke."

"The one who was talking about your wife's book?"

"Yeah. Sean McNulty."

"Can't say I know much about him – but I've definitely heard the name."

"Well- looks like he's got a part in it. And him and Kay are together."

Denise paused a moment to take a drink. "So, did he say that?"

"Didn't have to. Could see it a mile off."

"And you're absolutely sure? There's no chance you might be jumping to conclusions?"

"No, love- he's with her. I just know."

"Male intuition, eh?"

"Yep - something like that." He smiled sadly. "Thing is, it's not like I've not been out with anyone else. Our Jac set me up on a blind date with this mate of hers. Debs, her name were - her fella had died in a car crash a few months before. It weren't that long after me and Kay split up – and I know Jac meant well, but it were way too soon. We had a laugh – helped us both get through things. But when it came down to it, Debs were nowhere ready to move on from Ian – and I don't reckon I'll ever be over Kay.

"'Course, I knew she'd meet someone – why wouldn't she? But, I dunno - I s'pose I thought it might all come out in 'wash - you never know..."

"But not now?"

"Well - a bloke like him – not got a cat-in-hell's chance, have I? But it's not just that. I knew she used to write when she were younger. It all stopped when her brother passed on. I were always saying she should get back into it again. But that's been and gone, she'd say – no point looking back. Then, soon as I'm gone, she does all this..."

"And you wonder why she didn't do it when she was with you? Just a thought – but sometimes, people create – write, paint, compose – when life's not going so well. In fact, it's often when they do their best work." She glanced at the clock. "Anyway – I'm sorry, Philip, but our time's just come to an end. Would you like an appointment for next week?"

He shook his head. "No - I'd just be going over 'same ground, and it won't change owt. But thanks, any-rode, love."

"Well – if you change your mind, our door's always open. Take care, Philip. Hope all goes well."

Chapter Fifty-two

It was time, Sean decided, to buck his ideas up. The play had finished now, and on Sunday he'd head back to London. He and Katie were still no further in moving things on – he wanted it more than anything, so what was wrong with him?

Perhaps he imagined it, but she seemed to light up when she spoke about Phil; and there was the feeling that, if he suddenly put in an appearance, she wouldn't be in a rush to turn him away. She shared so many memories, mostly happy; like seeing Motorhead with him at the MEN – not really her thing, but she'd got into the spirit of it. She'd also gone to Donnington with him – but then, he'd been with her to see Paloma Faith and Norah Jones, and of course, the opera at Verona. Compare that with Suzie, who wanted her way, her terms, or nothing at all.

It shone through in the book, too. After watching the play, she said she realised she'd based Pat on Phil – instinctively, not intentionally; and although she'd created all her characters with love, Pat was portrayed with such warmth. Maybe they should never have split up. Torn apart – not through death, like Pat and Maggie, but through circumstance – and pushed to the limit, they'd made a mistake that both were too proud to put right.

Perhaps, then, Sean was right to hold back – and instead of making a move, should encourage her to go back to Phil. And yet...where *was* he? Over two years, and still no sign. A strong man would surely be fighting tooth-and-nail to get her back –

unless, of course, he'd moved on with his life.... For whatever reason, he wasn't here – and Sean had never felt so happy, or so well, in such a long time. Why should he give that up? No – enough with the messing about, the "faffing", as his Da called it. Time to get his act together.

****

On his last night, Sean surprised Kay with a meal at the Carriage Works, which he knew she'd been wanting to try. Over salt-marsh lamb (washed down with a deep, serious Malbec) and duck-egg custard tart, they talked about how quickly the time had passed - and how they'd loved every minute.

"Although," she said, "it still all seems a bit surreal. It was strange to sit and watch it. And Kitty made me realise what a martyr I've been!"

"Hey, c'mon. Give yourself a break, Sure, I know it's a cliché, but hindsight really is a wonderful thing."

"I saw a counsellor a while back – not long after Mum. I was beating myself up for pretty much everything, and she said something along those lines. That we're all doing the best we can, in that moment – and that's all we can ask of ourselves. And that thing about the oxygen masks…"

"Fit your own mask first?"

"Yeah – because if you end up dead, what use are you to others? Time after time, Phil would say just what Pat does – slow down, don't make yourself ill – and I shot him down in flames."

"You know," Sean said, "Phil sounds a lot like Jim. And he said all those things to Ma."

"Your poor Mum. Did she find it hard to accept help?"

"Absolutely! Wouldn't hear of Da going in a home at first. But in the end, there's no choice – they need someone 24/7. Jim was right, of course – but sometimes he's a bit black-and-white. His heart's in the right place, though. He's the one who holds everyone together."

"I think there's one like that in every family. The backbone."

"Yeah – that's just what he is. And being there onstage – especially the funeral scenes – it wasn't that hard to do. I just thought of how Jim was feeling, when we buried Da. Stayed strong throughout the mass – even when we were leaving the chapel, and they played "My Way" – it was one of Da's faves. Pure finished me and Kieran off. 'You okay?' my nephew Kev asks Jim. 'Aye, son, I'm fine,' Jim says. 'Don't worry.'

"We brightened up a wee bit when we got to the pub – a few drinks down us, remembering the good days, and it carried on when we took Ma back home. 'Just popping out for a cig,' Jim says. I noticed he'd been gone a while, so I went out to the garden to find him. He was standing at the very edge of the lawn, the furthest end from the house, facing the back wall. 'You alright, Jim?' I asked. No answer. I tried again. 'How you doing, fella?' Then he turns round, the tears streaming. 'Quick,' he says. 'Let's get in. I don't want Ma finding me like this'

"So, that's Jim. I wouldn't mind, the telling-off he gave Ma for not looking after herself – he's the world's worst for it! It bothers me sometimes, that it'll all get too much for him. After everything with Da, I really don't know what I'd do if anything happened to him."

"Well," Kay said, "it's good you were there when he was so upset. You know, when I think of that time I saw Dad in tears over Andy – the thing I remember most was how *lonely* he looked. At least Jim's got you."

"I hope he knows that." For a moment, Sean seemed to choke up, but then he smiled. "Anyway – enough with the morbid stuff! Seeing it's my last night, and it's all gone so well, I say we round it off with some champers. What d'you reckon?"

"You don't do things by halves, do you?" She laughed. "Yeah – why not?"

Then, once they'd settled up, they headed back. Not to the hotel bar, this time; but, at last, to his apartment.

Part Four: Landing

Chapter Fifty-three

Several hours later, she awoke in a sudden panic from a nightmare; sat bold upright. "Phil?"

She looked frantically around, forgetting for a moment where she was; then, as she focused, became aware of the elegant, surroundings of the aparthotel room, and Sean snoring happily away beside her. Her phone was in her hand, which confused her – memories of the night before were blurry, but she had a vague idea she'd put it on the bedside table. Then, when it started ringing, another wave of panic. She looked at it again – Jen's number. It was just before 4am, so why would she be calling now, if it wasn't bad news...?

"Phil," she said again; but then, why would the police contact Jen? It didn't make sense – unless something was wrong with Jen herself...?

"Jen? What's happened? Is everything okay?"

To her relief, Jen laughed. "I'm fine, hon, but shouldn't I be asking *you* that? You rang *me*?"

Kay looked again at the phone – so *that* was why she was holding it. Somehow, in her dream, she'd reached out for it; and perhaps, as in real life, she'd looked to Jen for moral support.

"Jen," she stammered, "I...I'm so sorry. I must have leant on it in my sleep. I feel awful for waking you."

"Aw, don't worry- I couldn't drop off anyway. But look, Kay, are you alright? You sound shaken up."

"Just a bit of a nightmare, that's all. I'll be fine when I've calmed down. Now, you get some sleep. Speak tomorrow."

Next to her, Sean began to stir. "Hmmm…?" he mumbled; then settled down again, his arm around her waist. They were both still fully dressed, and lying on, not in, the bed. As much as she tried, she couldn't get comfortable; felt tense, agitated, chest burning with reflux. Couldn't get Phil off her mind; whatever had happened in her dream, he was probably in it. But she shouldn't be thinking – *or* dreaming – of Phil. *This* was what she'd longed for. Hours earlier, she'd berated herself for being so damn *passive*, and waiting for Sean to make the move; there was nothing to stop her asking him to *her* place. Yet somehow, the idea of him – *them* – being there just didn't feel right….

Perhaps, she reasoned with herself, it was the fear that happened when things change, even in a good way. It might help her to focus on her evening with Sean - but it all seemed so far away.

Their meal was still clear enough, but their night together afterwards was hazy. Gradually, the more she focused, it began to come back. Sean had a well-stocked fridge and cracked open a magnum of champagne. "Well, he smiled, "it's like you said – I never do things by halves." It seemed to be gone in no time; and as they neared the end, he opened a Chilean Malbec that seemed even richer and heavier than the one they'd had at dinner. Then things began to hot up. After all this time alone, she quickly grew wet at the thought of what was to come – how good it would be, to feel a man's touch, once more....They moved over to the bed.... Where, almost at once, he crashed out!!

As for herself, she'd felt quite lively – but by that point, her head was starting to spin. She couldn't remember exactly when she'd dropped off but guessed it must have been soon after.

So - no further on, after all. To be fair, they were tired; probably a little nervous, too; and they'd both had a lot to eat and drink. Perhaps they'd built it up too much. Next time would be different, she told herself.... Then nausea hit her suddenly, as the acid in her chest continued to burn. She swallowed hard and, for a moment, it seemed to pass. At the end of the day, she thought, she should be making the most of this, not wishing she were anywhere but here. Okay, perhaps last night had turned out disappointing, but there'd be other chances. She needed to stop dwelling and *enjoy*.

That might be easier if she didn't feel so sick. But it kept coming, each wave stronger than the last – and it didn't help that she was lying on her bad elbow. Very gently, she moved Sean's arm from her waist, turned over, and tried to remember her dream.

It came back in fragments. The more she recalled, she realised that it was only a "nightmare" in the sense that it unsettled her. Not frightening, exactly – just the overwhelming feeling of trying to get somewhere, do something, *say* something, and going round in circles. At one point, she was on the underground, stuck on a train that wouldn't move (which *was* quite scary!), and trying desperately to find a way out; a broken-down bus, in the middle of nowhere; and then, at last, back home with Phil, and looking everywhere for her phone.

"Don't worry," he said. "It'll turn up."

"I know, Phil, but I need it *now*, to ring Jen…to warn her about that Maria…. Oh, Phil, where *is* it? And can you turn the telly down? I can't think straight!"

In the background was some weird music, like a sinister merry-go-round. That was it – the theme from "Picture Box[xliv]", which had always spooked her as a kid. Phil tried to turn it off, but as he pressed the remote, nothing happened. "Battery must've gone," he muttered.

"Oh God, what next?!" she almost sobbed. "My head's about to explode!"

"Panic over!" Phil grinned, pointing to the phone on the bedside table. "It were there all along!"

And then…of course! Still dreaming, she'd picked it up and started calling Jen…

She'd thought remembering would help. The panic did start to subside, but in its place came a deep sadness. For one, why had Maria, of all people, come to mind? It had been years since she'd seen, or even heard of her. Those old anxieties – rejection; exclusion - she'd battled so hard against them and had honestly thought she'd turned a corner. Everyone had blips, she reminded herself – but why now, when life was going so well?

The other thing was that, throughout the dream, her constant thought was that she needed to get back to Phil. And now she was awake, it was just the same. All she wanted was to turn the clock back; to have not let him leave. To be in her own house – her own bed; Phil alongside her, cats snoozing at their feet. And the book, a distant idea that would come to nothing....

It was no good – she couldn't ward off this nausea and was starting to feel really ill. The smell of last night's stale booze turned her stomach, and she headed for the bathroom without further ado.

Chapter Fifty-four

Afterwards, she bathed and dressed quickly, feeling stronger already; thanks mainly, she guessed, to the invigorating, monsoon-style power-shower. She groaned inwardly as she noticed a streak of vomit on her blouse, but luckily, the apartment had a washer-dryer. It shouldn't take too long, she thought; and in the meantime, was sure Sean wouldn't mind her borrowing a red plaid shirt he'd left draped across a chair.

Sitting down with a weak mug of tea, she put her headphones on and tried to calm her thoughts. Of course, she didn't really regret writing the book – or anything that came from it. The idea had been in her head for years; it was only a matter of time before she put it down on paper, so why the sudden self-doubt? What was the problem?

Nothing - apart from Phil, who wouldn't leave her mind…She tried to make it stop by thinking about Sean, but the more she did this, the stronger Phil seemed to appear. But why now? It was crazy. Over two years, and she'd achieved so much – why the hell would she want to go backwards?

She reminded herself of his faults. Loud. Untidy. Never looked at things properly or stopped to *think*…. But at the same time…kind, gentle, generous; treated her like a queen. In her attempt to get over things, she'd forced herself to forget all that – and for a time it worked. She thought, suddenly, of those who'd spent months, maybe years in a coma, eventually coming round to find their loved one gone. Much worse, Kay thought, than anything *she'd* been through – but perhaps she could relate, in some small way, to the feeling of having just woken up; and wanting him back, more than anything.

In Sean, it felt as though she'd found the best of both worlds. Clever and creative (the qualities which, however mistakenly, had drawn her to Stu) combined with a warmth and humour that reminded her more than a little of Phil. She'd be lying if she'd said it didn't. But, as last night had shown, some things just didn't come close.

She thought back to her first time with Phil – her first time *ever* – remembering his patience, and how scared she'd been. A mixture of fear and anticipation – excitement for what was to come, but afraid of the unknown. It might be painful – or, even worse, he might dump her afterwards, or laugh at her inexperience. Perhaps she could just bluff it, she wondered – but she'd always been a terrible liar. He'd soon suss things out, so she'd have to come clean and hope for the best. They'd been together a few months before they finally got the chance of some time alone, when Pete and Jackie took the lads for that week in Center Parcs. She grew slightly tearful before they went upstairs, as she found herself blurting out just how stupid and naïve she felt. He did all he could to reassure and put her at ease, and they took it gradually, exploring each other's bodies bit by bit; she learned so much.

The more she relaxed, the more she loved being in his hands – he seemed to know, instinctively, just what she needed. She enjoyed the feeling of his strength and weight on top of her; of his beard and rugged chest, bristling against her skin…. It got better each time; and once they were married, it happened most, if not every night. They'd shower together afterwards, holding each other as the warm, soothing water poured down. "I never knew life could be this good," he said once; and neither did she.

He'd kept her grounded when she beat herself up. "There's enough folk out there to give you grief," he'd say, "without you doing it to yourself." He'd go over to help her parents at the drop of a hat; and while cooking and housework weren't his forte, he'd tried his best for *her*. Whatever went wrong that day at the Crem, he couldn't have done it on purpose. It wasn't in him.

The days before the funeral had been so confused, but like everything else, they were now becoming clearer. He was with her for every step — telling the family, registering the death, the undertaker's…. And that night, when all was over, he'd held her in bed, telling her how sorry he was to have let her down. She remembered now.

"I panicked, love," he'd said. "I think it's because I weren't expecting it — and I knew how much it meant to you, so I didn't wanna mess up. Then I felt so stupid — that's why I kept away from everyone afterwards. But I were wrong for that. I should never have left your side."

Oh God, she thought, oh God, what had she done?

Chapter Fifty-five

Her thoughts turned back to Sean. She felt awful for what she was about to do. He wasn't a bad person; he was sensitive and kind, and they'd had so much fun. Until that point, she'd painted a rosy picture of what their life together might be like. The actor and the writer; a slightly off-beat, bohemian couple who'd support and inspire each other in their work. Sean, like herself, was a keen cook, and she guessed the kitchen in his house in Ireland would be amazing. They'd spend lots of time in it, as well as beautiful walks along the Antrim coast....

But how would things look a few years down the line, when she (like Suzie) fell from her pedestal? Sean worked with women all the time – beautiful, confident women. He was a tactile person; and, by his own admission, something of a flirt. Or maybe it would be the drink. She knew it must have been bad, for him to end up in that cell for the night – with Jim's help he'd got himself together, but she could tell he was still fond of the booze. It was hard to keep up with him when they were out; no wonder last night ended up a non-starter! Not that she and Phil hadn't enjoyed a drink, of course. But with Sean, it seemed somehow like he needed it, in the way he needed holidays, nights out, women.... all for the same purpose; to believe his life was happier than it truly was.

Perhaps she was being unfair. Everyone was guilty of kidding themselves, sometimes – of seeing only what they chose to see. Herself included – hadn't she done just that with Stu? But the more she learnt about Sean, she got the feeling it wasn't just sometimes, and he'd done this his whole life. His father's illness, for instance – he'd honestly believed that Gerry still knew him and could live indefinitely with Alzheimer's. There was always shock and disbelief at losing a parent, no matter how unwell they'd been, or for how long – but it would have been so much worse for Sean, because he'd convinced himself that somehow, Gerry would always be around. As for Suzie, could he really have been with her for that long, and not got at least a *glimpse* of the cold, cynical side? The woman had told him, in no uncertain terms, that she wanted out. He'd responded by proposing!

It seemed he only dealt well with the messy, complex stuff, when he wasn't being *him*. A man who ran from real life yet was at his best in his portrayals of the gritty, genuine, down-to-earth everyman. The emotions he brought to the roles were *true* emotions – *his* – but he was only brave enough to feel them as Pat, or Stephen; or anyone but Sean.

Perhaps it had had rubbed off on her; or perhaps she'd ignored the red flags and her instincts, not wanting to fall back into her old way of expecting the worst. But it was almost as if, when she'd had the nightmare, she'd returned to reality; and as tough as that was, she'd have been happy to stay and face it – she and Phil. Then, when she'd woken, she was back in Sean's dream - where she no longer wanted to be.

At face value, she and Sean had come from almost identical backgrounds – solid, "affluent", skilled working-class. During their time together, they'd shared so many memories from childhood. She'd laughed as she told him the stories of Andy, and the scrapes he got into - but at the time, it wasn't so funny at all, too often ending in tears. Unless Frank was around, Dot always seemed to blame *her*. Like the time Andy fell in the Dell – "It's your fault, Katie – you wanted to go there and feed the ducks." Sean had said that he and Jim got in trouble for Kieran's misdemeanours; but then admitted it was really just Jim….

Someone tried to bully him at school – no problem. Jim came along and sorted it. Years later, when his girlfriend dumped him and he went off the rails, Jim sorted it again; and at their father's funeral he'd stayed strong for them all. In fairness to Sean, he'd been there for Jim when he'd broken down afterwards; but still, it was clear that he relied on Jim to make everything right and saw Kay in the same role. "I feel safe with you," he'd once told her. She'd taken it as a compliment; but did it really mean someone else to lean on….?

Caught up in her thoughts, she was unaware that Sean was awake and dressed.

"You're looking far away, there," she heard him saying. "Did you sleep okay?"

"Oh…. Yeah …" she stammered, "well, no…. I had a bad dream and couldn't drop off again. I wasn't too good, to be honest. I didn't make it to the bathroom, I'm afraid. Hope you don't mind me borrowing your shirt?"

"Ach, don't worry about that – it's just an old rag to knock around in. But are you alright? You're very pale."

"Better than I was. I just needed a shower and a cuppa – think I may have overdone it last night."

He grinned mischievously. "I'm not saying I'm God's gift or anything, but it's the first time I've made anyone throw up! I'm not *that* bad, am I? Aw, I'm just kidding – don't get upset."

"I'm so sorry," she said tearfully.

"What for?" he laughed. "Don't be so daft – happens to me all the time!"

"I know…it's not that, it's…. I'm so sorry," she said again. "I feel terrible. You're a lovely person…"

"Oh, God!" He chuckled, but she could hear the sadness behind it. "This sounds like one of those "not you, it's me," speeches."

"Yes…I mean, no, it's just…."

"Phil?"

"Yeah," she almost whispered. "I didn't realise till now, but yes…it is."

He hugged her. "Don't worry – I think I knew deep down, even if you didn't. And it's absolutely fine."

Chapter Fifty-six

He made some toast; she only managed a slice, but it did seem to settle her stomach. As they ate, he said he'd picked up on it when she'd first spoken about Phil – and had guessed she'd based Pat on him.

"I hadn't meant to," she said. "I just did it without thinking."

"And that's how I know you care for him. You just wrote from the heart."

What could she say? Perhaps she'd got him wrong. Maybe he was stronger, wiser, than she gave him credit for - and *she* was the one lying to herself, to justify what she was doing….

"I just feel I've led you on," she said sadly.

"No. If anyone's at fault, it's me. I could see you still love Phil, but I went for it anyway. Sure, it'll be fine, I said – she'll forget him. I just turned it round to how *I* wanted it to be. That's what I'm like, you see, Katie. I bury my head in the sand."

So, she *wasn't* wrong – he knew his own failings.

"Look," she said, "don't be hard on yourself. We all do it. I know *I* have – pretending to myself that I was over Phil. I think it's just a way to cope."

"Yeah, but I *don't* cope, that's the thing! Like with Da. Jim tried many a time to warn me how things would end up, but I wouldn't have it. He's not that bad, I'd say – just a wee bit confused. It always blows up in my face in the end, but I never seem to learn. Catch yourself on, as Jim tells me – the Irish way of saying, stop being a bloody fool!"

"Oh, Sean," she sighed. "I'm not letting you blame yourself like this. I mean, I didn't exactly push you away, did I?"

"Now, this is getting like Mrs. Doyle[xlv] and her pal in the café!"

"Where they nearly kill each other over who's going to pay?"

"That's the one!" They laughed.

"I'll miss all this, you know."

"Well, there's no reason it can't carry on," he said. "I hope we'll stay friends?"

She smiled. "I was afraid to suggest that in case you thought it was have-your-cake-and-eat-it. But as long as it's what you want, then yes. I'd love to."

She took a cab home. He'd offered to drive her, but best not, she said – with them drinking so much the night before. Once in, she sat down a moment; her head felt fit to burst. Jazz and Jet jumped down from the window-sill and onto her knee, eager to see her – and for their breakfast, of course! Once she'd fed them, they followed her upstairs. The next hurdle was getting in touch with Phil – and before she could think of that, she'd need more sleep.

Chapter Fifty-seven

She awoke mid-afternoon, after several hours of deep, uninterrupted, "dead-to-the-world" slumber; no dreams this time.

It would be scary, of course. She had no idea where he was living (she'd only guessed it was still with Pete), or what he was doing. Anything could have happened, these last few years; he could be ill, or with someone else – or just want nothing to do with her. That was the chance she had to take, and until she called, she'd never find out – it was now or never.

She scrolled though her phone. Phil's mobile was there, but that probably wasn't the best idea – she had no idea how he'd react if he her name come up (assuming he'd kept her number!). Easier to ring Pete and Jackie's landline; and if he wasn't there, at least she'd know the score…Heart-in-mouth, she pressed "call". It rang out straightaway, and she felt more and more jittery, the longer it went on. Perhaps they were away. She was about to hang up, when suddenly, a male voice, which threw her; she'd expected Jackie.

"'lo?"

"Hi…is that Pete?"

"No – it's PJ. Who's this?"

She took a breath. "It's me, Phil."

"Kay?!" She could hear the shock in his voice; then silence.

She thought her worst fears were confirmed, and he'd hang up any minute. "Are you still there?" she asked.

"Yeah," he answered. "Still here, love. You just took me by surprise – it's been a while."

"I know – and I hope I've not done the wrong thing, calling like this – out of the blue. I don't want to put you on the spot."

"No, don't be daft, love. It's good to hear from you." Well, at least he sounded friendly. That was a start. "So - how are things?"

She kept it light. "Not so bad. I've got a different job now – teaching assistant. I really enjoy it."

"That's brilliant, love. Sounds right up your street. And then you've got your book, haven't you?"

"Oh!" It was Kay's turn to sound shocked. He was never a big reader – didn't have the patience, he said – so it hadn't crossed her mind that he might know. "How did you find out?"

"Saw it on "Granada Reports". And I'm chuffed for you, love – it's what you deserve."

She felt herself tearing up. But then, that was him – he might be hot-headed, but he didn't have a nasty bone in his body. How could she have got things so wrong?

"Thanks so much," she said, composing herself. "That means a lot. Anyway – how about you?"

"Oh, you know – fair to Middleton." He chuckled. "Remember Dave Tucker?"

"From the old gang?"

"Yeah. So, you know he's a paramedic? Well, he got me a job as a porter. Been there a year now. I love it."

"That's great, Phil – a big change, but sounds like a good one."

"Oh aye – keeps me out of mischief, if nowt else!"

"Now, that I can't believe!"

They both laughed, then all went quiet again.

"Look," she said, "I need to talk properly – face-to-face. Could we meet up some time? When you've got a minute?"

Another pause. Was he going to say no?

"You're right," he said at last. "We've got a lot to sort out. I've not long finished work, so I'm free now, if you want?"

It was as good a time as any; and best to know sooner, how things would pan out....

"Great. Shall I meet you somewhere?"

"No, love, I'll come to you – it's easier."

"Okay – then I'll do something to eat." She took another deep breath. "See you soon."

Chapter Fifty-eight

It had gone much better than expected, but – how to explain it? It was crazy; but he'd been so light and relaxed, and had he sounded just *slightly* angry, she might have felt more reassured. Not too much, of course. Not enough to stop him forgiving her; but enough to show he cared, in the way he'd cared before. And "a lot to sort out" – did that mean trying again, or did it mean divorce?

Oh well – she'd find out soon enough, she guessed. Meanwhile, she'd promised him a meal, so she'd focus on the task in hand.

∎∎

Phil's head was spinning. It was so good to hear her voice – he'd begun to think he never would again. But his heart sank at the same time; he had a gut-feeling what this was all about....

She'd sounded so bright and breezy. He was glad she was happy, that went without saying – but he wanted her happy with *him*! He'd kept his tone light, to match hers; but when he got there, he'd tell her how he felt, and see what came of it. No use getting too deep over the phone; it wasn't easy to say much, with Pete stood there, listening in....

∎∎

She hadn't had time to shop this week, but what she *did* have in was plenty of pasta. In the fridge she found chorizo, sun-dried tomato-paste, a garlic bulb, mixed peppers and an onion; and from the window-box, she pulled handfuls of basil and sage.

Italian was always her go-to; it never failed to lift her. Switching the TV off, she put on a CD of the bluest blue-note jazz she could find. She cooked (and wrote) her best to this; and as she chopped and peeled, she felt the negativity slip away.

■ ■

"So," Phil said to Pete, "are you gonna stop staring at me, or what?"

"It were *her*," Pete scowled. "Weren't it?"

"What's it to you?"

Pete laughed bitterly. "You fucking dope! Clicks her fingers, and you go running!"

"If you must know," Phil snapped. "I think she wants a divorce. Now do us a favour and stop going on. I'm not in 'mood."

"Well, good riddance," Pete smirked. "And I hope that poncey actor-bloke treats her like shit!"

"You know what, Pete? Go fuck yourself!"

■ ■

It was all about finding the best, Kay thought, as she flung the veg into a roasting tray, drenching it in olive oil. Not just hoping but *believing*. She'd been sceptical of Jen's books, but they did work; and now wasn't the time to close her mind.

■ ■

He was always a scrapper, so why would that stop now? Enough was enough – he needed her back. Perhaps she wouldn't want to know; he had to be prepared. But, however things turned out, he couldn't go on like *this*; living here, with Pete, who resented him for anything – any*one* – that brought him joy.

Michelle was there, as ever, and Craig was round with his girl, Sophie, for a late-afternoon Sunday lunch; their baby was due any time soon. Jac had just dished up the roast, but they all stopped eating and watched as Phil, without a word, went through to get his jacket.

"Look at that," Michelle said, as he slammed the door. "He's left his dinner again!"

■ ■

The sauce was looking good – rich, glossy and deep red from the chorizo oil. A dash of Worcester Sauce; a glug of Merlot, which she'd serve with the meal; and to finish, the rustic-cut herbs.

It had started raining – tapping gently on the window at first, but soon hammering away. It was just after 4, but the evening was already drawing in; the house felt cosy from the warmth of the oven, and she hoped the cooking smells would give an inviting feel.

Not long now.

■■■

The train pulled out of Huyton –only a few more stops. Thing was, Phil asked himself, if McNulty was just some bloke from Kay's office, what would he do? Try to win her back, of course – it wouldn't occur to him to do anything else.

Never say never – that was what his mate Dave had said, when he'd ended up telling him last week in work.

"I mean," Phil said, "who would *you* choose – me or him?"

"Dunno if I'd choose either, to be fair," Dave smirked. "No offence, pal, but you're not my type!"

They roared with laughter. Dave always cheered him up.

"No, but you know what I'm saying? Think of 'life she'd have, with someone like that."

"Well, she wanted for nowt with you, lad – and 'two of you were happy. I still don't get why you broke up in 'first place!"

"Nor do I, mate," Phil smiled sadly. "Worst mistake ever."

"Look," Dave said, "from what I remember of Kay, she weren't struck on owt too flash – it weren't her style. So, I wouldn't throw 'towel in just yet – not till you know owt for sure."

And he was right – it *wasn't* Kay's style. Never one to show off; look at how she'd been on the phone. Wouldn't even have mentioned her book if *he* hadn't....

They pulled into Broadgreen. The rain was battering down as he left the station, and he was glad he'd decided against coming here on the bike. Hurriedly crossing the main road (and drenched already), he headed for the estate; and as he approached the house, was welcomed by the amber-gold glow of the porch-light. He could faintly make out some music – the kind of bluesy-jazz she loved, and he recognised as Nina Simone's "Feelin' Good[xlvi]".

He rang the bell. A few seconds, and there she was; he wanted to laugh and cry.

"Look at you," she said, smiling warmly. "Let's get you in."

Chapter Fifty-nine

He hadn't changed much. Soaked through; wild and windswept, like the wild man of Borneo – and she wouldn't have him any other way.

She led him through to the lounge. He'd sounded chipper on the phone, but now he looked intense, agitated, deadly serious; and *that* was what she'd wanted to hear – a bit of fire!

"Come on," she said, and they went up to the bathroom, where he dried his hair vigorously over the sink.

"How long were you out in that?" she asked.

"Only a few minutes," he said, "walking across from 'station."

"What about the van?"

"Got rid of it a while back. Don't need it so much these days."

"Well, I'm just glad you didn't set out on the bike."

"Yeah – I were thinking 'same thing." He smiled, catching sight of the Thai Buddha tattoo on her right forearm. "When d'you get that done?"

"About a year ago. D'you like it?"

"Love it."

They looked at each other. "I've missed you," they both said at once, and laughed; then were in each other's arms again....

She enjoyed the friction of his beard against her skin, as he softly kissed her lips, face, neck, breasts.

"Thought I'd lost you for good there, love," he said hoarsely. "When you said you wanted to see me, I just put two and two together and…"

"So did I – you said we had a lot to sort out and I just thought… well, why would you want me back, after the things I said? I'm so sorry, Phil. I wasn't right after losing Mum, but it's no excuse. I was a bitch to you, and you didn't deserve it."

"No, love – it were my fault. I kept stuff back that I should've told you." He paused; and she wondered briefly, what this "stuff" might be. So much to ask him, but it would keep. She had her man back – and, in this moment, that was all she needed. "I know one thing, though – now I'm home, you're stuck with me for good!"

"Oh, don't worry – you're going nowhere, Mister. I won't be letting you out of my sight anytime soon!"

They kissed again, and she peeled off his sweater, which was sticking to him – he was still damp. She grabbed the towel and tenderly dried him, then buried her face in his chest; his broad, magnificent chest with its forest of thick, dark hair.

And then he lifted her – carried her to their room – where he placed her gently, but firmly, on the bed.

****

As Pete sat, slumped and sullen in front of the box, Jackie threw away the leftovers, washed up and mopped the kitchen floor. She felt despondent; it always ended up like this, and she was sick to death of being spoken to like crap in front of folk.

Craig had just gone – not before tearing a strip off his dad, for whatever it was he'd said to PJ. From what she'd heard, it was Kay on the phone, and she guessed it was something to do with that. After PJ had walked out, they'd eaten their roast in stony silence. Another thing that annoyed her; she'd spent hours making it, to have it ruined, yet again. "You look tired, babes," Craig had said to Sophie – whose due date was less than a week away. "Best get home in a bit, eh?"

"Listen to you!" Pete mocked. "'*Let's get you home, babes!*' Bloody soft-arse – you're as bad as *him!*"

Craig looked at him in disgust. "You're having a pop at me, after how *you've* carried on! You're a class act, Dad, I'll say that for you."

"It's nowt to do with you."

"Well, that makes two of us, doesn't it?"

"I mean it, lad, you're pissing me off now. So, go on, if you're going – fuck off out of me sight!"

Michelle muttered under her breath; Jackie sighed.

"Look, Pete, I've said this before – it's no way to treat him. It's like he's some bloke down 'pub who's doing your head in. You're his *dad* – start acting like it!"

"Wouldn't know it though, would you?" he snarled back. "And *you* can stop poking your nose, too – you interfering bitch!"

"*Dad!*" Craig warned.

"Leave it, son," Jac said– she'd noticed Sophie starting to look tearful. "You get yourselves off – we'll talk later."

"I'll call you tonight, Mum – after I've rung Uncle P. I'm worried about him."

"And we can't have *that*, can we?" Pete sneered.

Pete's jealousy – that was always the problem. He resented the lads' relationship with their uncle, and anyone PJ cared about, that wasn't *him*. The sad thing was, Pete adored his brother, and thought the world of his sons. If he only could have found a better way to show it…. The lads were small, like him, and he was afraid they'd be bullied. He was hard on them, he said, so they'd know how to handle themselves - because he didn't want them going through what he had. Trouble was, it did nothing but make them withdraw – and eventually hate him.

It was this that caused the row on PJ's stag-do. Earlier that day, the lads had got upset about their uncle leaving to get married.

"Come on," PJ said to them. "Your faces'll be on 'floor if they get any longer!"

"We don't want you to go," Craig said tearfully.

PJ laughed. "It's only Liverpool, not Australia!"

"But we won't see you anymore…"

"'Course you will! And you can stay over with us, whenever you want."

"Will Auntie Kay not mind?"

"No – she'll be made up. Now listen to that," he chuckled. "I'm turning scouse already!"

Craig managed a smile.

"That's more like it."

"It's just we'll be stuck here with Dad – and he's horrible to us."

"I know, son. He's out of order for that. But don't fret – I'll keep an eye on you."

Unbeknownst to them, Pete was listening at the door, fuming. He said nothing at first; just waited till they got to the pub where, with a few drinks in him, he accused PJ of trying to turn his kids against him. Then Col had a go at Pete for spoiling the night; by all accounts, it nearly ended in a punch-up.

"What happened?" Jackie asked PJ.

"I'll tell you another time, love," he said wearily. "I'm gonna get some kip – else I'll be in no fit state for tomorrow."

Pete, meanwhile, had staggered upstairs – where Jackie found him in the lads' room, having woken them to tell them it was *their* fault. *They'd* caused the row, by being wusses, whinging on about their uncle leaving home. Why did they care? They had *him*, didn't they…?

"Get yourself to bed, Pete," Jackie said sternly, "and leave 'em alone."

She knew it was hard for Pete; but it made her mad to think how often she'd warned him. "They won't be kids forever," she'd say. "They'll grow up one day and remember all this." But nothing ever changed. He'd snap at them for nothing; they'd get upset and turn, as always, to Uncle P, who said the same to Pete as she did. "You wanna watch it – you'll turn 'em against you, if you're not careful." And it was true. The lads had no time for him – didn't respect him – and saw PJ as the dad they wished they'd had. PJ didn't *want* to take them away from Pete; it just happened that way, because Pete made it so hard for them – for *anyone* – to love him.

Then there was the way he spoke to *her*. Through the years, she'd learned to give as good as she got. She'd sometimes get in there first, shout and swear before he got the chance, but that was only because nothing else worked; and sometimes, being the "bigger person" started to wear thin. Come to think of it, what she did now didn't work, either, but at least she was sticking up for herself, instead of being a bloody doormat!

She'd thought of leaving, but why should she? She loved this house; it was *her* home, and if she went, she'd most likely end up in a flat, which would be nowhere near as nice…. Then, she'd need a job, of course – and what could *she* do, after all this time? She was 50 now, and the last time she'd worked was at 16, for a year or so after leaving school, at a sewing factory. She'd hated every minute and was so glad when she'd left to have the twins.

She was at that place when she met Pete – he and PJ were on building job over the road, and they all drank in the same pub after work. She'd turned 17 by then, and Pete was 19; they'd only been going out a few months when she fell pregnant. She was barely 18 when Craig and Carl were born. From then on, her life was taken up with them, as well as helping Michelle with their disabled mum.

Now Craig was going to be a dad. It couldn't come quick enough. This wouldn't be Jackie's first grandchild – Carl and his wife Julia had three in all, but they'd lived down south for the past three years, and life seemed so empty without them. She often felt bad for how down she got - thinking of how her own parents had scrimped and struggled, before her dad died at 53, and her mum was wheelchair-bound at barely 60. At least she had her health, and everything she needed; Pete was a good provider, and for all his faults, never laid a finger on her. But she'd give anything to be *happy*…

As she finished her cleaning, she was unaware of him coming in.

"Are you not watching 'telly with us?" she heard him ask.

"No," she said flatly; didn't turn to look at him. "I'm fine here."

"Want a brew?"

"Yeah…if you're making it."

Different story, she thought, when no-one else was around.

In all honesty, she hoped PJ would sort things out with Kay – for her own sake, as well as theirs. As much as she liked PJ, it did no good to have him and Pete under the same roof. Pete's shitty attitude riled him; he took things to heart, far more than folk realised, especially when he thought he – or anyone – was being belittled. Jackie knew why this was; she'd guessed his secret years ago, ever since he'd started asking her to write Kay's cards. As for Pete, well – it didn't matter who was there; PJ, Craig, Carl, Michelle – he *had* to show off, and let them know he was top-dog. It wasn't so bad when it was just *them….*

"Come on," he said. "You know I don't mean owt. It's just how I am."

"Yeah. It *is.*"

He gently kissed her cheek – reminding her of the other reason she stayed. Despite everything, she still loved him, because of these rare moments – when he was *him*, and stopped putting on the act.

She sighed. "Why can't it always be like this?"

"I don't know, love," he said sadly. "I don't know.

Chapter Sixty

The sauce tasted as good as it smelt – and tossed through penne, washed down with the Merlot, it worked a treat. As they ate, she told him about Sean, and was surprised – slightly shocked – to find he'd already worked it out.

"Look, love," he said. "I need to ask. It is definitely over with him? Because if I build my hopes up, just to lose you again…"

"I told you – you're going nowhere! And yeah - it's over for good. I'll be honest, Phil, I did care a lot for Sean. Perhaps I thought it might be – well, not exactly the same, but maybe *something* like you and me. But nothing could replace that. Lovely as he is, Sean's in a dreamworld - and that's no good to me."

Phil, in turn, was upfront about Debs. "Thing is, we were both lonely. Her fella died, and I didn't know if I'd ever see you again. I suppose it were a way to get through things – for her, as much as me. But if I'd thought there were any chance of us…."

She looked serious for a moment – then, to his relief, she smirked. "So – I guess you'd call it 'Last Tango in Haydock[xlvii]'?"

"Bloody hell, love," he laughed. "You had me worried! You and your jokes. You're a case!"

He washed up and made a brew – just as if he'd never been away. They curled up together on the sofa, as they always had, her head resting on his chest.

"There's more I need to say."

"Oh no – don't tell me – 'Last Tango in Thatto Heath'?" They laughed again. "Look, whatever happened when we were apart – there's no need to explain. We were both free agents, after all."

"It's not that. I wish it were, in a way." Then that same tense, troubled look as when he'd first arrived.

"Hey," she said. "It can't be that bad, surely?"

"I hope not."

Then she listened as he told her everything – about just how much he'd struggled at school; why he couldn't follow shopping lists or recipes; how every card he'd ever given her was written by Jackie; and why he hadn't been able to read Dot's eulogy. It was only after going to counselling that he'd finally got help.

"Oh, sweetheart," she said. "I *wish* I'd known."

He broke down, then. She swapped them round, so his head lay on her breast now, and she held him, stroking his hair, kissing his beard, as he sobbed, "I've let you down, love…I'm so sorry…I've let you down."

"No," she whispered. "Of course not. It's alright…It's alright."

She made more tea. He'd calmed down by now but looked exhausted; drained. It broke her heart to see him so vulnerable.

"You do know you could have told me, don't you?"

"Yeah," he nodded, "I knew all along, but…" His voice was still tearful. "'More I left it, 'worse it got, I suppose. I know I should've been honest in 'first place, but I were just so ashamed. I mean, who can't read and write, in this day and age?"

"More than you think. You'd be surprised."

"Yeah – I know that now, from going to them classes. But before that… I'd heard of dyslexia but didn't really know what it were – not properly, any-rode. Wouldn't have crossed my mind I had it. I thought I were just thick. Still do, sometimes."

"Now listen, Wainwright," she said sternly, "you can put a stop to that, once and for all! Think back to what you always told me – about there being enough folk out to put you down. I've learned loads from you. Remember our first time?"

"As if I'd forget!"

"I was terrified – and you were so patient – so kind. How I hope I am for you." It was her turn to tear up. "What I said to you that night – I didn't mean it. And if I'd known what you were going through, I'd never have…"

"I know, love. It's all forgotten. Don't worry."

"Just as long as you know I'm sorry. Because you're more than good enough." She smiled. "You're the best there is."

THE END

Notes

[i] Mr Magoo, created at UPA animation studio, 1949

[ii] Peter Pan, created by JM Barrie, 1902

[iii] "Come Fly With Me", Frank Sinatra, 1958; written by Jimmy Van Heusen and Sammy Cahn

[iv] "I'd Like to Teach the World to Sing", the New Seekers, 1971; written by Bill Backer, Billy Davis, Roger Cook, Roger Greenaway

[v] "Top of the World," The Carpenters, 1972; written by Richard Carpenter and John Bettis

[vi] "Jesus Christ, Superstar", 1971, written by Tim Rice and Andrew Lloyd Webber

[vii] "Terrahawks," 1983, created by Gerry Anderson and Christopher Burr

[viii] "Blue Peter", 1958; executive producers Biddy Baxter, Edward Barnes, Rosemary Gill

[ix] "Jilted John" by Jilted John, 1978; written by Graham Fellows

[x] "Etch-a-Sketch", 1960; invented by Andre Cassanges, manufactured by Ohio Art Company; now owned by Spin Master, Toronto

[xi] "Playdoh", 1955; invented by Kay Zufall, Brian Joseph McVicker, Bill Rhodenbaugh; owned by Kutol (1955), Rainbow Crafts (1956-71), Kenner (1971-91), Hasbro (1991 to present)

[xii] Ancestry.com ,tm 1996; founded by Paul Brent, Allan Taggart; owned by GIC and Blackstone Group

[xiii] Irwin's - chain of Liverpool Stores

[xiv] From "Keeping up Appearances," 1990; created by Roy Clarke, Harold Snoade

[xv] "Grange Hill", 1978; created by Phil Redmond, produced by BBC

[xvi] Center Parcs", founded 1987; Martin Daulby

[xvii] "Sweet Child o' Mind", 1987; written by Guns n Roses

[xviii] Beefeater, tm, 1974, founded by Whitbread

[xix] Royal Doulton, tm, 1815; founded by John Doulton, John Watts, Martha Jones; owned by Fiskars Oyj, WWRD Holdings Ltd

[xx] Smooth Radio, tm, 2010, owned by Real and Smooth

[xxi] "The Secret", 2006, Rhonda Byrne; published by Atria Book, Beyond Words Publishing

[xxii] "The Boys from the Blackstuff", 1982; written by Alan Bleasdale, produced by Michael Waring (BBC)

[xxiii] "Chocolat", 1999, Joanne Harris; published by Doubleday

[xxiv] Brookside," 1982; Phil Redmond, Mal Young, Mersey Television

[xxv] YouTube, tm, 2005, founded by Chad Hurley, Steve Chen, Jawid Kirem, owned by Alphabet, Inc

[xxvi] "Morning in the Streets," 1959, BBC; directed by Denis Mitchell and Roy Harris; researched by Frank Shaw.

[xxvii] "Hard Labour," 1973; written by Mike Leigh, produced by Tony Garnett (BBC)

[xxviii] Facebook tm, founded2004, Mark Zuckerberg

[xxix] "Great British Bake Off," 2010, produced by Love Productions; BBC and Channel 4

[xxx] "Hard Times," Charles Dickens, 1854

[xxxi] Twitter, 2006; Jack Dorsey, Noah Glass, Biz Stone, Evan Williams

[xxxii] "Muriel's Wedding", 1994, written and directed by PJ Hogan, Ciby 2000, Film Victoria, House and Moorhouse Films

[xxxiii] "Granada Reports", 1956 to present, Lucy West; MediaCity

UK (ITV Granada)

[xxxiv] "Rainbow", 1972, created by Pamela Lonsdale; Thames Television, Carlton Television

[xxxv] "Playschool", 1964, created by Joy Whitby; produced by Cynthia Fagan, BBC

[xxxvi] "Child's Play", directed by Tom Holland, produced by David Kirschner, Metro-Goldwyn-Mayer, from a story by Tom Holland, John Lafia and Don Mancini

[xxxvii] "Othello", William Shakespeare, 1603

[xxxviii] "Tainted Love", Soft Cell, 1981, written by Edd Cobb, produced by Mike Thorne; Some Bizarre/Warner Brothers

[xxxix] "When you were Sweet Sixteen", The Fureys with Davey Arthur, 1981; written by James Thornton, 1898;

[xl] "She Moved Through The Fair," Padraig Colum and Herbert Hughes; published by Boosey and Hawkes, 1909

[xli] Co-op Stores, founded 1863, Manchester

[xlii] "Three Steps to Heaven," Eddie Cochran, 1960; written by Eddie Cochran, Bob Cochran; produced by Snuff Garrett; Liberty (USA), London (UK)

[xliii] "Cathy's Clown", the Everly Brothers, 1960; written by Don Everly, produced by Wesley Rose, Warner Brothers

[xliv] "Picture Box", 1966, (ITV Schools)

[xlv] "Father Ted," 1995, created and written by Graham Linehan, Arthur Mathews; Channel 4

[xlvi] "Feelin' Good", Nina Simone, 1964; written by Anthony Newley, Leslie Bricusse; produced by Musical Comedy Productions

[xlvii] "Last Tango in Paris," 1972, directed by Bernardo Bertolucci

Printed in Great Britain
by Amazon

A WAVE OF
AFFLICTION

By Elliot Robinson

Dedication

I would like to say thank you to all of those who are and have been involved with the Trevor Gibbens Unit.

I would also like to thank the Friends of Mental Health for all the good they do.

And thank you to all at the Voluntary Services and all the volunteers at KMPT.

WWW.KMPT.NHS.UK

Chapter One: The Test

Nine AM and Annabel walks through the school gates, she is early as usual and so she sits down on a bench and reviews her workbook.

She has an important test today.

"What a nerd!" Annabel freezes and looks around examining the students around her.

Ha, she doesn't have a clue.

The bell rings and Annabel makes her way to class, looking over her shoulders.

She sits down at her desk as her Teacher addresses the class, "Right everybody, as you all know you will be sitting through a maths test today, and I do hope you have been revising".

"Annabel has, Boffin". Annabel is startled and looks around the class with blank faces as she stares at each student.

"Are you ok?" Her teacher asks. "Erm yes Miss" She replies. Laughs come from the class.

"Quiet everybody! Today is very important and will have an effect on your futures, so please everybody use the next few hours to revise quietly and we will have a question and answers time before break".

It is break time and Annabel opens her lunch and pulls out a chocolate bar.

"Fatty!" She hears as she opens the packet. She look around but cannot see where it could be coming from, she walks to the bin and throws the chocolate away. "That was silly, you'll be hungry".

Annabel starts to sweat and shake, "WHO IS IT?" she shouts a group close by turn to look at her. "Is it you?" she says. "Us what?" says one of the group. "Aww don't worry." Annabel says as she storms off crying. She walks into the toilets checking there is no one around; she looks into the mirror at her tear covered face.

"Ha what's she crying for?" Annabel storms around looking for who it could be, checking each cubical. She hears giggling getting close to the toilets, so she enters a cubicle and locks the door. A pair of girls walk into the toilet, Annabel hears them talking, one of the girls is saying how she hasn't revised at all, Annabel thinks to herself about the test.

The end of the break bell rings. Annabel comes out of the cubicle, and hears laughing as she passes the two girls; she hurries out of the toilets.

Everybody is making their way into the sports hall, there is laughing and then silence as the students see the rows of single desks bordered by teachers.

"Find a desk and sit down everyone, chop chop". "Yeah chop chop Annabel". She starts to make her way to the back desks, by the time she gets there all the back desks have been taken, Annabel looks around for a desk. She ends up sitting near the middle, 'great' she thinks to herself.

"Right everyone, you will be handed your papers shortly, do not turn them over until you are told to, does everybody have a sharp pencil, rubber and a calculator?" One of the teachers asks.

"Of course Annabel does, Geek!" Annabel puts her head down.

"You will have forty five minutes to complete your tests. You cannot ask for help, you will not be allowed to leave until you are finished. If you leave, you will not be allowed to re-take the test. Right, if everybody understands...

START!" "Yeah start, hurry up, chop chop Annabel".

"What's she waiting for; doesn't she know this is important?" "I know this is important!" Annabel says.

"No Talking!" Annabel looks up and sees it has already been five minutes. 'I haven't even opened it yet, I'm so hungry' she thinks to herself.

"Shouldn't have thrown that chocolate bar away." She lifts her head up. 'Did I just hear that' she wonders, 'or did I just think it?'

Annabel opens her test. 'Right, Question One'.

Paul has two pound and fifty three pence. He needs to buy six apples at thirty three pence each, how much change will he have?

'Six times thirty is, one hundred and eighty'…

"One hundred and eighty, Bulls eye" She hears.

'Three times six is eighteen, one hundred and eighty plus…"

"One hundred and eighty, Bulls Eye" She hears.

'Plus eighteen is one hundred and ninety eight'…

"Oh I thought she was going to get it wrong!"

Annabel looks around, 'who could it be?' she thinks.

'Two hundred and fifty three minus one hundred and ninety eight'…

"That's tricky, she'll never get it. Yeah that's hard".

Annabel concentrates.

'That's fifty five, fifty five pence change'. She smiles.

"She's such a nerd".

Annabel looks around at all the heads down at their papers, 'who is it?' she thinks to herself. She looks at a teacher close by. 'Surely it couldn't be?' She thinks.

"Heads Down!" says the teacher.

She looks down at her paper.

"Come on, question two Annabel". 'I know', she thinks to herself.

"Well quickly then, this is important". 'I know', she thinks to herself.

"God just leave me alone" Annabel says out loud.

"Quiet Annabel" says one of her teachers, shaking her head at her.

Annabel starts to sweat and shake again, her hands are clammy and she feels her heart racing in her chest. 'Calm down just ignore them this is important' she tells herself.

She looks down at question two. "Question two, question two" she pretends not to hear.

She reads a question in her head. 'Michael buys five packets of nine chocolate bars'.

Annabel thinks of the chocolate bar she threw away. She thinks how stupid she was to listen to... well whoever it was. 'I'm not fat' she tells herself... her belly rumbles.

"How many chocolate bars does Michael have Annabel"

"Five times nine Annabel"

 She tries to ignore it, 'Five times nine.. .' she thinks to herself… 'Five, Ten, Fifteen, Twenty, Twenty Five'.

"Come on we don't have all day Annabel"

"FIFTEEN minutes left everybody. Don't forget to check your answers" Says a Teacher.

'Fifteen minutes...' Annabel thinks to herself. 'I haven't even finished the second question.

"Well I told you this was important didn't I?"

Annabel stands up in the middle of the hall, everybody looks up at her, and she is looking around at them, tears in her eyes and breathing heavily.

A nearby teacher places their hands on her shoulder. "Are you alright?" they say.

"Alright? Am I alright? No I'm not, no one can shut the hell up!" She screams, as she throws her chair over and runs across the hall, banging at the door.

A teacher opens the door for her, "calm down" they say, "just calm down, come with me". 'Calm down?' Annabel thinks to herself.

She hears laughter in the background as she is escorted to an empty classroom.

"Oh no, I've failed the test' Annabel thinks to herself as the teacher leaves the room.

"Just sit here I'll be back in just a moment" they say. "I'm just going to get your teacher".

Annabel cries into her hands.

"She's definitely failed, of course she has she couldn't even get through two questions".

"I know I've failed I'm not stupid!" Annabel screams as the two teachers walk into the room.

"What's wrong Annabel, why are you so worked up? Sit down and talk to me" says one of the teachers. "What's wrong?" She says, "I'll tell you what's wrong, everybody's laughing at me, everyone thinks I'm just a fat geek, I've been trying to study for weeks and now I've failed, what am I supposed to tell my parents?"

"I'm sorry Annabel but you don't know if you've failed yet"

"Yes I do, I didn't even complete question two."

"Oh Annabel, I didn't realise, I'm sorry."

I didn't realise how much stress you were under."

"I'm not stressed", says Annabel, "It's just I can hear people talking about me and I couldn't figure out who it was, I couldn't concentrate and I got…"

"Got what Annabel? Stressed out?"

"Oh you don't understand."

The teachers look at each other and one nods to the other, "well Annabel you can't go back to finish the test and it will be lunch time in a little while, you sit in here until then, we've got to get back to the hall, just try and calm down".

Annabel watches as they leave, she dries her eyes.

"oh boo hoo, what a baby".

Annabel runs to the door, she looks down the hall , she sees the backs of the teachers walking off.

'Screw this, I'm going home' she says to herself.

As she makes her way down the corridor her heart beats faster, she is panicking.

"Where is she going? She's going to bunk off"

Annabel looks in the classes as she walks down the corridor, she walks out onto the playground and she looks around.

The bell for lunch rings, her heart is pounding in her chest as she is caught up in a sea of students rushing outside.

"Ha look there's Annabel" She hears.

"Freak" they call her.

Annabel doesn't acknowledge it, her heart still pounding, she feels her eyes start to fill with tears, and so she runs for the gate.

"Umm she's done it, she's bunking off, what will she tell her parents, failing a test and leaving school early, she's a bad kid"

Annabel thinks about what she hears, 'they're right. I can't go home early, I'll have to go to the park'.

Annabel's heart beats slower the closer she gets to the park, she sees a couple with their children, never having been out of school early, and she begins to wonder…

'What if they call the school, or worse the police?' As she walks past the couple she hears…

"That girl's truanting, little rebel, should we call and tell the school?"

Annabel turns her head from view and walks to a bench, she sits down. 'What if they do call my school' she thinks, 'what do I do if the police turn up at the park, should I…"

"Run" she hears.

She watches as they couple push their kids on the swings.

'Well they don't look like they mind me being here' she thinks to herself.

Feeling hungry, Annabel opens up her bag and brings out a sandwich.

As she goes to take a bite from her sandwich, she notices she has caught the attention of the family's dog, which comes bounding over tail wagging.

"Well give it to the dog then"

Annabel looks over to the family by the swings. The lady is looking over… "Can I feed your dog?" Annabel asks.

"No, No please don't. Come here boy." The lady shouts.

Confused, Annabel thinks 'why did you tell me to give it to the dog then? Unless…'

Annabel looks around wondering if it could have been someone else. There's no one around, perhaps they've gone; as she is looking she sees a police car through the fence making its way down the road.

"That's her in the park, quick get her".

Annabel springs to her feet and begins to sprint across the park, dropping her sandwich as she runs.

As Annabel runs she hears "quick she's getting away". This only makes her run faster.

She reaches the far end of the park and begins climbing over the boundary fence.

"She's going over the fence".

As Annabel jumps over the fence she catches her jumper, she pulls at it...

'I'm going to get caught' *Rip* goes her jumper. No time to think, she continues to run off up the street, she turns the first corner and carries on running.

Finally she's away and exhausted so she slows to a fast walk.

"Look, that girl should be in school, and she's ripped her jumper!"

'Oh no! My jumper!' Annabel thinks as she looks in the windows of a house, 'My mum is going to kill me!'

'What a day. I've failed my test, bunked off school, ran from police and ripped my jumper'.

As Annabel walks down the road, she takes off her jumper and puts it in her bag.

She must be cold, it's freezing out.

Annabel starts to run again, 'I need to get off the street' she thinks to herself.

As she runs further up the road, she sees a shop coming up, there are a few older kids from another school.

"And where are you going" asks one of the older boys. Annabel hesitates.

"What's it got to do with you?" says a girl. "Leave her alone, are you alright?"

Annabel looks up at the girl and breaks out into tears, "I'm being chased by the police" she cries.

"Police?" says one of the group… "We better go"

"Come with us" says the older girl, "we won't let them get you".

"Come on everyone, let's go".

Chapter 2: The Theory

Annabel scans the group trying to decide whether or not too trust them. She looks up at the girl who has a wide smile and bright eyes.

"Come on" the girl says, offering her hand to Annabel. "We've got a secret place, they will never find us" she insists.

"Unless you wanna get nicked" says one of the boys.

"Great bring the little geek with us"

"If you don't want me to come, I won't" says Annabel.

"Of course we don't mind you coming, what's your name?" asks the girl.

Annabel looks at the group and tells them her name.

"That's a nice name" says the girl, "what you bunking off for anyway?"

"She thinks she's a rebel that's why"

"I don't" she says

"Don't what?" asks the girl

"Never mind, anyway, where are we going?" asks Annabel.

"It's a secret" says one of the boys. "Top secret" says another.

The girl laughs and turns to Annabel, "don't worry it's not a secret, it's just an abandoned factory, it's not far and nobody ever goes there.. Not even the police."

The group is alerted to a siren in the distance, "come on everybody, run"

"Yeah run Annabel, run!"

As Annabel's little legs struggle to keep up, she focuses on the group as not to lose them.

She looks down at her feet just for a second, when she looks back up, as if by magic they are gone.

Annabel looks around, an alley veers off to the left, but it is empty.

"Where have they gone" she wonders.

"Great, I'm lost"

Then she hears a rustle in the bushes to the right.

The older girl appears, "come on Annabel"

"Ah I thought I'd lost you, I was running then I couldn't see you" says Annabel.

"You haven't lost us, come on it's just through here" she says, "not far now"

The pair walk through the bushes and through a hole in a buckled up fence.

They are greeted by the two boys who are standing outside of a huge abandoned building with grey walls and smashed windows.

"Well we tried ditching her"

Annabel hears and responds "What? What did you say?"

"What's she on about" says one of the boys. "Don't worry" says the girl "come on, let's get inside".

"How do we get in" Annabel asks, looking for a door.

"That's the secret part" say the boys.

"Top secret right?" says the girl laughing.

"Come on Annabel, it's just round here" she offers her hand and says "Just keep hold of my hand and don't let go".

Annabel takes hold of the older girls hand as she leads her around the side of the building to a pair of cellar doors at the back, the group crowd around.

"Who's going first" one of the boys asks as he pulls one of the doors open.

"You go first" says another boy. "No I went first last time" argues the other boy".

"Come on Annabel, we'll go first" pulling her hand as she begins to walk down the stairs.

Annabel resists, "come on" says the girl "just don't let go, it's dark down here"

Annabel begins to walk down the stairs, 'It's dark' she thinks, 'really dark'.

They get to the bottom and start walking, Annabel looks forward but can't see a thing.

"Now get her, go on, now!"

"What?" Annabel says, her heart beat races and she pushes the girl in front to speed her up.

"Quickly" says Annabel.

Suddenly light appears at the top of a flight of stairs ahead.

"See that wasn't so bad" says the girl as she squeezes Annabel's hand.

"You got scared then didn't you?" she asks.

"Well what do you expect" says Annabel. "One of the boys said, 'get her get her'".

"What?" says one of the boys, "we didn't say anything" "no we didn't say anything" says the other.

"You boys are horrible" says the girl. "Leave Annabel alone, she's only young"

"But we didn't say anything" claims the boys.

"Whatever, forget it" says Annabel, "where do we go now?"

The girl slaps the boys one by one as they lead into a large room with chairs laid out in a circle.

The boys rush in.. "I'm getting the big seat" one boy says as they wrestle for an arm chair.

"Boys" the girl says as she giggles, smiling at Annabel. "Come on, we'll sit over here" leading her to a couple of chairs in the corner.

"So Annabel, why are you bunking off" the group goes quiet. Annabel looks around.

"Well you'll just think it's silly" she says.

"Well if it's silly, even more reason to tell us, could do with a laugh" says one of the boys.

Annabel laughs, "well" she says. "I had a test today" "oh that says it all" says one of the boys, "let her talk" says the other.

"Anyway..." Annabel continues, " I heard people making fun of me and I stormed out of the test, the teachers took me into a room and then I heard them talking about how I had failed the test so.. Well.. I ran out of school and I couldn't go home so I went to the park, then a couple with their kids and their dog must have called the police, then I ran off and that's when I ran into you lot"... "Oh and I ripped my jumper".

"Wow" says the girl, "you've had a bad day".

"Pathetic, what a wimp".

Annabel looks up "I'm not a wimp!" she says angrily.

"What? No-one says you're a wimp" says the girl.

"Anyway, don't worry about it, we was all scared the first day we thought there would be homeless people in here".

"Not all of us were scared" "yeah I wasn't scared" says the other.

"Oh yeah, so why were you both holding hands" laughed the girl.

Annabel lets herself laugh. "See you're alright now" says the girl, as she pushes Annabel.

"I'm going to be in so much trouble, my parents are going to kill me says Annabel". "Oh I wouldn't worry too much" says the boy. "You'll probably just get grounded for a couple of days"

"Or a week" says the girl. "That's what happened to me".

"My dad didn't even care" says the other boy.

"Oh I don't even want to think about it, what is there to do here?" asks Annabel.

The group laugh. "Nothing" says the girl.

"Come on lets go for a wander" "Come on Annabel, come with us" the girl offers her hand to Annabel once again.

The boys run ahead as Annabel is lead through a corridor and into an enormous opening with a walkway high up, there are tables and strange looking pieces of metal everywhere.

"bang bang bang" the boys are armed with pieces of wood, and are playing golf with whatever they can see.

"I want to go up there" says the girl, pointing to the walkway way above "come on".

"Is it safe?" says Annabel. *'It doesn't look safe'* she thinks to herself.

"Told you she was a wimp"

"I'm not a wimp, it just looks very old" Annabel explains to the girl.

"Oh don't start all that again" says the girl. "Come on, I've been up there loads" she says as she directs Annabel up a rusty looking staircase.

Annabel watches as the girl starts to climb the staircase, listening to the clanks and squeaks as she climbs higher.

"Come on!" the girl shouts.

Annabel puts her foot onto the first step, the staircase wobbles a little.

"Oh I don't know about this" she says quietly to herself as she takes the next step.

'Come on Annabel, they'll think you're a wimp, take it slowly' she thinks. So she continues up the stairs holding onto the rail with both hands, freezing every-time the metal squeaks.

As she reaches the last few steps the two boys come running up the stairs behind her, racing with one another to get to the top. Annabel loses her footing and falls backwards.

"aaaaaaaah" screams Annabel as she falls.

"Got ya" one of the boys grabs her. "That was close" says the other boy "are you alright?"

The older girl runs back to see what's going on, "what happened" she asks.

"They made me fall" yells Annabel, "they came running up behind me and I fell".

"Hold on" says one of the boys. "We never made you fall, we saved you".

"Should've let her fall"

"What? You should have what? Let me fall? Well perhaps you should've"

"What?" says the girl "look Annabel, they might be a pair of idiots but they wouldn't have done it on purpose, just calm down".

Annabel glares at the boys, then follows the girl up the walkway which leads into an office. The girl takes a seat behind a big wooden desk.

"Let's throw stuff off the walkway" says one of the boys, "good idea" says the other as they get looking for things to chuck.

"Come and sit in the boss's chair" says the girl gesturing to Annabel.

As Annabel takes a seat she sinks into one of the cushions.

"Comfortable isn't it?" remarks the girl as she walks out towards the boys.

As the boys throw things over the walk way a procession of bangs and clanks fill the air.

Annabel can hear the three talking.

"What else can we throw? Let's throw Annabel".

'Did I hear that right?' she wonders as she gets up from her chair.

"We shouldn't have brought the little geek".

Annabel moves closer to the door, "she'll tell about this place, let's throw her".

Annabel storms out onto the walkway, "I won't tell anyone about this place, I promise, please, don't throw me off, please please I promise" she insists.

The bangs and clangs stop, the building goes deathly quiet.

"Don't be silly" the girl says as she walks towards her.

"Please don't come near me" says Annabel, nearly in tears.

"Okay I won't come near you, no-one's going to hurt you, you don't need to cry".

"Aww she's going to cry"

Annabel looks over to the boys, "I heard you, and I heard you saying you want to throw me off the edge because you think I'll tell about this place"

"What?" laughs one of the boys "you're crazy" laughs the other.

"But I heard you" cries Annabel "I heard you".

"Look" says the girl, "No-one said anything like that, I don't know what you think you heard but it wasn't that, I promise, and we don't think you'll tell anyone about this place, you won't.. Will you?" she asks.

"No I promise I won't tell anyone" answers Annabel.

"Let's go back downstairs if you're that scared" laughs one of the boys. The other boy laughs with him.

Annabel looks over the girl who has a big smile for her. "Oh leave her alone you two, she's only young". "Come on Annabel, let's go back downstairs".

As the group gets closer to the staircase the girl puts her arm on the hand rails to block the boys.

"Go on Annabel, you can go first".

Annabel hesitantly edges towards the first step.

"Quick push her hahaha"

Annabel turns to look at the three behind her, "Don't, please" she says.

"No-one's going to do anything" claims the girl "Just goes on.."

Annabel takes another step. "Now!" she hears.

Without hesitation Annabel runs down the staircase.

Annabel runs of the last step and heads for the staircase leading into the cellar.

"Quick get her"

"Wait, Annabel where are you going?" she hears in the background. She doesn't stop, she quickly gets down the stairs and everything goes black.

'There's no time to be scared' Annabel thinks to herself, *'just get down the stairs'*

"Wait, Annabel, Wait" she hears getting louder.

Annabel sprints for the light in the distance, getting closer and closer, with all of her strength she pushes the cellar door up and throws it down behind her.

"I'm out" she says aloud as she tries to remember where the hole in the fence was.

Remembering the three just behind her, she runs across the grassy grounds and hides behind a stack of wooden pallets.

The two boys and the girl climb from the Cellar as Annabel watches.

"Where did she go? Annabel where are you?" shouts the girl.

Chapter 3: The Truth

Annabel stays hidden while she watches the three disappear around the corner.

'How do I get out of here without them catching me?' she wonders. What feels like an hour passes, and Annabel decides she's waited long enough. She cautiously climbs to her feet and looks around. *'They're gone, now how do I get back to school?'* she thinks.

Annabel wanders around the building trying to remember where it was that she comes through the fence, when she stumbles across a hole in the wall.

Well it wasn't where she got in, but she thought at least she would be out, and surely someone would be able to give her directions.

Annabel squeezes through the gap and is confronted by a huge field with a big hill in the middle.

'If I climb the hill I'll be able to see where I need to go' she thinks to herself.

She starts to head towards the hill trudging through the long grass.

As Annabel reaches the foot of the hill she hears someone talking.

"She's over there" she hears.

"Oh no" Annabel thinks, 'They found me'. She looks in all directions. 'Where are they? They must be hiding in the grass'.

Annabel ducks into the tall grass and makes her way to the side of the hill.

Walking on her hands and knee's keeping her head down, and stopping every few steps to listen out for them. After a few minutes, Annabel decides to stand up and see where they are. She watches across the field to see if any of the grass is moving.

She decides she has gone far enough and starts to head up the hill. As she gets further up the hill she notices it is getting darker. 'It must be getting late by now' she thinks 'I must be getting home'.

Finally she reaches the top of the hill. At one end she sees the abandoned building she has just escaped from, and at the other a busy main road and just field in both directions.

"Great" she says aloud as she takes in the view. 'I'll *never get home'* she thinks. She looks down the hill to see if anyone is there.

She sees no-one.

'Maybe they have given up and gone home, they must have' she thinks as she breaths a sigh of relief.

'Home' she thinks. Annabel sits down exhausted after the climb, she looks through her bag. She pulls out a bottle of drink and an apple.

As she takes a bite of her apple she hears "Look fatties eating". She jumps to her feet and searches the area where is that coming from? "Who's there?" she shouts.

"She hasn't got a clue"

Annabel continues looking around, "I know you're there!" she shouts, "what do you want from me!" she screams.

She gets no answer.

"Show yourself!" She shouts.

"I'm here" Annabel jumps and spins around, "where?" she shouts, "Where are you?"

Annabel's heartbeat increases and she starts to panic, "I've got to get home" she says.

Annabel decides the best option is to head for the main road. *'At least there will be cars going past, cars mean people'* she thinks to herself. *'Then whoever's following me might back off'.*

She starts to make her way down the side of the hill, heading towards the busy road. She hears a rustle in the bushes as she passes them.

"Where are you going? Quick, get her"

Annabel starts to sprint, faster than she's ever ran before, hoping to lose whoever is behind her.

She can hear the busy road getting louder and louder as she wades her way through the tall grass.

Finally she crosses a small ditch and up a small mound which leads her onto the road.

"I made it, I made it" she thinks to herself as she looks across the field.

There's no-one there.

It dawns on her, "I'm lost, which way do I go.. It must be getting late" as she looks into the sky, "at least I'm not alone".

She decides to head in the same direction as the traffic. As she is walking she sees a sign stating the town centre is in three miles. "But I live miles away from the town, I'm going to be in so much trouble" she thinks.

She carries on for what seems like forever.

A car slows down and pulls up behind her, she turns to look blinded by the headlights she panics and freezes, not knowing whether to run.

"Annabel, are you Annabel" she hears. The headlights are turned off, and there is a police woman "are you Annabel?" she asks.

"Yes yes I'm Annabel" she sighs relief as she runs towards the police woman.

"We've been looking for you" the officer says "your parents are very worried about you".

"I'm so sorry" says Annabel, "I got lost and someone was following me, and I didn't know what to do."

"Someone was following you?" asks the officer.

"Well.. " Annabel says "I heard someone but.. "

"But what?" asks the officer as she directs Annabel into the car.

"But I couldn't see anyone", Annabel starts to go quiet as she thinks back about her day.

"So why did you run out of school?" asks the officer.

Annabel looks up at the officer, "my parents know, don't they?" she says.

"Yes, they do and we're taking you home now. I'm sure they'll just be happy to know you're safe" says the officer with a smile on her face. "Don't you worry".

Annabel sits quietly looking out of the window as they drive.

She starts to recognise the houses as they get closer.

The police car turns into Annabel's road and up to her house, and they stop.

"I'm in so much trouble" Annabel insists.

"Well I'll come in with you, to make sure everything is alright" the officer says.

The police woman gets out and holds the door open. Annabel slowly gets out, as she does she sees the curtains move through the front window.

The front door flies open and Annabel's mum comes running, grabbing and lifting Annabel up in her arms.

"my baby, oh my baby I'm so glad you're okay" she says as she kisses Annabel. "Where have you been? "She asks.

"Can I come in with you?" The officer asks.

"of course, come in" replies Annabel's mum, "your fathers not back yet" she says to Annabel as she ushers her indoors.

Annabel, the police officer and Annabel's mum are sitting around the dining table.

"When we found Annabel she said that someone had been following her, however she did not see anyone" says the officer.

"Well who was it, how do you know you was being followed Annabel" says her Mum " you must have seen someone".

"well.. " Annabel stutters. "I..." "I.. heard someone.. they were trying to get me and calling me fat."

Annabel's mum and the officer share a look.

"Why did you leave school" asks her mum "why did you walk out of your test? You know how important it was... you've been such a little book worm lately."

"I'm a geek, I know.. just a little nerd I know.. " cries Annabel.

"What? Where did that come from?" asks her Mum.

"Calm down and tell us what's going on" says the police officer.

Annabel tries to calm down. "they were calling me fat and calling me a geek" Annabel cries "so I threw my lunch away, and they were making fun of me during the test.. I couldn't take it so I ran out."

"Who was making fun of you Annabel?" asks her Mum.

"I don't know, I couldn't see who it was and when the teachers left me in the little room I heard them saying how I had failed the test, so I ran out of school.. I'm sorry Mum." Annabel wipes the tears from her eyes.

"Oh my darling, don't worry" says Annabel's Mum.

The officer stands up and pushes the chair in "well Annabel, you're safe now, we will run a report but unfortunately if you did not see anyone we cannot do anything about it.."

"We will notify your school about what you have told us, so have a good night both of you" says the officer as she walks towards the front door.

Annabel's Mum gets up and follows the officer to the door "honestly, I can't thank you enough for all your help".

"The officer responds saying "Happy to help, we're just happy she is safe" and with that she leaves.

When Annabel mum shuts the door, Annabel gets up and walks into the hall where her Mum is.

"Mum I'm so sorry, I couldn't take them making fun of me, and when I ran out of school I thought I was going to get arrested so I ran away from a police car and.. and.. I ripped my jumper.. I'm so sorry" says Annabel.

"Oh Annabel, don't worry about the jumper" her mum laughs. "I'll wait for your father to get back home and then we will go over what has happened. Don't worry, you're not in trouble. Now are you hungry my dear?"

Annabel's eyes light up, "yes mum I am hungry, I dropped my Sandwiches".

"Well you just sit down and watch some television and I will see what I can rustle up for you". Her mum goes into the kitchen.

Annabel walks into the living room, sits down and reaches for the remote control. Just as she is about to turn on the TV, she hears laughing and a voice saying "We will get her tonight". Annabel runs into the kitchen "Mum! Mum!" she shouts, "They're here! They're here!".

"who's here?" Her mum asks.

Annabel is shaking "the people that were following me, I heard them saying they were going to get me tonight".

"Calm down dear, there's nobody here. Must be your imagination" she says.

"Mum!" Annabel shouts. "I heard them, I'm telling the truth".

"ha ha ha" she hears.

"Did you hear that?" Annabel asks, "I heard them laughing, how can you not hear that?"

Annabel's mum stops what she is doing, "right Annabel, come on, we are going to have a look around.. There is no-one here but me and you." She takes hold of Annabel's hand and leads her around the house.

They check every room downstairs, and then they head upstairs. Just as they are checking the last room, the front door slams shut.

"See, they've gone out the front door" she shouts as she runs to the window.

She looks out the front of the house but she sees nothing.

"I'm home!" shouts a voice from downstairs.

Annabel's mum lets out a sigh "it's just your father", now come and sit down and we can all have something to eat.

Annabel looks up at her mum "but.. but.. she says".

.

Annabel walks downstairs holding her mums hand, as she gets close to the bottom she lets go and seeing her Father, runs towards him.

"Daddy!" she says as she jumps into his arms.

"Well somebody's had a busy day haven't they?" says her Father with a stern voice, "what was you thinking?" he asks.

"Look we will all sit down and talk about things over dinner" says Annabel's mum.

Annabel looks at her with a look of relief and she mouths the words "thank you" over her Fathers shoulder.

As they sit down and eat together Annabel is asked to go over all that she'd heard and all that she'd done through the day right up until she was picked up by the police officers.

As Annabel is talking, she stops to put the fork into her mouth.

"Eat up fatty" she hears.

Annabel goes bright red and freezes. Her parents notice and look at each other.

"What's the matter Annabel?" asks her Mum.

"I just heard someone call me a fatty" says Annabel.

"Nobody said anything Annabel" says her father.

"But I heard it Dad, Mum please believe me" Annabel pleads.

Annabel's father stands up and calls her mother into the living room.

Annabel tries to make sense of the whispers.

"You're in trouble now" she hears.

Annabel looks around "where are you?!" she screams and starts to cry, tears flooding from her eyes.

Her parents run back in and her Mum is crying as well, "oh my poor darling" she says as she grabs hold of Annabel.

"Annabel my dear" her Father says, "we need to talk, come and sit down on the sofa".

"Am I in trouble dad?" Annabel asks as she tries to understand what's going on. Her father looks into her eyes and begins to talk. "No you're not in trouble, we think you might be under a lot of stress dear. Me and your mother are very worried about you, and this is going to be very hard to understand."

"Sometimes..." he continues.. "Sometimes when people are under a lot of stress from work or school, they can hear things that aren't there."

"But dad.." Annabel cries, "They are real".

" I know this is hard to take, but me and your mum think you need to see a Doctor. What you're hearing may seem very real, but there is a possibility it is your imagination.".

The next morning Annabel is taken to the doctors by her mother and father, Annabel's father explains what has happened to the Doctor, he tells the Doctor about the voices.

The doctor nods his head and begins to ask Annabel some questions, the Doctor tells her parents he believes Annabel has developed a mental illness. The doctor diagnoses Annabel with Paranoid Schizophrenia due to stress.

The End

Dear Reader,

If you have had similar experiences to Annabel, or you know someone who is hearing voices or noises that are hard to locate or maybe they are seeing things that are not there.

I recommend that you keep a diary of anything you hear or see, and book an appointment with your GP at your local surgery.

There can be many reasons for developing a mental health issue and it can affect anyone at any time.

Please look through the contacts on the next page; hopefully we can point you in the right direction.

We wish you all the best with your mental health in the future.

Thank you for reading.

Elliot Robinson

<u>Mental Health Charity Contacts:</u>

www.time-to-change.org.uk

www.sane.org.uk

www.mind.org.uk

www.dbsalliance.org

www.healthyplace.com

www.healthfulchat.org

www.thinkpacifica.com

www.nice.org.uk

www.helpguide.org

www.samaritans.org

Printed in Great Britain
by Amazon